PRAISE FOR M. L. BUCHMAN

Tom Clancy fans open to a strong female lead will clamor for more.

— *DRONE*, PUBLISHERS WEEKLY

Superb! Miranda is utterly compelling!

— *BOOKLIST*, STARRED REVIEW

Miranda Chase continues to astound and charm.

— BARB M.

Escape Rating: A. Five Stars! OMG just start with *Drone* and be prepared for a fantastic binge-read!

— READING REALITY

The best military thriller I've read in a very long time. Love the female characters.

— *DRONE*, SHELDON MCARTHUR, FOUNDER OF THE MYSTERY BOOKSTORE, LA

A fabulous soaring thriller.

— *TAKE OVER AT MIDNIGHT*, MIDWEST BOOK REVIEW

Meticulously researched, hard-hitting, and suspenseful.

— *PURE HEAT,* PUBLISHERS WEEKLY,
STARRED REVIEW

Expert technical details abound, as do realistic military missions with superb imagery that will have readers feeling as if they are right there in the midst and on the edges of their seats.

— *LIGHT UP THE NIGHT,* RT REVIEWS, 4 1/2
STARS

Buchman has catapulted his way to the top tier of my favorite authors.

— FRESH FICTION

Nonstop action that will keep readers on the edge of their seats.

— *TAKE OVER AT MIDNIGHT,* LIBRARY
JOURNAL

M L. Buchman's ability to keep the reader right in the middle of the action is amazing.

— LONG AND SHORT REVIEWS

The only thing you'll ask yourself is, "When does the next one come out?"

— *WAIT UNTIL MIDNIGHT,* RT REVIEWS, 4
STARS

The first...of (a) stellar, long-running (military) romantic suspense series.

— *THE NIGHT IS MINE,* BOOKLIST, "THE 20
BEST ROMANTIC SUSPENSE NOVELS:
MODERN MASTERPIECES"

I knew the books would be good, but I didn't realize how good.

— NIGHT STALKERS SERIES, KIRKUS
REVIEWS

Buchman mixes adrenalin-spiking battles and brusque military jargon with a sensitive approach.

— PUBLISHERS WEEKLY

13 times "Top Pick of the Month"

— NIGHT OWL REVIEWS

AIR FORCE ONE

A MIRANDA CHASE ACTION-ADVENTURE
TECHNOTHRILLER

M. L. BUCHMAN

SIGN UP FOR M. L. BUCHMAN'S NEWSLETTER TODAY

and receive:
Release News
Free Short Stories
a Free Book

Get your free book today. Do it now.
free-book.mlbuchman.com

Other works by M. L. Buchman: *(* - also in audio)*

Action-Adventure Thrillers

Kate Stark
Final Taste
Ice Burn
Knife's Edge

Miranda Chase
*Drone**
*Thunderbolt**
*Condor**
*Ghostrider**
*Raider**
*Chinook**
*Havoc**
*White Top**
*Start the Chase**
*Lightning**
*Skibird**
*Nightwatch**
*Osprey**
*Gryphon**
*Wedgetail**
*Air Force One**

Science Fiction / Fantasy

Deities Anonymous
Cookbook from Hell: Reheated
Saviors 101

Contemporary Romance

Eagle Cove
Return to Eagle Cove
Recipe for Eagle Cove
Longing for Eagle Cove
Keepsake for Eagle Cove

Love Abroad
Heart of the Cotswolds: England
Path of Love: Cinque Terre, Italy

Where Dreams
Where Dreams are Born
Where Dreams Reside
*Where Dreams Are of Christmas**
Where Dreams Unfold
Where Dreams Are Written
Where Dreams Continue

Non-Fiction

Strategies for Success
Managing Your Inner Artist/Writer
*Estate Planning for Authors**
Character Voice
*Narrate and Record Your Own Audiobook**
Beyond Prince Charming: One Guy's Guide to Writing Men in Romance

Short Story Series by M. L. Buchman:

Action-Adventure Thrillers

Kate Stark Stories
Miranda Chase Stories

Romantic Suspense

Antarctic Ice Fliers
US Coast Guard

Contemporary Romance

Eagle Cove

Other

Deities Anonymous (fantasy)
Single Titles

The Emily Beale Universe
(military romantic suspense)

The Night Stalkers
MAIN FLIGHT
The Night Is Mine
I Own the Dawn
Wait Until Dark
Take Over at Midnight
Light Up the Night
Bring On the Dusk
By Break of Day
Target of the Heart
Target Lock on Love
Target of Mine
Target of One's Own
NIGHT STALKERS HOLIDAYS
*Daniel's Christmas**
*Frank's Independence Day**
*Peter's Christmas**
Christmas at Steel Beach
*Zachary's Christmas**
*Roy's Independence Day**
*Damien's Christmas**
Christmas at Peleliu Cove

Henderson's Ranch
*Nathan's Big Sky**
*Big Sky, Loyal Heart**
*Big Sky Dog Whisperer**
*Tales of Henderson's Ranch**

Shadow Force: Psi
*At the Slightest Sound**
*At the Quietest Word**
*At the Merest Glance**
*At the Clearest Sensation**

White House Protection Force
*Off the Leash**
*On Your Mark**
*In the Weeds**

Firehawks
Pure Heat
Full Blaze
*Hot Point**
*Flash of Fire**
Wild Fire
SMOKEJUMPERS
*Wildfire at Dawn**
*Wildfire at Larch Creek**
*Wildfire on the Skagit**

Delta Force
*Target Engaged**
*Heart Strike**
*Wild Justice**
*Midnight Trust**

Night Stalkers Reload
*Guard the East Flank**

Emily Beale Universe Short Story Series
The Night Stalkers
The Night Stalkers Stories
The Night Stalkers CSAR
The Night Stalkers Wedding Stories
The Future Night Stalkers

Delta Force
Th Delta Force Shooters
The Delta Force Warriors

Firehawks
The Firehawks Lookouts
The Firehawks Hotshots
The Firebirds

White House Protection Force
Stories

Future Night Stalkers
Stories (Science Fiction)

ABOUT THIS BOOK

Brace for the ultimate plunge! The seemingly invincible *Air Force One* suffers a catastrophic engine failure. When it plummets into the Atlantic with the U.S. President and Chairman of the Joint Chiefs of Staff aboard, the world dives toward a peace-shattering crisis.

Enter Miranda Chase, the high-functioning autistic air-crash genius, and her extraordinary NTSB team. Faced with an impossible deep-sea salvage operation of the 747, Miranda must rely on her unparalleled intellect and her diverse crew: the fiercely loyal Holly, methodical Mike, brilliant Jeremy, and resilient Andi, along with the enigmatic Taz.

This meticulously researched, hard-hitting, and suspenseful thriller unveils a deep-seated conspiracy that threatens global stability and challenges the team's very definitions of loyalty and survival. Can Miranda's and the team's skills help them survive exposing the truth before the world unravels?

———

A list of characters and aircraft may be found at:
https://mlbuchman.com/people-places-planes
Scroll down to: Miranda Chase
And return afterward for a free bonus story
and a recipe from the book.

FOREWORD

This title and the initial events were planned long ago as a natural evolution of the Miranda Chase series. The events of this book were never intended as a political statement on past, present, or future administrations. This is a work of fiction about the world inhabited by Miranda Chase and her associates.

PROLOGUE
TOMORROW

"Hello. This is Miranda Chase. This is actually her and not a recording of her," Miranda answered her phone in her typical quirky style, which gave Drake brief comfort.

"You need to come find us."

"Is this like a game of Hide-and-go-seek, Drake? I haven't played that in years, but I was intrigued by it as a child. I enjoyed the counting and developing the most methodical and efficient search patterns. Though because of my autism, I couldn't bring myself to count out loud until I was five."

"No, Miranda. Not the game. I'm still on *Air Force One*. You have to find out who killed us. Promise."

"I promise, Drake. But if you're dead, how are you—"

"Thank you, Miranda. I know I can trust you. I must call Lizzy now. Take care of her for me." He hung up, wishing he had time left for Miranda's convoluted conversational style. For a thousand of her questions and curious diversions. But he didn't.

There was, however, one person he was going to miss far more if he did indeed die aboard *Air Force One*.

He dialed his wife and listened to the most mundane sound in the world, doubting that he'd ever hear it again—a ringing phone.

1

THE PRIOR EVENING

"Is this really happening?" To Miranda, the pitch of Holly's voice sounded atypically high—almost squeaky.

"I do not see anything fake. We are in the President's living room of the White House Residence." As confirmation, the Truman Balcony wrapped around outside the tall windows; the early January evening spreading a few ice crystals on the glass. For the moment, it was being used as the bridal suite, but that was also real, albeit temporary. "Well, technically, I suppose it is fake. Many early administrations were prone to selling off the old furniture and buying more modern furnishings. Then most of what remained was sold off or discarded during the Truman renovation of 1948 to 1951. Congress refused the additional funds to purchase historically correct furnishings. It wasn't until First Lady Jackie Kennedy's 1963 renovation that anyone attempted to recreate the proper look."

There was certainly nothing authentic about the glass coffee table or the dark red leather of the Chesterfield couch and armchairs. The big-screen television was decidedly anachronistic for any period of the White House excepting the most recent decade. Of course, it was the President's personal living room on temporary loan to the bride, so perhaps he enjoyed the anachronisms. She'd have to ask him.

"That's not what I meant. I meant...this." Holly waved Miranda's wedding bouquet of daisies and winter jasmine about so negligently that Miranda decided it would be better if she took it herself rather than continuing to trust Holly's self-control. Roy had offered a rose bouquet from the White House collection, but she'd always felt they bragged too much. She preferred these, especially as neither flower had a scent, which she rather liked. They were just their pretty selves and didn't need to prance about fluffing their petals at everyone.

"This?"

"Wedding. How? Why?" Holly was stuttering worse than an engine running on the wrong fuel. Miranda was rather pleased by that metaphor; it was so rare that her autism allowed her to create such a cogent one.

"Because I want to spend the rest of my life with Andi. So does Meg." Miranda pointed down at her Glen of Imaal Terrier with the two wedding rings tied to her therapy dog harness.

"But..." Holly seemed to give it up. "I just don't understand. Why are you two getting, you know..." She flailed about but couldn't say the word.

For once, Miranda actually did know. Anytime the word marriage came by, Holly's old military training displayed a great desire to kill it. Miranda liked the sound of the word, though the silent *I* bothered her at times. Of course, without it, the word would be marrage, and she had no wish to be marred by anything in particular. Or in general. She tried to think of how to explain it.

"You've been together with Mike for six years," Miranda started out.

"Five and a half. No, wait, barely over five and a quarter. And don't mention that."

"And you renovated your new home together."

"Or that."

Miranda had never understood Holly's refusal to admit the reality of her relationship with Mike Munroe. In Miranda's experience, Holly Harper was a stark realist on all other topics, whether her elite warrior past with the Australian Special Air Service Regiment or her air-crash investigator present.

"It's not as if you're the one getting married." First Lady Rose Cole entered the temporary bridal suite from her and Roy's bedroom. She stopped close by Miranda but knew not to offer the friendly touch that she gave to most people around her. Miranda almost wished she didn't so mind being touched because Rose made it seem so pleasant...but she did.

Rose normally towered five inches over Miranda's five-four. Today she wore three-inch heels, a skill Miranda had never wanted to master, making her two inches taller than even Holly. Her evening dress was much frillier than Miranda's own sleek silk—not fancier, just frillier. She found Rose's dress a little unnerving as parts of it seemed to move with a mind of their own.

Miranda looked away quickly and focused on Holly. "It's good that you aren't getting married today—"

"Or ever!"

"—with the way you hate clothes." Miranda had rather enjoyed finding a dress that wasn't annoyingly annoying. Clothes were always a challenge as she couldn't stand the touch of synthetic fabrics. Or clothing tags. Or too many seams, like Rose's must have. Or washed with scented soaps.

"Perhaps she should have a casual beach wedding." There was something about Rose's smile that said she was having... fun? Oh, perhaps she was teasing Holly? Another thing Miranda's autism rarely allowed her to identify.

"That is a good idea." Whether or not it was a tease. Holly said she'd burned her military uniform the day she left the Australian Special Air Service Regiment, and she'd never worn a dress and wasn't about to start now. She had finally accepted the idea of a nice pantsuit—after Andi had made some dire threats if she showed up at the White House in her normal jeans, t-shirt, and ball cap for the Australian women's soccer team.

"What part of never getting married didn't you understand?"

Rose touched Holly's arm in that way she did. "I'm finding it curious that you're more nervous at Miranda's wedding than she is."

Miranda nodded. That *was* curious. She was simply glad to be here, though it had included an odd series of events.

She'd called Lizzy to ask if she and Drake wanted to come to her wedding. Miranda had been Lizzy's maid of honor, so it only made sense. That they were one of the top Washington, DC, power couples—as the future and present Chairmans of the Joint Chiefs of Staff—had never entered her thoughts until Mike had pointed it out later. She'd worked with both of them until they became friends.

But when President Roy Cole heard, he'd insisted on being the officiant and had proposed shifting the wedding to DC in January. She and Andi had planned on a backyard spring wedding, but Roy's second term of office ended in three weeks. Andi had been glad to move up the date, so they'd all come east. They *had* kept it small. Which was good, as Miranda had never much enjoyed crowds.

General Drake Nason had insisted on the privilege of giving her away. He looked very impressive in his Army uniform with the four stars on his lapel and all the medals he'd been awarded over the years. Drake, too, was retiring at the end of Roy's presidency. Roy himself had opted not to wear his old Green Beret uniform. *Because,* he'd said, *I don't wish to be outranked at your wedding day by a mere upstart of a 75th Ranger turned four-star general.*

Miranda didn't understand. The President was the Commander in Chief, and he was the one who had promoted Drake to being the Chairman of the Joint Chiefs of Staff; there was no question of who outranked whom in this case. Yet they had always fomented a rivalry between the Rangers and the Green Berets, though the President hadn't served in over thirty years. Whatever the explanation, Roy instead opted for a three-piece suit that First Lady Rose said he looked *positively yummy* in. Why she used an adjective appropriate for food products rather than people, Miranda decided she'd rather not know.

"I'm not nervous," Holly began pacing from one side to the other of the living room, like a caged...Holly.

Sometimes metaphors were *not* Miranda's friend. This one eluded her.

"I'm allergic to weddings."

With a complete lack of histamines, Miranda couldn't imagine what immuno-suppression vector that would require, but she'd never researched the possibility. She reached for her personal notebook, except her dress didn't include a pocket for one. It was a major oversight. Without her notebook, she would now be distracted throughout her own wedding, making sure that she remembered to delve into that question at her earliest opportunity. But then how could she possibly remember her lines for the ceremony at the same time?

"Holly, can you do something for me?"

"Sure. What? Is it far away? Where's the antipode; can you send me there? Please!"

"No. Besides, the antipode is very wet. The opposite side of the Earth from the White House lies in the Indian Ocean, twelve hundred kilometers southwest of Australia, so why would I send you there? No, the favor I need is that I don't have my personal notebook, and I need to remember to research how it is possible for you to be allergic to weddings."

"I'm not allergic to weddings."

"But you just said— I'll never understand neurotypicals."

Rose laughed. "Holly Harper may be many things, Miranda, but typical is not one of them."

Holly's protest was unconvincing even to Miranda's ear. Holly began picking at her maid-of-honor blazer's sleeves like they were...covered in fleas? That wasn't a nice metaphor; Miranda edged away a step just in case it was true.

Rose braved the metaphor and gave Holly a gentle hug that didn't appear to do anything to calm her down. What was the point of being able to tolerate a hug if it didn't calm a person down?

Miranda wanted to ask, but Drake joined them to say that Roy and Andi were ready for them.

Before leading the way into the Yellow Oval Room on the second floor of the Residence, Rose started the player with the lovely Bach *Goldberg Variations*. Much prettier than Mendelssohn's overused "Wedding March."

Miranda waited for Holly to follow Rose, then she stepped through with Drake on one side and Meg trotting along on the other.

———

MIRANDA AND ANDI HAD AGREED THEY WANTED A SMALL, SIMPLE ceremony. She'd invited the rest of her team: Jeremy, Taz, and Mike. The President had invited the President-elect and VP-elect, Sarah Feldman and Carl Crawford, respectively.

These are the two you'll be working with after I'm gone. It will be a good chance for you all to get to know each other better.

Miranda knew neither one very well, but if Roy thought it was a good idea, she knew it was. Jeremy had worked more with Sarah than she had. But Miranda had been surprised that Andi didn't know VP Crawford, he was a former Army general after all.

He retired into politics while I was still lieutenant. There were over a million of us in the service, you know.

One-point-three-four at the time you left, Miranda had corrected her.

She and Andi had spent much of yesterday visiting Terrence in the hospital, her mentor since her first day with the NTSB. His hip replacement had gone well, mostly, but complications were keeping him in the hospital through her wedding. Tante Daniels, who'd been her childhood therapist and then governess after Miranda's parents died, had a bad flu. They were streaming the wedding for the two of them and they'd already planned a party when both were doing better.

Despite Holly's whining, Miranda had also invited the Director of the CIA, Clarissa Reese at the First Lady's suggestion. They had worked together so often and Clarissa had always been nice to her.

Even this morning, after Terrence and Tante Daniels had cancelled, Holly had lobbied against Clarissa. They had never gotten along. *She's the unlucky thirteenth!* But that wasn't accurate. Firstly, statistically, thirteen was *not* any unluckier than other numbers. Second, with the White House photographer—who had groused about the images being for archival purposes only—and several Secret Service agents circulating as well, they were more than thirteen. And that didn't count Meg at all. Her therapy dog might not count to others, but she definitely counted to Miranda.

The moment that Miranda forgot all about that was when she saw US Army Captain Andi Wu in her blue service uniform with all her medals on display. She might be a petite five-foot-two Chinese-American, but she looked terribly impressive— even if the top of her head didn't reach Roy's shoulders as they waited at the head of the Yellow Oval Room.

Rose and Lizzy had each warned her that the ceremony would go by in a blur. She had largely discounted that as they were both neurotypicals...yet they'd been right. In fact, the dinner in the President's Dining Room and making married love with Andi as guests in the Lincoln Bedroom that night had also been a blur. One she'd very much enjoyed, but still a blur.

By this morning the effect had dissipated by at least fifty percent, though she estimated by less than sixty-five percent. It was so hard to judge her own emotional state. Others she simply didn't understand, but she kept hoping that someday her autism would allow her to understand herself. Not yet.

Over breakfast with the First Couple, Roy kept teasing Andi about sharing Lincoln's bed. Andi rarely blushed but she certainly did now. Miranda pointed out that the bed there probably wasn't Lincoln's. And the room had been his office in the 1860s and not his bedroom, so it was unlikely he'd had sex with Mary Todd in that room.

"You never know, Miranda," Roy told her. "He was only fifty-six when he died. Trust me, I'm a decade older and I can tell you that he'd still have plenty of interest. Especially with the right lady."

Rose offered a happy hum that sounded like agreement—even though Miranda hadn't made a study of hum sounds—as she leaned over to kiss him.

"And you have to admit that married sex is a definite improvement over merely engaged sex."

Miranda considered. "It is. Measurably."

"Miranda," Andi whispered as even the tips of her ears turned red.

"Young things like you two probably had plenty of energy," Roy continued. He winked for reasons that were unclear.

"We did."

"Miranda!" Andi hissed out her name—and turned even redder.

"But it's true. You were amaz—"

"Just...stop, okay?"

"Okay." She stopped.

It was only as they were leaving the White House that she fully descended from the heady event and felt as if she once again inhabited her own body. Perhaps it was the freshness in the air of the unusually spring-like temperatures in January, snowdrops were already peeking out around the bed edges in the Rose Garden and the crocuses were exploring the above-ground world with the first tentative spears. The thin cirrus clouds stretching across the brilliant blue sky were very…she wasn't sure what, but she liked them, too.

It didn't matter what. Everything felt…better. She looked down at herself. It was her own body, but with a gold band now on her left ring finger. She'd never worn jewelry of any kind before, but it looked pretty and it matched Andi's, so that too was a good thing. Andi had been right about that.

She'd also been right about the idea of traveling to meet the wild horses of Chincoteague Island for their honeymoon. Especially the rescue and rehab center, as that's what Miranda had turned her former island home into. Miranda had never had horses on Spieden Island, but she missed her sheep, deer, and flocks of birds that had been stocked there years before she'd inherited it.

Sadly, the wildlife near their new property in the Cascade foothills in Washington State visited her only rarely. Their property backed onto tens of thousands of acres, and the animals could wander away at any time they wished. She had yet to make friends with any of the deer or elk, though there was a rabbit she was growing close to. It probably deserved a name, but she hadn't found the right one yet.

This morning, they'd journeyed out to Andrews Air Force Base in the Marine One helicopter that smelled of lemon-scented cleansers with the slightest overtones of hot grease from the engines. They waited to see Roy and Rose off on his final foreign relations journey as President—a European and

African goodwill tour. Drake stood by the airstairs as he was joining them aboard *Air Force One*.

After the President and First Lady worked the press line, all of the reporters rushed to the back stairs to board the plane. Anyone not in their seat when the President boarded got left behind. There were more still on the ground, waiting to take the usual departure shots, but the Secret Service kept them back as she, Andi, and the First Couple moved to the foot of the front stairs before stopping to chat.

"You know," Roy paused with his foot on the bottom step, "If you'd gotten married today, you could have had the wedding in the Rose Garden." It was thirty-six degrees warmer than yesterday, an April temperature in January, so it was comfortable to do.

"But Roy, there wouldn't have been any roses in bloom for months yet."

In answer, he returned from the step, kissed her on the forehead, shook Andi's hand, and ascended the stairs. Rose's hug had turned out to be very nice—and thankfully brief. She couldn't tolerate contact lasting more than a few seconds other than from Andi. Miranda and Drake traded fist bumps, which they'd recently worked out between them as being both personal and the briefest possible contact. He'd saluted Andi very formally, and she'd saluted back.

When Miranda asked why she was crying, Andi just shook her head and wiped away the tears.

Then the Beast, as the President's limo was called, which had been sent ahead as a diversion of possible attack at the same time as the Marine One flight, waited to take them to the nearby Potomac Airfield. There they'd pick up their rental helicopter to fly out to Assateague Island. Miranda felt a little disappointed not to have the rest of the motorcade travel with them, as she was curious about what that looked like from the inside.

2

THE MOST CAREFULLY MAINTAINED AIRPLANES IN THE WORLD ARE a pair of highly modified Boeing 747-200Bs that were built in 1986. First flying in 1987, they were not completed until 1990 due to numerous wiring issues. Those were well in the two planes' past.

Once completed, and designated as US Air Force VC-25As, these two aircraft were assigned to the Presidential lift mission. When they did so, their call sign changed. Normally SAM—Special Air Mission—28000 and 29000, they were called *Air Force One* when the President was aboard.

For thirty-five years and thousands of flights, there was no reported instance of either aircraft *not* being mission-ready.

The President decided at the last minute, at least by Presidential travel standards—a mere three weeks earlier—to take a final trip. He led his long-time friend General Drake Nason and First Lady Rose Cole aboard *SAM 29000* at 0914 Washington, DC, local time. Per standard operations, within three minutes after they boarded, all four engines were started and safety checks completed. With a favorable northwesterly wind of fifteen knots, *Air Force One* taxied one-point-two kilometers from its custom hangar to the near end of Runway 01 Left in just eighty-four seconds.

They received immediate clearance and exclusive use of the airspace within ten kilometers, briefly altering flight paths for Ronald Reagan Washington National Airport and grounding all aircraft at several smaller fields.

After performing the few steps required by the Pre-takeoff Checklist, pilots Colonel Sandra Ames and General John Owen advanced the throttles on all four engines.

Takeoff and departure proceeded per plan, wheels up a minute early at 0919, and air traffic restrictions at the local airports were lifted by 0921. The VC-25A included over fifty tons of additional weight due to modifications ranging from built-in airstairs both forward for the President's use and aft for everyone else's, luxury seating, communications gear capable of running a global war, and anti-missile defenses. The aircraft was still fifty tons lighter than its commercial airline counterpart because it carried three hundred fewer passengers, minimal luggage, and no additional dead-space cargo. With a fifty-five percent fuel load to reach Africa, it saved another eighty-one tons.

With such a favorable thrust-to-weight ratio, *Air Force One* climbed quickly as it flew slightly south of east. In just fifteen minutes, it reached a cruising altitude of forty-five thousand feet and cleared the coast. Within thirty, it passed two hundred kilometers offshore.

The order of travel was unfortunate.

The original plan, for what the media had dubbed the President's Final Farewell Tour, had included stops at London, Brussels, and Paris before proceeding to Senegal to speak at the African Union meeting. All fifty-five African leaders would be in attendance, making it an excellent opportunity for President Cole to investigate the best leverage opportunities with the various leaders. Major General Ralph Eubanks, the recently promoted director of the White House Military Office responsible for all Presidential travel, had feared that placing the African Union as the ultimate stop on the final tour of a very popular American President might insult the European nations. He therefore shifted the trip's timing enough to reverse the order of the visits.

Under the original plan, *Air Force One* would have flown along the US and Canadian east coast for the first twenty-two hundred kilometers. Under the revised schedule, the plane flew directly east, striking for the distant African coast with the first land being the Canary Islands, which lay five thousand, five hundred and twenty-three kilometers from Washington, DC.

3

———

They were a very convivial group in the President's onboard office, helped along by mimosas and generous bowls of hothouse strawberries, pre-cut and doused in clover honey. Roy sat behind his desk. Drake sat in the seat across from him and Rose upon the curved couch that faced her husband.

Drake had never trusted Rose's first husband, Senator Hunter Ramson, though Drake had spoken many times before the Senate Armed Services Committee that the man had chaired before his fiery and—in his and the FBI's opinions— fully deserved demise. But it was impossible not to like his widow, Rose. She'd long been dubbed the First Lady of DC for her keystone position in the social set. Over the last year as the President's girlfriend and then wife, she'd proven herself to be a major asset both socially and personally.

"Pity that we'll be losing you as First Lady in three weeks. Of course, then the country would have to keep putting up with Roy here. Nobody's ready for that. I'd have suggested that you run for his office, but there's no way I'm going to stick around for another four years, even for you, Rose." Drake's mandatory retirement after thirty-five years of service had already been extended twice by President Cole—he was done.

"You will not escape that role so easily, Ranger," Roy grinned at him. That too was new; a lighter spirit that Rose had brought to the main man. "Not with your wife bringing home the worries of the office."

"And what is a former Green Beret going to do with his retirement...golf?"

Roy made a disparaging sound; neither of them had played a round of golf in their lives. "I'm sure that my lovely wife will have a brilliant idea or two."

"Make him Sarah's ambassador to the UN." Drake turned his attention to Rose.

"Oh, you must think me very cruel," she managed with a bright laugh.

"No, I—" That's when Drake noticed the shifting sunlight through the plane's windows. The oval blotch of brightness moved across the dark mahogany of the President's desk and highlighted the President himself. They were barely thirty minutes into the flight. The first turn shouldn't be for another five hours.

Drake picked up the phone without asking and punched through to the flight deck. The copilot answered.

"Report."

"We had a failure in Engine Four and have been unable to restart it. We're turning back for the US coast to—" Then Colonel Sandra Ames cursed in a very unladylike but very military manner. "Sorry, sir."

Drake didn't have to ask. Despite the heavy sound insulation of the President's onboard office, he could hear the strange cascading scale of another engine winding down. He hadn't heard the first one go.

"I won't keep bothering you, but keep the line open." Drake

switched to speakerphone and tapped the mute button so that they could listen without being heard.

"Roger that."

He and Roy exchanged a glance, and Rose didn't miss it.

"Should I be worried?"

"She'll fly comfortably on two engines. Tricky to control, as both failures are on the same side, but—" He kept listening to the pilot chatter in the background.

They spoke few words, and those were in some sort of pilot code. He wished Miranda was here to translate as he and Roy had only ever been ground pounders. But he'd picked up enough of the lingo from her to know that things were not going well.

"Negative restart on Three and Four."

That part he understood.

"Calculate best glide settings."

Glide? As in powerless glide? He'd always assumed that a 747 was more in the flying-brick category. Or was that the space shuttle? This bird had big wings; she must have some ability to glide.

"There goes Number Two."

Sure enough, the descending note of another engine fading in a long glissade sounded from the other side of the plane. He knew that a 747 couldn't maintain altitude on a single engine, but would it be enough to reach land?

Roy Cole moved out of his seat behind the desk and buckled in on the couch beside his wife.

That left Drake alone by the desk with the President's phone. He unmuted it as the last engine began its decline. The plane became eerily quiet with only the roar of the wind over the smooth lines of the fuselage. They still had power, so the auxiliary power unit must be running, but it was no more than a generator somewhere in the plane's tail.

"Report."

"Four-engine failure." This time it was General Owen who replied. "It may be possible to restart them once we descend into thicker atmosphere below fifteen thousand feet, but I don't want to sacrifice any altitude to test that sooner rather than later."

"Cause of failure?"

"Unknown. It doesn't make any sense. They simply shut down. We still have over fifty-percent fuel load, and I can verify that by the gauges as well as the feel of the aircraft."

"How about dumping fuel? Will that get us back to land?"

"Slower but not farther. Glide rate remains constant. Nice try, General, but unless we can get a restart, she's going to come down where she's going to come down. Sandra is talking to the ground for troubleshooting."

"If you can't restart?"

"We *technically* have the glide slope to reach the Delaware shore with some leeway."

Drake could hear the *however* and waited for Owen to continue.

"But the jet stream is driving hard today. It was giving us a hundred-and-thirty-kilometer-per-hour advantage. That is now a disadvantage. She's not as good a glider as the new birds."

"The ones that are five years behind schedule."

"Right. We will descend out of the jet stream effect closer to land, but the tradeoff of dropping altitude now versus distance…"

He left it hanging, and Drake didn't push him.

"Do your best, General Owen."

"Roger that, General Nason." It was far too much like saying goodbye. Owen must have thought the same as he didn't leave the call connected.

General Owen's open announcement five minutes later over

the PA echoed down the length of the massive jet. Though *Air Force One* was full of civilians, it was a military jet. He did nothing to sugarcoat his words—or their chances.

It confirmed that today the general's best wasn't going to be good enough.

4

DRAKE WAITED AS LONG AS HE COULD STAND IT, ABOUT TWENTY
seconds, before excusing himself from the crushing silence that
enveloped the President's office. The First Couple deserved
some quiet time together, especially if it proved to be their last.
He mumbled out something about going to see if he could be of
any assistance. They all knew he couldn't.

He and Roy kept it to a simple handclasp for their decades
of friendship and eight years of service together. Neither of
them had any words.

Rose unbuckled her seatbelt and stood with the innate
elegance of the great hostess she was and gave him an
unexpectedly hard hug. She also bestowed a kiss on his cheek
before returning to her husband's side. Even she found nothing
to say.

He made sure the door latched behind him so that they'd
be left alone. Stepping past the shell-shocked secretary perched
in a seat outside the President's office, he saluted the colonel
who carried the nuclear football. Sufficiently well-trained in
end-of-world scenarios to advise the President and execute his
orders in far worse conditions, the man returned the salute

sharply and only then offered a grim soldier's nod. Drake returned it and climbed the stairs to the command center on the 747's upper deck. They both knew a soldier's life came with few guarantees.

The senior comm officer was stepping out of the cockpit. He latched the door open and offered a sharp salute before waving a hand asking if Drake wanted to meet with the pilots.

He shook his head. Drake didn't need to go to the cockpit to confirm their status. The five officers who could run a global war from the upper deck of *Air Force One*—staring at their displays in grim silence—answered that. There was nothing he could do in the cockpit except get in the pilots' way.

The officer approached but didn't appear able to speak at the moment.

"I need to place some phone calls. May I have a private line?"

The man indicated the empty seat normally reserved for the President. A girl, a woman—God, they were all so young—seated at the next station over handed him a headset and then tapped the screen to bring up a keypad display.

Drake dialed as she turned back to contemplate her own, now useless, screen.

5

———————

Andi and Miranda stepped out of the Beast limo at Potomac Airfield. Meg jumped down after them and sniffed the air. Miranda did too. It smelled like...air. Actually, as illogical as she'd always found it, it smelled like coming rain. Even though rain was water, which she knew had no smell—but it did. The high clouds were already shifting to a heavy overcast, which didn't bode well for their honeymoon trip down the coast, though the temperature remained near record warmth.

Potomac was a quiet little airport for private aircraft with only a few flights each hour on a weekday. It would be busier on the weekend. They were fetching their luggage from the trunk when Miranda's phone rang.

"Hello. This is Miranda Chase. This is actually her and not a recording of her." She answered precisely as she always had since the day she'd been accused of sounding like a recording.

"You need to come find us," Drake said, getting straight to the point as he always did. Miranda appreciated that about him. Except this time she didn't understand.

Andi leaned close. Miranda must remember to answer using the speaker in the future. Not only was Andi her wife now, but she'd proven herself very useful when a call turned stressful. Miranda couldn't tolerate people yelling at her when they were upset; for reasons Miranda literally was incapable of understanding, Andi didn't seem to mind.

"Is this like a game of Hide-and-go-seek, Drake?" Miranda asked. "I haven't played that in years, but I was intrigued by it as a child. I enjoyed the counting and developing the most methodical and efficient search patterns. Though because of my autism, I couldn't bring myself to count out loud until I was five." Her first words ever had been a discussion with her live-in therapist, Tante Daniels, about the niceties of a well-played round of Hide-and-go-seek.

"No, Miranda. Not the game. I'm still on *Air Force One*. You have to find out who killed us. Promise."

"I promise, Drake. But if you're dead, how are you—"

"Thank you, Miranda. I know I can trust you. I must call Lizzy now. Take care of her for me." And he was gone.

"Please tell me I heard that wrong." Andi slid a hand around Miranda's waist. Andi remembered to make it a firm gesture; she never forgot. One of the many things Miranda had written on the list of what she appreciated about Andi when deciding her answer to Andi's marriage proposal. It was quite a long list, which had decided the matter. The list of what she didn't appreciate still remained empty.

"That was Drake. He said that someone killed him and Roy. Rose too, I suppose. He's calling Lizzy now. That was a paraphrase, not an exact quote. I've been trying to get better at that."

"Uh, you are. But that's making even less sense than usual."

"I'm sorry. He literally said, *You have to find out who killed us. Promise.* And when I did, he said—"

"Don't worry," Andi only cut her off when she was going down the wrong logical path, a very useful tool once Miranda had identified it. "The paraphrase worked fine. And you're sure it was Drake?"

"It sounded like him. And he knew my name and phone number."

"Should we call him back?"

Miranda tipped her head one way, then the other before answering. "He sounded..." she made a guess though she was generally very poor at judging emotions even when the person was present, "...a little busy. Or maybe stressed is the right emotion. Or... I'm sorry, I just don't know."

Andi looked to the east, so Miranda did as well. *Air Force One* would be at least thirty minutes aloft by now. That put them two hundred kilometers off the Delaware coast, probably at forty-five thousand feet. Not knowing the type of emergency, it was difficult to determine the possibility of the plane returning successfully. Based on Drake's assessment, there was no chance—she'd learned to trust him.

The Secret Service agent helping them extract their packs from the trunk of the Beast—Miranda was disappointed not to see a vast array of auxiliary weaponry stowed there, only the backup communication and air supply systems—seemed to turn to them in slow motion.

"Excuse me, ma'am. What did you just say?"

"Drake just called and said that he and Roy had been killed."

"General Drake Nason and President Roy Cole?"

"Yes."

"Killed?"

"That's what Drake said."

"Don't move an inch!" He strode away and raised his wrist microphone to his mouth.

"An inch is a very restrictive distance," Miranda started to look down, then gasped and moved her head back to its former position.

"All he means is, stay here," Andi told her.

"Are you sure?"

"I'm sure. You can turn to look at me or even move a little. Just don't go far."

"How far?" She turned the least amount possible to look at Andi just in case she guessed wrong about how far *too far* might be.

"Stay here by me," Andi pointed at the ground, "And we'll be fine."

Miranda moved to stand where Andi had pointed, even though it placed them so close together that they were at risk of knocking each other over. Andi hugged her. "If you stand that close to me, you get an automatic hug."

"Thank you, that's useful information. But how am I supposed to start investigating his death if I can't move?"

"I'm thinking there must be some communication mix-up. We should know soon what is actually—"

The Secret Service agent blasted into them from behind and separated them by the simple expedient of grabbing both of their upper arms without breaking stride. "Apologies, I need you to come with me. We need to hurry."

In three steps, they were at the side door of the car. Without so much as asking, he shoved them into the back seat and closed the door. Andi pushed the door open long enough for Meg to jump in with them, then closed it again. The agent circled around to the passenger door at a full sprint, slamming the trunk loudly as he passed by.

"Where—" Andi started to ask.

"That means Drake is right. He is dead." It was confusing to receive a phone call from a dead man. She'd never heard of such a thing.

Wait, she had. Some passengers on the hijacked airliners during the 9/11 attacks had phoned loved ones, knowing they were probably dead. So Drake's syntax was not precise, they weren't dead, but in his professional estimation they *were going to be.* That made much more sense.

Miranda thought about *Air Force One's* typical flight level. High enough to take a long time to descend even under disastrous circumstances. Four minutes and thirty-six seconds if they didn't exceed a parachutist's terminal velocity, calculating the six seconds to reach terminal speed. That was if she didn't factor in the coefficient for the wind drag at forty-five thousand feet to reach terminal velocity. However, at that altitude, they were above eighty-four percent of the atmosphere, so the additional drag was hardly worth calculating until they were lower in the atmosphere, especially as she didn't know their precise cruising altitude, descent angle, or wing configuration.

Miranda stopped her brain, then exhaled slowly.

Rabbit hole. Rabbit hole. Rabbit hole. She whispered it three times to herself to shift her mind away from a pointless calculation or consideration. It always made her think of small rabbits snuggled all warm and cozy in their dens, which was a good thing.

So four and a half minutes minimum descent time— another deep breath—approximately. At a best-practices fifteen-to-one glide slope and a speed of three hundred knots, they'd be aloft for a maximum of thirty minutes with a most-likely first-order approximation of twenty-six.

Either a catastrophic descent or a controlled one would allow Drake time to call his wife to say goodbye. Miranda pulled out her personal notebook.

"What was that note?" Andi leaned over to look as the Beast squealed its tires in a sharp turn outside the airfield's gate.

"If I'm ever in that situation, I want to make sure I remember to call you." The car's motion made it very difficult to write legibly.

Andi grabbed her hand and kissed it before holding it to

her cheek, making it even harder to finish the note with her other hand—but she managed.

As the Beast cleared the airport, they picked up a police escort.

Before they reached the White House grounds, an armed helicopter flew low above them.

"What are we doing here? If Drake and Roy are crashing out to sea, that's where I should be."

Andi didn't answer, instead holding her hand tighter.

Meg settled in for a nap across her toes in the footwell.

6
___

Sarah Feldman had been in the Oval Office many times, but none of them helped her now.

She'd been here for meetings as the UN Ambassador, then as the National Security Advisor, and eventually as the Vice President. Now she stood here as the President-elect.

But this was the first time since the election that President Cole was out of the country. In two weeks, this would be her office. That chair behind the Roosevelt Desk would be her chair.

For now? She remained paralyzed two steps into the Oval. One of the secretaries had the decency to quietly close the door and leave her to face her fears in private.

"What am I doing here?"

She had no answer and, as she was the only one in the room, she was left with that lack. Having had terrible taste in men, twice, she was alone on that front as well. Which was a pity, she could really use a strong shoulder other than her own at the moment.

Over the last eight weeks since the election, she'd made every effort to form a coherent government as well as formulate an action plan. Bless Roy Cole all the way down to his shoes. He'd gladly answered her endless questions, walked her through the hidden ramifications of every security briefing, and helped stave off any incipient panic attacks by the simple expedient of assuring her they were perfectly normal.

He'd also refused to answer any policy questions. *Need to ask those of yourself and your team, Sarah, not some old gaffer twenty years your senior.* In his mid-sixties, he still boasted one of the sharpest minds in the business. She'd half-circumvented his stance by asking the reasoning behind his various past decisions; the ones he'd included her in and especially the ones he hadn't. He'd permitted the workaround with one of his annoying-as-hell all-knowing half smiles. Though she figured that he'd earned it fair and square. After eight years in the chair, he was the most all-knowing person alive about the duties and challenges of the US presidency.

She had every intention of keeping his post-presidency phone number on speed dial.

For the next five days, she'd be pinch-hitting from the front lines while he traveled.

Pinch-hitting, hell! She could hear the military snap that Roy Cole had never quite left behind—at least when the cameras weren't directed his way. He'd made sure that she'd been in on every decision since the day of her election, especially the hard ones. And for the next five days he'd said that he wanted to travel and do the Final Farewell Tour—and not worry about anything else. As if. But she'd try to at least keep the worst of the nonsense off his plate.

She'd stood this side of the Roosevelt Desk so many times over the years. But today she would sit in the President's chair if it killed her. Per her schedule, she should have a quiet hour to perform one of her favorite tricks.

Sarah liked to sit in the *Other Chair.* When she couldn't do it physically, she did it mentally. Before any key meeting, she would do her best to sit in the other person's chair, even when it was the chair in front of her own desk. She would imagine she was the French ambassador, the Secretary General of the UN, or even General Drake Nason having a meeting with her. Then she'd start asking herself questions.

What was *their* view of this meeting?

What was their most likely agenda?

Biggest fears?

Greatest hopes?

This was her first chance to sit in the President's chair uninterrupted and think about how the nation and the world looked from the highest seat. It encompassed both a view of the thirty-five feet of the Oval Office and of the entire world beyond.

What was *their* view, the ubiquitous *they,* of the first female President? The first Jewish one as well. What would they think of a forty-six-year-old woman who had ridden into office on Roy Cole's strengths, the women-and-youth vote, and a shortsightedly fear-based campaign by her opponent that her people had managed to deflect until it fed on itself instead of the voting populace?

After several deep breaths, she'd managed two of the six steps toward the chair—which just might be glowering at her presumption—when all four doors of the Oval Office burst open at once.

"What did I—" Thankfully she didn't have a chance to complete the daft question of her possible guilt for daring approach the hallowed seat before two agents took her arms and ninety percent of her weight. The others encircled her with their weapons drawn.

She knew a White House crash when she saw one. Except usually it was about staying in place, well back from the bulletproof windows, until whatever suicidal fence jumper had been apprehended and read his rights while lying face down in the South Lawn. Because the Oval Office faced the South Lawn, they almost always came in over the far wider expanse, leaving plenty of time to stop them.

Not this time.

Her protection detail formed a phalanx with her at the center. The head of her detail, Kali Singh, took the point position as they raced left down the corridor outside the Oval. At the Chief of Staff's office, they took a sharp right. Felicia Cowell stuck her head out to see what was going on.

"Grab her," Sarah shouted at one of the agents.

The squeak of surprise and the sudden clatter of heels told her that her right-hand woman was now in tow.

They slammed into the lift and plummeted down into the relatively new PEOC—Presidential Emergency Operations Center—that a prior administration had built beneath the West Wing's Situation Room.

Five stories down, through the first bank-vault-thick door, a twenty-second hold while the air was flushed by a high velocity fan. It would strip away most contaminants. The airlock was also a kill zone. It, as easily, could have been evacuated of all air if someone managed to get this far.

Then they were through the second equally massive door.

Once inside, everyone ground to a halt. Sarah almost smiled. They were milling around the security foyer like a herd of cats. Even the PEOC's security guards looked at a loss to explain the sudden influx of personnel into their quiet domain.

"Well?"

Special Agent Kali Singh had been decisive since the moment she took over Sarah's protection detail—the same day that Roy Cole had nominated her to replace the murdered Vice President. Sarah had liked having Kali—the goddess of time, death, and destruction—protecting her. The woman barely broke five-five but Sarah had watched her take down men twice her bulk on the practice mats—well-trained men. As the daughter of two Marine Corps officers, Sarah knew a top fighter when she met one.

Now, Special Agent Singh looked lost.

"Kali?"

"Yes, ma'am?"

"Pardon my language but—What the hell?"

"I wish I was knowing, ma'am. We received word that President Roy Cole and General Drake Nason were dead."

For lack of any chairs, Sarah shoved aside some forms and sat on the head of security's desk. What it lacked in decorum, it made up for in a welcome solidity that her knees could no longer claim. "And how did we receive this word?"

Kali blushed, her mid-tone skin turning beet red. "I'm told that General Drake Nason reported their deaths."

"Should I repeat myself?"

"No, ma'am. I fully understand your expletive." In three years, despite the goddess she'd been named for, Kali had never cursed in her presence. "We are awaiting further information."

"Has anyone tried calling them?"

"Calling them?"

"They're on *Air Force One* together."

"They are the ones who placed the call." Kali stopped abruptly. "Yes. That is correct. I am sorry. I was so very focused on moving you to safety. That was my first priority. I was told that General Nason called Miranda Chase with orders to find out who had killed him and the President. I told the agent who overheard the conversation to bring her here immediately, then I moved you to safety. That is all the information I am so far having."

Any other source, Sarah might laugh off. But Miranda, however convoluted her myriad personality quirks might be, was invariably careful in her communications. Sarah rather hoped that her *accuracy* was in question.

7

———

BEING THE DAUGHTER OF TWO MARINE CORPS OFFICERS, SARAH also knew how to choose her priorities and called out orders to Kali as she moved. "If Miranda Chase is en route, make sure they let her in. And, no, I don't care if we've crashed the White House or not—get her inside."

If she was the last person to talk to *Air Force One*, Sarah wanted to wring out every detail she could extract.

She barely heard when Kali reported that *Air Force One* had declared an emergency. *No shit, Sherlock.*

"Go to COGCON 3." That would require key government officials to notify the Watch Office of their locations. The first step down from peacetime in the Continuity of Government Readiness Condition scale. But it didn't feel like enough. "Find Vice President-elect Crawford and the Speaker of the House, make sure they are both safe and separately well away from here. Do *not* go to COGCON 2, we don't want to cause a panic until we know more." DC newsies would recognize an evacuation of Congress, the Supreme Court, and the White House. It would be splashed on every screen in the country within minutes.

That took care of the civilian government, not the military.

"Go to DEFCON 4. Get General Elizabeth Gray-Nason on the line ASAP." Elizabeth had hyphenated her last name at Sarah's suggestion, because Sarah was tired of mixing up communications between the two General Nason's. "Better yet, get her here as well. I need her advice on whether we go to DEFCON 3."

Sarah had to stop and double check her memory that she got it right. Why couldn't they have numbered COGCON and the military's Defense Readiness Condition with the same scale?

She waved Kali away and stepped into the President's PEOC office. There was no time for slow approaches or personal fears now; she dropped into the President's chair, waved for Felicia to close the door, and tapped the intercom key. "Get me a direct line to *Air Force One*. Preferably the President."

The Marine Corps officers that the National Security Council placed to monitor the Situation Room and the PEOC swung into action. While she waited she stared at the blank white walls of the rectangular room. Her desk sat at one end, facing a small group of chairs and a bank of monitors. In the middle stood a conference table with ten chairs and at the far end, a podium with the Presidential seal on it. Behind it was a dark blue velvet curtain and in front a pair of video cameras for addressing the nation. She definitely wouldn't be doing that.

Sarah managed not to cry out with relief when she heard Roy Cole's voice sound over the phone less than thirty seconds later. "In my chair yet, Sarah?"

"Not the one upstairs, but I am in PEOC. It's not as comfortable as I'd imagined. But it's very good to hear your voice."

"You're in the hot seat; never let it become too comfortable and you'll do okay. Sadly, there's a fair chance that it's yours now."

"But—"

"Four-engine failure. You need to get Miranda Chase to—"

"Apparently General Nason already took care of that."

"She's an easy woman to doubt. Take my advice—don't."

Sarah had barely met the woman other than at yesterday's wedding. They'd only worked together tangentially, except for once, and that had lasted under thirty minutes—four years ago. That scattered her thoughts in several directions. One of Sarah's strengths was processing all those different paths simultaneously—or close enough that no one had been able to prove to her satisfaction that she did otherwise.

The President had chosen to give Miranda and Andi the first White House wedding in eighteen years. Okay, Miranda Chase needed listening to, at least until Sarah could make up her own mind about the woman's reliability.

An attack? Or a maintenance issue? Assume the worst, hope for the best, and shoot down the middle. She needed to get the military moving, at least at the command level, so she had to keep this short.

"I assume that you're attempting to return to the coast, Roy?"

"So I'm told. It's only been five minutes, but I'm told we won't make it."

"I'll make sure a rescue team is headed your way." She waved a hand at Felicia, who sat at the conference table, picked up another line, and began issuing orders.

She heard Felicia say, "Give them no reason, Admiral, we need to keep it the hell off CNN. Just get their asses moving."

Felicia gave her a helpless look and held out the phone in her direction.

Sarah didn't even bother taking it. Instead she half shouted, "Do it, Admiral. On my authority as Vice President and—" she swallowed hard "—*acting* President Sarah Feldman."

Felicia listened for a moment, nodded, and hung up. Then

she dialed again to make sure a couple of escort jets were scrambled in *Air Force One's* direction.

Sarah turned her attention back to the President.

Roy Cole actually had the wherewithal to laugh briefly. "You'll do great, Sarah. Maybe we'll get a Miracle on the Hudson moment."

She didn't manage to join in his laugh. Captain Sullenberger had managed to ease an Airbus A320 down on the perfectly calm surface of the Hudson River after a bird strike had killed both his engines. He was also a glider pilot and truly had performed a modern miracle, saving every single life. Along with every other New Yorker, she'd been transfixed by the coverage for hours—which had included numerous experts saying that what he'd done was technically impossible.

Sarah tapped the mute key and selected the intercom again. "Get me the current sea state off the Delaware coast."

The Marine responded immediately, which meant he'd been monitoring the call. "It's a Four, ma'am." This time she'd take the efficiency over any privacy concerns. From the family vacations of her youth out to Montauk at the tip of Long Island, she knew exactly what that meant. Sea State 4 translated as two-meter-high waves ready to catch a wing tip and shatter a 747.

She released the intercom and unmuted the line to *Air Force One.* "We'll hope for the best, Mr. President."

"Plan for the worst and shoot down the middle, as you always say. I'll gladly take the middle on this."

"Me too, Mr. President. Is there anything else I can do for you?"

"Yes, Sarah Feldman. Trust your people, but moreover, trust your gut. Goodbye."

It took her a moment to manage, "Goodbye, Roy."

But he'd already hung up the phone.

8
____

"I'm sorry. The order only stipulates the admission of Ms. Chase."

"No. No. No! No!" Miranda wrapped both hands around Andi's upper arm as the guards tried to separate them. Meg set up a loud whine and leaned hard against her calf.

The Beast had descended into the parking garage under the Treasury Building and dropped them at the entry to the tunnel that led to the White House basement.

"The President-elect wishes to see you, Ms. Chase, immediately."

"No. No. No! No!" She held on tighter. Meg's whine escalated. It was a sure sign that she wasn't imagining things, but was actually in a high-stress situation. High stress and her autism were never a good combination. Meg's validation did offer some comfort by confirming that what she was feeling was actually her real feelings, but not enough for her to let go of Andi.

"It will be okay, Miranda." Andi kept her voice calm. "I'll go to NTSB headquarters and find the others. We can—"

"No! Drake is dying or dead already, and he is separated from Lizzy. I won't be separated from you."

The guard stared at her as if he'd just been...poked with something very sharp. She liked that metaphor, but it didn't make her feel any better about not being with Andi. This time she wouldn't be freeing up a hand to pat herself on the back.

"I will not be separated from you." Miranda knew she was repeating herself. Interesting. The repetition *did* serve the purpose of reinforcing her initial statement. Maybe she'd finally found the purpose of repetition, though that didn't appear to be how most people used it. "I—" No, a third repetition would serve no discernable purpose. So she just held on tight and said, "I refuse." It was a repetition of sentiment but not a literal restatement. That too worked...appropriately.

Another car pulled up behind the Beast and Lizzy stepped out. Her face... Something was wrong with her face, but Miranda couldn't tell what. And she wasn't letting go of Andi's arm to pull out her notebook with the emotions reference page to figure it out.

"Hi, Miranda. What's wrong?"

She briefly envied Lizzy's ability to read emotions without a cheat sheet. "They're trying to separate me from Andi."

"Pull out your IDs."

Miranda released one hand from around Andi biceps long enough to hand over her ID. Then held onto Andi again. Andi stopped Meg's whining by leaning down to scoop her up. She swarmed so strongly into Miranda's arms that she had to release one hand from Andi's biceps but she kept hold with the other. Meg lay her head heavily on Miranda's shoulder, which felt nice.

Lizzy took their IDs and her own to the security desk. "Three people with Yankee White clearance to enter the White House." Yankee White wasn't merely cleared to be near the

President; they were all three cleared to be armed in his presence.

"I'm sorry, General. The White House is crashed, locked down, and that isn't good enough to get through."

"I'm not going into a crash without Andi. I don't care if it's a plane or the White House. I'm not." Miranda knew she wasn't making the most sense but kept her grip on Andi—though she didn't tighten it further as she didn't want to cut off the blood supply to Andi's arm. Andi was the only thing that did make sense at the moment.

Lizzy pulled out her phone, dialed a number, and tapped for the speaker.

"General Gray-Nason. How close are you?" Miranda recognized the President-elect's voice.

"Stuck at the Treasury Building Tunnel entrance with Miranda Chase and Andi Wu. They aren't letting Captain Wu through as she's not on the cleared list. Miranda is finding that upsetting."

"Well, shit! Tell whatever agent is blockading them that if they don't want a personal ass-kicking from the President-elect, i.e. yours truly, they'd better clear her damn fast. Better yet. Kali," she called out, "Kick whoever's ass for me."

That was enough for the guard to beep all three of their IDs. Two agents led them through the barrier and into the long tunnel. A pair of massive doors closed behind them, sealing off the tunnel. The tunnel itself was comforting; Miranda liked the feeling of being enclosed. It was wood-paneled and as well-lit as a hotel corridor—the nice kind.

"We're on our way." Lizzy disconnected the call.

As they were let through, one of the guards whispered, "Is the Chairman of the Joint Chiefs really dead?"

"Maybe. Roy too." Miranda answered because she finally *did* recognize Lizzy's expression—she was very close to being violently sick.

"The *President?*" The security door slammed shut behind them, so she didn't have a chance to interpret the odd tone of his voice—it had sort of...squeaked.

The tunnel from the Treasury Building to the White House was long enough for Miranda to scrape back some degree of internal equilibrium. Enough, at least, for Meg to slide down and once again trot along beside her.

They entered the White House grounds underneath the East Wing, passing through it, the Residence, and the West Wing to reach the PEOC. The Secret Service all knew something bad was happening, but the rest of the White House appeared to be operating relatively normally. Phones rang, people talked, but no one was allowed to move from their desks. As the three of them were escorted past every lockdown barrier without a single hesitation, she could feel their eyes following her.

Miranda didn't like being looked at, but as long as Andi held her hand, she would stay focused on that.

9

THE TWO-HUNDRED-AND-SEVENTY-FOOT-LONG, MEDIUM-endurance US Coast Guard cutter *Bear* stood ten meters off the pier at USCG Base Portsmouth, Virginia.

"Long damn cruise, Skipper." His XO made it sound as if it had been five years instead of three months.

"We got it done, Zeb." But it felt good to be home. Just like his father before him, he'd been sailing out of Portsmouth for most of twenty years. He breathed in the atypically warm air rich with evergreen and dead leaves. Damp, without the heavy humidity of the southern reaches felt as good as a shower. Even the busy industry of Portsmouth Base brought along the familiar taste of metal hot from welding and ship's paint. It smelled like nowhere else in the world.

Commander Randy Davidson kept an eye on the helmsman. After twelve weeks at sea, patrolling the shipping routes as far south as Rio, an overeager docking might be in the books. But the man brought them in clean, coming to a dead stop exactly in place—not an easy task in a boat almost as long as a football field. She'd been built for seaworthiness and speed, not for cruise-ship-level stability underfoot, which also made her as twitchy as a sullen teenage girl asked to be civil in public. Gods above and below, were his twins really going to be teenagers in high school next year?

He gave the man a clap on the shoulder for a job well done for bringing the ship in so neat and clean. Not a chance of his handling the twins half so well.

A glance at the deck below and he could see the ABs, the able-bodied seamen, getting ready to toss the monkey's fists across to the pier. The light polypropylene lines had their ends woven into six-inch balls ideal for casting ashore. They would be used to drag the bigger heavy lines across the gap. Once the shore crew looped those over handy bollards, the *Bear's* deck winches could haul them to the dockside.

He sighed. It would probably require another day before he could get off the ship. It took time to clear seven tons of cocaine and eleven prisoners. A haul that size would attract every DEA hack, media hack, and pain-in-his-ass Coast Guard hack to create a fanfare. It was his seventh major drug bust and the *Bear's* twenty-fifth, which made it old hat for both of them.

His twins were playing in a big school concert tomorrow. First and second viola; he'd been more of an electric guitar man himself. He'd been hoping to make it ashore for that; fifty-fifty at this point.

It would be easier if he was at sea—of course, almost everything was. If he was in port but missed the concert because of red tape and paperwork, they might not forgive him. Worse, Doreen might not. She'd known he was a career man when she'd signed aboard but each passing year proved harder rather than easier. Staffing was down across the services, which meant longer deployments to keep this coast guarded. At least the six-month forays to the Med and the Arabian Sea had tapered off...though Israel was now screwing that up by attacking anyone not wearing a yarmulke. Who knew what would happen over there now.

Not his problem today.

He watched the bow and stern monkey's fists fly free, trailing their nine-millimeter haul lines. One arced so high that it almost cleared the far side of the wide service pier. He wasn't the only one eager for this cruise to be done. Once he sounded shore leave, there'd be a hundred bodies racing to be first down the gangway. He'd wager a third would fall flat on their faces when they hit solid land. After this long a deployment, they'd all lost their land legs.

The distinct alarm bell of an encrypted high-priority message sounded.

Probably a welcome-home message from some shorebird who didn't understand the purpose of the system.

"What have you got, XO?" The ashore line handlers had gathered the fore-and-aft hauling lines. They were ready to begin pulling across the first pair of fifty-five-millimeter mooring lines.

"It's a little odd, Skipper. *Put to sea immediately. Head east-northeast until further notice.*"

"Let me see that." He picked up the handset and punched for the deck PA. "Hold all mooring operations. Repeat, hold all mooring operations."

Everyone on the deck and pier turned to look up at him on the bridge.

Zeb handed him the printout that a high-priority message always generated.

That was it—except for the bone-chilling phrase: *All haste!* He'd never seen that particular phrase outside of war.

"Is this some kind of dumb-ass drill?"

Zeb simply pointed out the window. Their sister ships, *Harriet Lane* and *Northland,* were both in port, and both were blowing the black smoke of an emergency start on their big diesels.

"Anything on the *gouge train?*" The USCG rumor mill was usually ahead of most nonsense.

"Nothing, sir."

Davidson took one last look down the line and saw that several of the forty-seven-foot MLBs—motor life boats—had crews on the scramble.

He hated himself for the moment of relief. Search-and-rescue. Big one if they were calling out all three cutters in port, and close ashore if they were kicking the MLBs loose. At least he wouldn't have to explain to Doreen and the twins why he hadn't been able to get off the ship sooner.

He again keyed the PA. "All hands. All hands. Retrieve lines. Prepare to put to sea immediately."

The blank stares were still directed up at the command bridge.

"I know people. Makes no sense. But we've got our orders. On the double." He kept the mike keyed open for the next order. "Helmsman, best speed to sea and damn any in-harbor limits. Move it!"

That lit the fire under the deck crew's behinds. The heaving lines were retrieved. By the vibrating deck beneath his feet, he could feel the seventy-three hundred horsepower of his own diesels plowing into the twin screws.

He beat the *Harriet Lane* and the *Northland* into the Elizabeth River—a lead he wouldn't be relinquishing. As he passed US Naval Station Norfolk, they were already making fifteen knots with five of the 47-MLBs at his side. Together they kicked a hell of a wake into the Norfolk Navy yard. Couldn't happen to nicer people.

Who the hell was important enough for all this?

He also noticed a distinct lack of activity in the US Navy's largest base anywhere. Commander Davidson could feel squids staring at him as he raced by, but he still had no answers.

10

"Ms. Chase, what can you tell me?" Sarah asked as the three women and one dog stepped into the President's office in the PEOC.

"Your conversational openers are as efficient as Drake's and more efficient than Roy's."

Sarah sighed. Just because *Air Force One* was on its way to crashing, didn't mean that Miranda would realize that was the only thing of importance at the moment. She didn't have time for patience.

"Elizabeth?" She'd never been comfortable calling a two-star general Lizzy. That would be even more true when she became a four-star if the Senate confirmed Sarahs' nominating her to replace Drake.

General Elizabeth Gray-Nason turned to Miranda and spoke in a calm, even tone that Sarah couldn't have managed at the moment. "Miranda, can you tell us the chances of survival of *Air Force One*?"

"Not without knowing all of their flight parameters."

"So find them out." Sarah pointed at a phone, one well off

to the side. "Punch Nine and the Marines will get you everything."

Miranda moved away with Captain Andi Wu in tow and the bright click of her terrier's nails on the parquet flooring following along.

Sarah turned her attention to Elizabeth. "I'm so sorry to not offer more sympathy, but what's the word from your husband?"

"Drake is in the command center of *Air Force One*, but this is out of his hands." Her voice was tight. Though she appeared to be a mild, slender, Japanese-Eurasian in her mid-fifties, she had commanded a combat flight of F-16s at one time and risen to be a two-star general in charge of the National Reconnaissance Office—one of the largest and most clandestine agencies of the US government. She knew how to keep it under control. "We didn't speak much about the flight."

"Understood. What's my tactical situation?" It just slipped out that way, as if she was already the President.

Elizabeth's light skin paled further, but she managed to sit when Sarah nodded toward one of the seats facing her desk. "Unchanged as far as we know. No sign of any launches or other overt activities among friend or foe. We're still inside the first thirty minutes, it only feels longer. I see you went to DEFCON 4 but not 3. I think that is an appropriate match for the current circumstances. I suggest we contact Director Reese at the CIA..."

Sarah pointed her joined index and middle fingers at Felicia, who immediately turned for the phone.

"...to further assess any back-channel chatter that may become relevant in—"

"Ninety seconds, plus or minus seven." Miranda spoke.

She'd moved so silently that Sarah flinched in surprise to see her standing beside the desk. No clicking dog nails in warning, as her therapy dog was now curled up and napping in one of the conference table chairs. Felicia stopped halfway through messaging Clarissa and stared at Miranda in abject horror.

"I'm sorry to interrupt, but time is of the essence at this juncture. I do not project a high chance of survival, but every crash is unique. As this one hasn't become a crash yet, I can't provide any accurate assessment—which we won't know as a fact—in approximately eighty-two seconds. A water-based landing tends to be far more abrupt than a land-based one—typically ranging between one and three seconds with the extreme outlier of nine seconds' duration for US Airways Flight 1549's landing in the Hudson River. Assuming a landing attempt at the edge of *Air Force One's* stall speed of a hundred and seventy miles per hour, in a worst-case scenario they would experience an eight-g deceleration, breaking many of their necks depending on their position in the aircraft and several other factors. The captain said—"

"You spoke with the captain during a flight crisis?" Sarah placed her hands flat on the desk to stop them from shaking.

"It seemed the most expedient way to gather the needed information to answer your question. I also spoke to Roy. He's always been very kind to me and my therapist taught me that it would be rude if I didn't say goodbye. The captain said—"

"You spoke to *President Cole?*" There was a ringing in her ears. There must be, because she wasn't hearing this right.

"Yes. The aircraft is—"

"What did he have to say?"

"Who? The captain or the President? The crash will occur in the next forty-three seconds. If you keep interrupting me, my analysis will become moot as it will be superseded by actual events."

"Do we have a visual on the aircraft?"

"Your conversational style is very difficult to follow, President-elect Feldman. Yes. Do you wish to see it?"

Sarah managed a *please* instead of a snarl. Miranda called

on the Marines to put an image on the big monitor. It was a split-screen view.

To one side was a pilot's view from *Air Force One*. It was overlaid by a whole array of numbers and little diagrams that Sarah had little basis for interpreting.

Elizabeth's sharp curse didn't bode well. Nice to know the woman wasn't wholly unflappable. She'd given little sign that her husband was aboard. If she was like Sarah, she'd grieve later—in private.

But the white crests on the too-visible waves and no hint of land in sight? *That* Sarah could interpret without a problem.

The other half of the screen was again split. The lower half a radar image, showing a single point of green light straight ahead. The upper half, she could tell by the shimmer of the blades sweeping across the top, was the view out the front of a helicopter. A tiny spark of white must be *Air Force One*—very low to the waves.

Sarah took a careful breath. "Ms. Chase, could you please interpret what I'm seeing. I'm not a pilot."

Miranda moved to stand beside the display and pointed at some numbers. "General John Owen has entered the final descent. He is presently flying at a hundred feet, bleeding speed for lift. This is particularly effective as he's low enough to ride the ground effect, such as it is over such rough waves. That's when air trapped between a surface and the bottom of a wing literally pushes back. It is giving him time to choose his landing but it will not assist him in reaching shore. As there is no chance of reaching shore, I had him turn toward the US Coast Guard ships that Felicia called out of port."

Miranda pointed to the two smaller views. "I had Andi ask the captain of the Medium Endurance Cutter *Bear* to launch his Dolphin MH-65 search-and-rescue helo toward the estimated impact location, which he was kind enough to do once she explained the situation. Though he did seem rather surprised by the aircraft model being a VC-25A."

Sarah sighed. Hiding *Air Force One's* identity had bought her over twenty minutes. Far more than she'd expected.

"General Owen is targeting the minimum landing speed to mitigate what he can of the impact. You can see by the numbers in the upper right that Colonel Sandra Ames is still attempting to restart the engines without success."

Numbers kept changing on the screen in a bewildering array, but she saw nothing to cause doubt in Miranda's interpretation.

On the radar view, the bright blip moved closer toward another of the static arced lines on the display. Closer to the helicopter, but she had no idea by how much or where the nearest land lay.

The view from the helicopter resolved from a bright spark to a blue-and-white toy model that quickly expanded into a 747 mere feet above the waves.

Another monitor lit up with two views. All they showed was an expanse of waves, but they were passing by *very* fast. Sarah assumed they were views from the scrambled fighter jets racing to the scene. It was only seconds before they raced overhead. Now they showed *Air Force One* like a giant cross shape barely above the rough ocean.

"There, that's his minimum speed, also called his stall speed," Miranda pointed at a *170* on the screen, not distracted by the new and alarming view. "Presently at fifty feet, his impact will occur in the next nine seconds."

Her voice was horrifyingly calm.

Sarah noted that she had risen to her own feet and planted her fists on the desk, but she couldn't release their clench. And if she stopped bracing against them, she might collapse face-first onto the desk.

"They'll be landing at..." Miranda pointed at a set of

numbers that were latitude and longitude. For three long seconds Miranda remained unmoving.

Then her eyes rolled back in her head, and she dropped to the floor.

Andi cried out and rushed to her side.

Above them, the right-hand image showed the tiny-with-distance plane catching a wave crest with one wing and pummeling into the sea.

The blip on the radar image flashed ten times brighter—the visual display showed the broad shape of an entire wing sticking vertically into the air—and then both the wing and the green dot disappeared.

Sarah held her breath through four long heartbeats that sounded absurdly slow—as if there was room between each to reach her hands out and undo what had just happened. But there was nothing to see other than the empty waves and the blank radar scan.

The view from *Air Force One*'s cockpit was black. After four more heartbeats, so drawn out that they hurt her chest, bright green letters appeared on the screen.

No signal.

11

____

Air Force One did not go quietly to her grave.

Out of options, John and Sandra had discussed the best landing tactic in between attempts to restart the engines and the call from the air-crash investigator. He'd heard of Miranda Chase though he'd never met her. It was a relief to have input from the outside. They'd spent precious seconds discussing extreme engine restart methods—two of which weren't in any manual he'd ever read but sounded promising. Neither had yet worked. He wished he'd thought to ask her opinion on one more point; with a Sea State 4 awaiting them on the surface, should they land with, against, or across the waves? The general rule was with, but these were not long, deep-ocean rollers; these waves were angry.

It was obvious that landing *with* the waves was better than against them. Even at a stall speed of a hundred and seventy knots, they'd be moving a hundred and fifty faster than the water; against the waves would be a hundred and ninety knots —two hundred and twenty miles per hour—relative speed to the water. They would also expend precious altitude executing a banked turn. If they landed parallel to the waves, they might put the fuselage into a trough and let the waves to either side exert even pressures against both wings. But they'd have to catch the trough perfectly. He'd seen the videos of a commercial jet that planted one wing first—the destruction had been horrendous.

General John Owen had captained *Air Force One* for four of President Cole's eight years in office. He'd never floated a 747 this far down a runway; it wasn't as if he was going to overrun the pavement. This was not how he wanted his record to end.

The stall buzzer sounded, yet he held the nose up mere meters above the waves. He glanced over at Sandra. She'd have made—would make...he hoped—a fine pilot to take over his role.

Her simple nod wished him luck.

He nodded back his thanks for all their flights together and turned his full attention to the landing.

Maybe if he nosed up hard at the last instant. Nosed up, using the belly of the plane and wings like a massive air brake the way the old Space Shuttle had. Then, when the tail caught the waves, he could commit a colossal belly flop into the ocean. To do that he had to—

12

A SERIES OF OCEAN WAVES IS NOT A SYMMETRIC, CONSISTENT medium. The period between waves is affected by wind speed and ocean depth. Gusts, currents, and distant storms can each add their own factors to the final ever-changing wave form.

The Elizabeth River of Virginia is not one of the nation's great waterways. No massive Ice Age drainage occurred to create a huge undersea delta across the continental shelf like the lethal sand bar guarding the entry to the Columbia River in the Pacific Northwest. Nor does the Elizabeth drain a great silt-producing watershed, creating an extended underwater landform far from shore like the Mississippi River Delta. Not even a deep canyon like the one New York's Hudson River sliced into two hundred kilometers of the continental shelf.

Generally overwhelmed by the effects from Chesapeake Bay, the Elizabeth River still had placed its own unique stamp upon the underwater landscape. The ten-kilometer-long tidal estuary that defines the Elizabeth River has existed for thousands of years. Its watershed includes a section of the Great Dismal Swamp. Most of these fine muds were swept aside, overshadowed by the effects of the great tidal pump of the Chesapeake Bay and its twelve thousand square kilometer watershed.

But the Elizabeth River did drive some the Great Dismal's fines out to sea with each tidal flush of the estuary. These were deposited as a gentle range of deepwater hills and valleys, trending northeast from the mouth of the Chesapeake. They extended along the deep coastal plain, only to be gradually swept north by the Gulf Stream currents.

A severely out-of-season hurricane had passed well to the south two days earlier. Only the forecasters and the climate-change deniers debated whether it was late season or early season, everyone else agreed there were no defined storm seasons anymore.

The storm's low pressure had allowed a massive storm surge to inundate the Georgia coast. Now, the post-storm rise in the barometric pressure pushed down on the ocean's surface, squeezing down as if a giant had stomped his foot on the ocean over a fifty-thousand-square-kilometer area off Savannah. It sent a pulse of water north over the continental shelf.

This pulse was forced toward the surface when it struck the low underwater hills created over the millennia by the Elizabeth River. The extra burst of water shifted a hundred million tons of fine sand to the north, some by meters, some by tens of kilometers.

Driving against the barrier of underwater hills, the water surge created a rolling wave crest, moving from south to north. No surface ship would have detected this without very sensitive equipment. The ocean in the area gradually became one-point-three meters deeper for the duration of the surge's passing.

The USGC cutters *Bear, Harriet Lane,* and *Northland* certainly detected nothing as they raced toward *Air Force One's* projected landing zone.

However, the generally east-to-west surface waves

approaching the coast interfered unpredictably with the rising crest of the deeper south-to-north pulse.

Sailors call it a *confused sea* when the regular pattern of waves is broken. Unlike Sarah Feldman, neither General John Owen nor Colonel Sandra Ames were sailors, not that it would have helped them once they flew into the affected area.

The neat lines of waves they'd been crossing above jumbled into chaos as *Air Force One* expended the last of its carefully nursed lift. In some places, waves disappeared as a peak met a trough and they canceled each other out. When two troughs met, deep holes bigger than any fishing boat could appear, only to be replaced seconds later by a towering peak of water when two wave peaks overlapped.

This was precisely what happened as General Owen prepared for his final last-ditch effort to create a survivable landing. He let the 747 settle until the biggest waves licked the bottom of the fuselage. He braced himself to heave back on the yoke and plant the airplane's tail hard in the water like an anchor. Or would the airplane's massive rudder act as a ship's rudder allowing him some modicum of control in how she belly-flopped? Only one way to find out; he kept his toes light on the pedals in case this worked.

General John Owen sent one last prayer for salvation aloft just in case God was listening on this overcast gray morning.

Warm air driven north by the storm had increased the temperature thirty-four degrees above the normal range for the first full week of January. If it hadn't, the denser, cooler air of a normal midwinter morning would have added fourteen more tons of lift throughout his descent. Though insignificant in comparison to the plane's overall weight, it would have lifted *Air Force One* clear of what happened next.

The low mud hills of the continental shelf drove the heart of the deep-running northbound storm surge to the surface beneath an already large wave. In a period of one-point-eight seconds, the two-meter wave rolling along steadily ahead of *Air Force One's* flight path grew to a towering six-meter giant called a rogue wave. The ten-meter width of the wave, generated by the interference pattern, heaved a million kilograms of water into the 747's path. At a thousand tons, the rogue wave out-massed the airplane by a factor of five times.

Had the fuselage plowed into it, it would have slowed the plane enough that as many as two-thirds of those aboard would have survived. However, the greatest mass of the wave rose directly ahead of the Number Four engine, hanging farthest to the right on the wing's underside. At a hundred and fifty knots, a hundred and seventy-two miles per hour, relative speed, the engine acted like an anchor tossed over the side of a speeding boat in shallow water.

It stopped in place.

The stress sheared the four breakaway bolts holding the engine to the wing and Number Four rapidly sank beneath the waves. But the damage was already done.

At the impact, General Owen instinctively yanked back on the control yoke to complete the maneuver he'd been nurturing in his thoughts. But with its right wing buried in the wave, *Air Force One* no longer had the lift to raise the nose clear of the maelstrom in one last desperate effort to save the lives of those aboard.

Though relieved of the burden of the Number Four engine, the right wing was twisted down by the impact. It acted like a propellor blade that drove the whole right wing deeper into the water. General Owen's final maneuver generated powerful lift in the left wing, raising it high above the waves.

Air Force One cartwheeled.

13

———

The strongest part of any plane is the wing box where the wings attach to the fuselage. With the right wing boring downward, the left wing—that shone so brightly and so briefly on the US Coast Guard helicopter's radar—stuck high in the air before the fuselage twisted around to plunge nose first into a wave trough. The trough formed by the same wave interference pattern close ahead of the rogue was also far deeper than normal.

Streamlined to fly through air, *Air Force One* dove cleanly into the ocean depths.

The skin of the airplane was designed to keep pressure inside the aircraft when exposed to the low-pressure environment of two-tenths normal pressure existing outside the airplane at its normal flight level. It was not designed to keep out water pressure measured in tons per square foot.

The fuselage of the 747-200B used as *Air Force One* measures two hundred and thirty-two feet long, over seventy meters. Before it achieved neutral buoyancy due to the air trapped inside, the nose of the plane reached forty meters below the surface. Had General Owen chosen to dump the twenty-eight thousand gallons of fuel from the wing tanks, they would have been automatically refilled with nitrogen to avoid a flashover fire like the one that destroyed TWA 800.

This would have had two effects. One was that the plane's glide, while landing in the same spot, would have taken seven minutes longer and the storm surge would have already passed through that area. The second was that the dumping of fuel would have made the plane a hundred and ninety thousand pounds lighter, which would have kept the plane from penetrating so deeply into the water.

He hadn't. Fuel is only typically dumped if an emergency is declared shortly after takeoff and the plane is too heavy to safely land.

The pilot's view from the USCG helicopter only revealed the tail section of *Air Force One,* which stuck straight up in the air. The fighter jets had overflown the mark and were circling back.

Outside *Air Force One's* cockpit, the water pressure reached five atmospheres—seventy pounds per square inch, five tons per square foot. The jet might have refloated...if the rogue wave hadn't continued moving. It overran the plane's position before collapsing once more to normal heights as the surge moved in one direction and the surface waves in another.

In that instant, what had been a deep depression became a towering pinnacle of water, burying the plane nine meters deeper. This added thirteen more pounds per square inch of pressure—an extra ton per square foot.

The copilot's side window imploded without warning; holding one moment and ripped from its frame the next. The acrylic panel beheaded Colonel Sandra Ames, providing a rapid death and sparing her any pain.

The single atmosphere of internal air pressure didn't measurably slow the in-rushing column of high-pressure water. It slashed across the cockpit with the force of a pile driver, smashing the upper half of John and Sandra's bodies fully sideways above the hips. John's death wasn't as immediate as Sandra's but not by enough to make his experience any different than hers.

The heavy cockpit door was designed to stop hijackers. It was the only door on the plane stout enough to confine the flood of water to the small compartment of the cockpit. As it had been left ajar by the officer of the communications center on the 747's upper deck—as a courtesy to General Drake Nason —the deluge continued unimpeded, sealing the plane's fate.

The inflow spent the next stage of its brutal power as it drove vertically upward through the communications deck. At the rearmost seat, now vertically the highest on the 747's upper deck as *Air Force One* remained nose-down, General Drake Nason had enough time to snatch a breath, but it was blown back out of his lungs by the force of the water striking him. He was knocked out when his head struck the console and was blissfully unaware of drowning.

High-pressure seawater flowed up the now vertical steps into the main cabin in a single arc like a massive fire hose. There it divided. The bulk tumbled like a massive waterfall as it collapsed into the air-filled nose of the plane normally forward of the stairs. Plunging along the starboard-side hallway, the impact killed those strapped into the seats that had marked them as vital personnel who must stay closest to the President. This included his secretary and the officer with the nuclear football.

Once the nose had been filled, the rising tide rapidly flowed upward, compressing the air toward the tail of the plane. This increased the air pressure rapidly, bursting the eardrums and most of the lungs of those who were not yet inundated.

Most of *Air Force One's* passengers didn't care because their necks had been snapped by the brutal impact. This is the reason that people are trained to brace for a crash landing with the head against the seat ahead of them, so that impact g-force and the commensurate instantaneous significant increase in a head's weight doesn't snap the neck. Few seats on *Air Force One* were arranged in the proper configuration for this, being placed around conference tables and work desks. Few aboard had viewed the Safety Briefing Card's helpful diagrams about how to properly brace for impact in other types of seating.

There were two compartments of typical aircraft seating aboard *Air Force One,* both at the very rear of the plane. There, two sets of fourteen business-class-style seats are arranged in typical rows.

Allyson Liddell had copped her first-ever flight in the port-side set of fourteen seats reserved on *Air Force One* for the Secret Service Protection Detail. Divided by the fold-down rear stairs, she sat opposite a similar fourteen-seat area reserved for reporters. When Rose Cole married the President, her protection detail had been automatically augmented. Allyson had called her parents the moment she'd been chosen for the team, and they'd celebrated together long distance to Adair, Iowa.

She sat in the second row from the back of the plane by the window. Allyson had asked for the window because she'd always dreamed of seeing Africa and didn't want to miss a moment.

One of the few aboard to have read the Safety Briefing Card, she wore her life vest and was properly braced against the back of Victor Conklin's seat. He'd made a very clumsy pass at her earlier in the flight—so clumsy it had been rather sweet. On consideration, she had decided to encourage him to try again after this mission.

The overpressure of the water driving in through the cockpit compressed the volume of air inside the plane into one quarter of the fuselage. High up in the tail of the bobbing aircraft, Agent Allyson Liddell was still breathing—though her ears hurt like hell. She would need hearing aids for the rest of her life if she survived.

But the increased pressure finally blew out her window. Despite fastening her seatbelt properly, she was ripped free and blown out the window by the hurricane-force release of compressed air. Because of her life vest, which automatically inflated once she was in the water, she traveled rapidly to the surface. Regrettably, she never recovered from a wave that inundated her and filled her lungs in her first gasp for air. Hers was the first body that the Coast Guard recovered.

The 747, which had briefly hesitated with its tail still showing above the calming waves, now flew straight down to the ocean bed—the bent right wing inducing a leisurely corkscrew spin. It struck the soft mud bottom, built from millennia of runoff from the Great Dismal Swamp, ten meters later. The broad nose of the 747 drove downward until it had buried the cockpit, the President's private quarters, and his onboard office in the marine sediments.

President Roy Cole was spared drowning as his neck was broken by the force of the initial impact. His final act hadn't been Presidential. Or even personal. It had been instilled into his reflexes by a long-ago Green Beret drill instructor—protect the innocent. By that deep-embedded training alone, Roy's twist to brace Rose at the instant of the crash had saved her but left his own neck at a vulnerable angle. It snapped with the eight-g impact that the plane had experienced—exactly as Miranda had predicted for a worst-case scenario.

The strength of the well-latched President's office door made First Lady Rose Cole the final survivor on the plane. Though it was only a matter of eleven additional seconds before the water pressure caved in the door, it felt far longer as she cradled her dying husband in her arms.

The aircraft remained vertically pinned in place by the nose section now embedded ten meters into the muddy bottom.

Once the storm-driven pressure wave continued to the north with the flow of the Gulf Stream, and the wind-driven waves again moved in east-to-west parallel lines, the tail of *Air Force One* was just visible in each wave's trough.

As the deep wave passed due east of Baltimore, the ocean rose in a long swell. The crews of several cargo ships experienced a jolt too minor for their experienced crews to note consciously—they just braced against the unexpected roll, then moved on about their duties.

Ironically, President Roy Cole's last-ever official act as President of the United States of America was to release federal emergency relief funds to the State of Georgia for recovery from the out-of-season winter hurricane. The same one whose passage had created the subaqueous pressure wave that killed him and his airplane.

14

———

"Is she alive?" Sarah leaned over the desk to look down at Miranda lying on the floor. Though she had no idea why she was asking about Chase's condition after witnessing the horror on the screen. It certainly wasn't a distraction she needed, no matter that her psyche had latched onto it as the lesser of two evils.

A moan answered her question.

"What happened, Miranda?" Andi had Chase's head in her lap. Her dog kept trying to lie on Miranda's chest and Andi had to keep pushing her off so that Miranda could breathe.

"Fifteen kilometers from shore," she managed a whisper. "Parents."

"Oh!" Andi must have noticed everyone else's attention. "Uh, her parents' plane went down fifteen kilometers off Long Island in 1996. The similarity must have been a shock."

"It was." Miranda sat up slowly, resting her head briefly against Andi's shoulder and petting her dog into silence. "Though it shouldn't have been now that I think about it. They died on a CIA mission in Russia and their bodies were secretly planted aboard after the crash to mask that. I find it interesting that I didn't recall that in time once I noted the parallel of Roy's plane crashing onto the continental shelf the same fifteen kilometers to sea as TWA 800."

Sarah didn't know if this was some tall-tale, screwed-up signal deep in Miranda's odd' brain, or a very unlikely truth. *Trust her* had been one of Roy's last instructions. She didn't make it easy.

Miranda glanced at the screen and then stood with Andi's help.

"Congratulations, Madame President."

"Congratulations?" Madame President? She supposed that much was accurate, but—"Con. Grat. U. *Lations?*" Her voice rose to a shout, something she prided herself in never doing—except with her two useless ex-husbands.

Miranda ducked behind Andi, then peeked out over her shoulder before hunkering lower because Andi was two inches shorter. "Isn't that the correct thing to say to someone who has just become President? I'm unsure of the social protocols."

"No. No!" Sarah answered before Andi could speak, then managed a quivering breath, but still couldn't release her clenched fists. "Maybe he is still..."

Miranda was shaking her head.

"...alive?" The pleading tone that slipped into her voice was wholly unintentional.

Miranda pointed at the screen behind her without turning or moving out from behind Andi. The same screen she'd barely glanced at before offering her congratulations. "Note the fixed position of the tail in the helicopter's camera. That indicates that the fuselage was breeched. This is not a submarine with multiple airtight compartments. If it hadn't been breached, it would exhibit sufficient positive buoyancy and currently be floating on the surface or at least bobbing about. The cabin is flooded."

Sarah looked at the screen. If not for the helicopter's view, it would seem as if the airplane's tail section *did* bob about in the waves and Miranda was wrong. But it didn't. The aftermost tip of the vertical tail rudder was exposed in each trough...but buried by each peak. From the stable viewpoint of the USCG helo, the tail remained fixed at the center of the screen and the water moved up and down past it.

"There is also debris on the water..." Miranda still didn't need to turn, apparently having captured everything in a single gestalt, "...and a body. I'll begin my investigation now. Would you like to ask the helicopter pilot to recover any floating evidence, or should I do so?"

Evidence! That was a dead person out there. A whole plane full of dead people. And she called it *evidence?* Sarah waved a hand at her weakly, signaling she could go.

Miranda turned partly away, then turned back. "You'll want to find a Supreme Court justice and make an official broadcast that you're in control of the government."

Sarah could only nod. She wasn't thinking that far ahead, but Miranda Chase was. "Did you think this all through just now?"

"Oh no. It was because Roy was at my house when he announced Vice President Clark Winston had been murdered."

"At your house?"

"Yes. Though it burned down in a forest fire since then, so you can't make your announcement from there. But you don't appear to recall, he stated that urgency was essential at the time."

Finally, Sarah's mind cleared enough to think. She *had* been there for that broadcast. Back then she'd been the newly appointed National Security Advisor, still dazzled by the wonder of it all, which seemed a lifetime ago. They'd all stood together in Miranda's living room on her private island in the Pacific Northwest: President Cole, General Drake Nason, and the core five members of the President's protection detail.

And of them all, she and Miranda were now the sole survivors.

15

———

MIRANDA WAS HALFWAY TO THE DOOR OF THE PRESIDENT'S PEOC office. She was unclear if that was technically correct as Sarah Feldman hadn't been sworn in yet, so perhaps it was still the President-elect's office—or was being Vice President a higher office? It didn't seem appropriate to ask.

"Ms. Chase," the President-elect / Vice President / President called out. Or should it be from highest to lowest possible offices: President / Vice President / President-elect?

Miranda had only just started thinking about contacting her team, so it wasn't too disorienting to delay her departure. "Yes?"

"Thank you, Ms. Chase."

"You're welcome..." except now it was a problem. "I don't know by which title to call you as you haven't been sworn in yet."

"You're right. You may call me Sarah. Felicia, find me a judge."

"The White House is in hard lockdown. That will take some time." A phone rang and Felicia answered it, said "Uh-huh," twice and hung up. "CNN has the crash from a flight tracker and is planning to go live in five minutes."

"That means we have to go live in four. People should witness me taking the oath. How the hell am I supposed to find a judge in that time?"

Miranda held up her hand.

"*What?*" Miranda once against retreated behind Andi. This time she remembered to duck lower from the start so that only her eyes and the top of her head showed. "I'm sorry. What do you have to say? And you don't have to raise your hand."

Miranda peered out carefully, though she didn't step clear. Her voice would be partly muffled by the back of Andi's shoulder. She hoped it was understandable as she wasn't moving an inch—

Oh! She finally understood the Secret Service agent's instruction when they'd received Drake's phone call. She went to pat herself on the back for learning something new, when she noticed everyone in the room was watching her. After a moment she remembered why.

"Article II, Section I, Clause 8 of the US Constitution places no restrictions on who can administer the oath; anyone can technically swear you into office. It was once even done by a notary public, when Calvin Coolidge's father swore him into office after word of President Warren G. Harding's death reached him at his father's home."

"Anyone here a Notary Public?"

No one answered.

Miranda whispered in Andi's ear, "Lizzy."

But she must have done it too loudly as Lizzy turned to look at them and began shaking her head. "No, I can't do it. Having it administered by the nominee for the next Chairman of the Joint Chiefs of Staff would send the wrong message. Besides," she waved a hand at the screen and mumbled softly, "Drake."

Miranda recognized a sad face without her reference page.

She'd been taught what to do about a sad face and said, "I'm sorry."

Lizzy nodded.

Miranda then gave Andi just enough of a push forward that she took a step.

She was fairly sure that the look Andi half turned to give her was panic, but that couldn't be right, because Andi never panicked except when attacked by her PTSD. And those attacks lay in her past.

"Uh, United States Army Captain Andi Wu (retired) willing to be of service, Madame President."

"Elizabeth is right. It still implies a military stance I'm unwilling to promote directly due to recent events." Sarah pointed at Miranda. She couldn't duck behind Andi because she'd pushed Andi ahead. "At the moment there are precisely three non-military personnel in this bunker. It can't be Felicia as she's my Chief of Staff and I can't swear myself in. You, Miranda are nominated. Someone find a Bible. Felicia, call CNN, FOX, and all the other majors. Get BBC, Al Jazeera, and anyone else you can think of. We go live in three minutes."

Before turning to the phones, Felicia tossed her a hairbrush, which Sarah caught neatly. Oh, the blast of air in the PEOC's entrance had made a mess of her hair.

Miranda tried to slip from the room three times. The first time Lizzy stopped her, the second time the scary-looking Indian woman named for the goddess of death and destruction, and the last time by her wife's gentle hand, firmly taking her arm and guiding her to stand beside the President-to-be.

It didn't make her feel any better that Meg had trotted along beside her each time, giving no indication that she sensed Miranda suffering an autistic meltdown. She wouldn't mind having one rather that what she knew came next.

16

———————

After the wedding, Holly and Mike had stayed with Jeremy and Taz in their Washington, DC, townhouse. They were enjoying a slow start to their morning. The post-wedding dinner in the White House Residence, too small to call it a reception or anything more formal, had run late. Food, alcohol, and memories had flowed freely among the small party.

"Can you believe that Clarissa was almost human?" After last night Holly just might be open to the possibility of the idea that she *maybe* only despised CIA Director Clarissa Reese's merest existence rather than wishing her to die a painful and immediate death.

"She actually let her hair down." Taz sounded as surprised as Holly was. Clarissa always wore such a severe ponytail that it made Holly's temples ache every time she saw it. Instead, it had been a lovely towhead fall to the middle of her back that spoke far more of woman than of power.

"Maybe she's mellowing with age. She actually spoke to me several times without any particularly vile insults." Taz raised her eyebrows in surprise.

"It won't last." Holly knew that much. "But it did make for a change of pace."

"I thought she was nice," Jeremy was nursing his second cup of hot chocolate as they lounged in the living room.

IKEA-inspired, this was far more Holly's style than anything she'd spotted in the White House. Of course, they'd added their own touches to it: all of Jeremy's techy stuff balanced out by a major section of the local toy store. One of them was seriously mushy about their kids and she was betting it wasn't Taz.

This morning, the four of them had taken it easy, except for Amy, Taz and Jeremy's two-year-old. She might look like a miniature version of her petite four-foot-eleven Latina mother, but she had the energy of Taz and Jeremy combined, which was impossible to imagine until witnessed. Amy had run Mike ragged before collapsing against him for a midmorning naptime. Taz was nursing Davito, their second, *and I swear last if I have to take a knife to Jeremy myself,* child.

"I never pictured him with a kid in his arms." Holly could feel herself smiling instead of sneering at Mike zonked out on the couch with a kid lying on his chest. He did look awfully sweet with the little black-haired girl curled up in his arms. She could imagine—

"What the hell!"

Taz and Jeremy turned to look at her.

"Nothing. No way. Nuh-uh!"

Taz grinned at her. "You pictured it, didn't you?"

"No. Absolutely not." Yet she could see Mike not being a dad...but being a superdad, maybe even with a capital S. He'd been great with Amy all morning and—

"Shit!"

"It doesn't go away once you see it. I'd bet hard cash that it would never happen to me and now I have two of the little terrors. Me!" The fierce little Latina went to thump her breastbone, found her arms were full of child, and smiled down at it. Maybe it *was* Colonel Vicki *the Taser* Cortez who had unloaded the inventory of several toy stores onto the living room floor.

Pure, unadulterated craziness! Madder than a tree full of kookaburras.

Holly turned to Jeremy. "I'm sorry, Little Padawan, but I'm going to have to kill your entire family for putting that into my brain."

He knew her too well and continued to nurse his hot chocolate.

"You included!"

He smiled at her.

Holly sighed. "Maybe I can get some brain surgery to remove—"

One of those National Emergency Alert tones blasted out of each of their cell phones.

"A test?" Holly hoped but had a nasty suspicion that it wasn't.

Mike and Amy slept through it, but the three of them pulled out their phones.

Jeremy read it aloud though they were all looking at the same thing. "An emergency announcement from the President will be broadcast on all major networks at 10:05 this morning. Please tune to your preferred news source or visit whitehouse-dot-gov for an important announcement."

"What? Are we suddenly at war?"

Jeremy turned on the TV. "It's 10:04 right now. We'll know in a minute."

Holly shook Mike's shoulder gently enough to wake him but not the sleeping Amy. Damn, but he did look sweet waking up slow and holding a little girl; it would just never be one of hers because no way, no how, never, nuh-uh! That was an idea that belonged way out in the never-never of the Australian Outback—out there and buried deep beneath the red sands until it rotted. Then a dingo could dig it up, eat it, and poop it out on the searing sands. After that...

A bright red *Breaking News* banner filled the screen. A scroller showed, *Important News from the White House* and a countdown timer already ticking into the thirty-second range.

War—or worse?

They exchanged looks. Every member of Miranda's team had ridden an air-crash investigation to the brink of open international conflict—several times. What if this was the time they were too late?

A text popped in from Andi. *Turn on your TV.*

Holly sent back a *Duh! Already there, Pint Size.* Andi sent back no answer to the insult. That was weird. So Holly added, *I thought you two were busy honeymooning? Maybe you're too busy having sex? Nada!* What did that teacup-sized helo pilot know that she didn't?

A news anchor came on screen to announce an emergency broadcast. But his timing was wrong, and he was cut off mid-opening when the image cut to Sarah Feldman's face. She stood at a podium fronted with the Presidential Seal. They'd seen her last night at the wedding and dinner. She looked quite different in the green power suit than she had in the flowing cocktail dress.

"This is Vice President and President-elect Sarah Feldman. I will keep this brief and to the point. Nine minutes ago, the President's plane, *Air Force One,* crashed in the Atlantic Ocean en route to a final, peaceful, goodwill tour. I regret to report that there is no chance of survivors. That includes President Roy Cole, his First Lady Rose Cole, and General Drake Nason, the Chairman of the Joint Chiefs of Staff, along with eighty other personnel. If you had friends or family on that flight, please accept my sincere condolences. You will be notified as soon as identities are confirmed."

Holly's breath, that she hadn't realized she was holding,

exploded out of her. She slid onto the couch and grabbed Mike's hand. His grip clamped onto her hand as hard as hers did his.

"A US Coast Guard team is already on site. In minutes, the nation's top air-crash investigation team will be launching. They will determine if this was an accident or an act of aggression."

"That had better be us," Mike snarled out in a rare angry tone.

Amy protested in his arms but fell back asleep when he patted her gently. Yep, Superdad to the core—*Bollocks!*

"I wish to assure the nation and the world that there is an absolute continuity of government. To that end, I have enlisted the aid of one of Roy Cole's closest friends and most trusted advisors." Sarah stepped to the side of the podium and the camera followed.

Holly laughed. There was nothing else she could do. The only ones who didn't look surprised were Amy, because she slept on, and Jeremy, because he was a total Miranda fanboy.

Andi stood at attention, the perfect US Army captain despite her casual attire, holding a book in front of her. She wore her favorite leather bomber jacket complete with sheepskin collar showing, so she somewhat looked the part—a petite Chinese woman in a World War I style jacket worked on her. Beside her, Miranda stood in a turtleneck and a fleece vest holding up her phone as if to take a photo.

Sarah placed her hand on the book—on the Bible, Holly realized—and Miranda read aloud whatever she was viewing. "Please repeat after me. I...um, it doesn't say to, but I think it would be more proper if you state your name after the I."

"I, Vice President and President-elect Sarah Feldman..."

"...do solemnly swear, or you can use the word affirm," she scrolled down, then up, "At least Franklin Pierce did in 1853. It's believed that the *affirm* option is in case you are a Quaker and don't wish to swear."

"...do solemnly *swear*. I'm Jewish, not Quaker, we swear plenty."

"Yes, I've heard you," Miranda replied without a hint of irony—because she *never* understood irony.

But Holly and the others laughed.

"...that I (meaning you)..."

"...that I (meaning me)..."

And so the rest of the brief oath of office continued. It would be hilarious if it wasn't so horrific.

Roy, Drake, Rose... Shit! Various prior investigations meant that Holly knew at least a dozen people who'd have been on that flight.

"How is this even possible?" Holly managed to ask.

No one tried to answer.

Once it ended, Sarah returned to the podium, but the camera followed slowly enough to capture Miranda turning to Andi and whispering, "Did I do okay?" And Andi rising on her toes to kiss Miranda briefly and whisper back, "You did great." The ultra-cute girl-couple swearing in the new President. Oh, but the conservatives were going to roll over in their graves at that one.

As the camera caught up to her, Sarah's half-smile to the side died as she again faced forward. "As President of the United States of America, I wish to convey that if this was an act of aggression, I have a recommendation for you. Whoever you are, you had best hide fast and hide deep, for we *will* be coming after you."

"Knew I liked her." Holly glanced at Taz, who nodded in reply. Sarah Feldman understood the military mindset just fine.

"Allow me to repeat," the new President continued, "that I have already met with my nomination for General Drake Nason's replacement, General Elizabeth Gray-Nason. Be assured, this is not a moment of weakness for our country or our national security. I will keep you updated as more is learned. This is President Sarah Feldman, signing off."

Over the next ten seconds, the news station replaced the blank screen with the *Breaking News* banner, then the news anchor, and again the banner. Off camera, the anchor stuttered with no idea what to say, then they finally cut to him. Someone must have whispered into his earpiece as he looked blank for a moment, then turned once more to the screen.

"I've just been informed that the, uh, unusual oath of office was absolutely legal, and Sarah Feldman is now this nation's newest President. We still don't have news as to who performed the ceremony, but we'll bring you that information as soon as we do." Again the pause for his director's feed to his earpiece. "It is now being called The Speech Heard Round the World."

It was clear that his director had just made that up, but it was good enough that Holly figured it just might stick.

"President Roy Cole's second term of office was due to expire in twelve days when..."

Jeremy muted the sound.

Holly's phone beeped with a message from Andi. It was only two words long.

South Lawn!

That was all Holly needed to know.

17

CIA Director Clarissa Reese had silenced the *Important News from the White House* national alert message. Leave it to Roy Cole to have to go out in a flurry. Wasn't he supposed to be gone on his happy little Final Farewell Tour already?

She almost deleted the next message from an unknown number. She hesitated only because so few even *knew* this number.

Find out who! SF

Who what? San Francisco?

She turned on her office television just as the *Breaking News* banner hit the screen. Powerless to do anything during the thirty-second countdown, she rattled her short-cut nails against her glass desk. All she could do was contemplate how glad she was to be almost done with Roy and Drake, and how she'd give her left arm for it to be *her* taking over the Presidency in two weeks. The fact that she'd avoided losing her life by seconds when it was snatched away didn't comfort her in the least.

Then Sarah Feldman—SF!—showed up on the screen. Yet it hadn't been from Sarah's private number. The President-elect had farmed the task of dealing with the D/CIA to some *lackey?*

Clarissa pounded the side of her fist against the desk. For eight weeks since the election she'd sucked up to the woman, briefing her on current threats and specialized operations, and pitching the power of the CIA if used to its full potential. Roy and Drake only ever came to her as a last resort.

She'd thought she'd built a rapport with Feldman but now some *lackey* was her handler? Ms. Jewish Princess-elect was about to find out that the CIA could be as horrific an enemy as it could be a major asset.

Then Sarah started to speak. As she delivered the news about *Air Force One*, Clarissa had to give the woman points. She had immense poise and delivered an unscripted speech without a single pause or stammer.

Considering the nine-minute timeline from crash to broadcast, maybe Feldman had only farmed out *sending* the message. The podium didn't fool Clarissa; Feldman wasn't in the Press Briefing room. She was locked in the deep underground vault of the PEOC, which meant her morning was busy indeed.

Then the camera cut to the left to show...

Clarissa's hands dropped limply into her lap.

Miranda Chase. How was that autistic nobody always at the center of things?

Rose!

Feldman had listed Rose as one of the passengers killed.

Clarissa clawed for breath, jerking open the high buttons of her blouse to no relief. Rose had been her one friend, her one trusted advisor. Rose had dragged her back from the brink after Clark's death had cost her the Oval Office. Even after Rose had married the President, they'd remained close. She'd been the only one Clarissa had invited to the memorial service when Kurt had gone down in the line of duty in North Korea. Rose alone knew that the head of CIA's Special Operations Group had been her lover.

Gone.

On her own again.

Well, she was the widow of a US Vice President and the youngest director in the CIA's history. Or had been when she'd grabbed power five years ago. She might be two years on the wrong side of forty now, but she could do this. She glanced at the phone message again as Miranda did a thoroughly predictable job of mangling the swearing-in ceremony.

Find out who! SF

If she assumed that exclamation point was specified by Feldman, perhaps the woman *did* see the real potential of the CIA. Now was her chance to prove it to the President. It was time for the CIA to regain its rightful power.

The instant the speech was done—nice threat, Clarissa wholly approved—she punched the intercom to her assistant.

"Set up an all-Directors' meeting in my office. It starts in five minutes and attendance is not optional."

18

———

"Your turn!" Heidi didn't want to talk to their bitch of a boss any more than Harry did. So they'd started taking turns answering Director Reese's calls.

Harry did one of his can't-hear-you things by pounding away on his keyboard.

Yeah, right! He'd pay for that later and he knew it. But Harry was never big on thinking about consequences; a bad habit they both had from their hacker days.

She started the payback by actually picking up the phone rather than using the speaker so that he could listen in.

"CIA Cyber Division, how can we be of service today?" She put on her sweetest voice, the one Clarissa seriously hated. It practically made her long Nordic-blonde hair curl each time. Of course, after so many years of working together, if she was actually civil, Clarissa would assume she was up to more than she already was.

"You saw it?" Not even a snarl back.

"Yeah, we're working on it already."

"You're excused from the meeting to—"

"What meeting?" Heidi enjoyed cutting her off.

Another line rang, forcing Harry to stop pretending and answer it.

"That meeting." Clarissa must have heard the ring.

Meeting? Heidi mouthed to Harry.

He nodded.

She signaled him with a slash of her hand across her throat. He acknowledged the call and hung up.

"Show me just how good you two are. And show me fast."

Clarissa hung up before Heidi could formulate some scathing remark. She waited a beat. Two. Nothing. *Crap!* She'd been on the inside for too long; her hacker brain was going stale.

Harry was back to buzzing away at his keyboard. He'd be fishing after any digital footprint in various databases, locked or not. She'd trust him to recover any tower communications, satellite tracking imagery, even flight profiles.

If her husband had one shortcoming, it was tunnel vision. To him the entire world lived down in the data. During her hacker days, before Bitch Clarissa had unmasked them both—and offered to recruit or bury them, their choice—she'd thought much the same. But trying to understand their most dangerous enemy, the D/CIA herself, Heidi had learned that there was a bigger picture.

Clarissa couldn't make a computer do jack shit, though at least she wasn't one of those helpless souls who needed to call tech support every hour. But damn, the woman sure knew how to cultivate and manipulate people.

Harry's brain simply couldn't go there, but Heidi had learned a whole new level of skills by reading through Reese's secure files. Easily done, as Heidi and Harry had written those security routines after breaking through the multi-trap code-beast that CtBR had someone out-of-house build for her. Clarissa-the-Bitch Reese needed a better acronym, but Heidi hadn't cooked one up yet; Cat-Brrr was far too cutesy and Caber too Scottish.

Just in case Harry wasn't faking it, she used the speakerphone this time. If he was actually that deep in code, he probably wouldn't hear the call anyway. He was her one-track man.

"Hey, Heidi." Jeremy answered on the first ring.

"You still owe me, Jeremy, just warning you."

"He still hasn't convinced you yet? Babies can be really fun."

"Remember, I was around for Amy's colic." Jeremy had planted the idea in Harry's head, but she still wasn't ready for having one of their own. Especially as Taz had described it: *Like having an alien grow in your body.* When she'd forced Taz to watch *Alien,* her sole comment had been: *Yeah, just like that.* Major ick!

"Davito is much mellower."

"Maybe, but with Harry and my genetics that so wouldn't happen. Anyway, are you on it?" She hated that she was echoing Clarrisa Reese.

"Give us a chance. We just launched three minutes ago and we're barely out the door."

She heard car doors slamming and engines starting. "Come on. Miranda was in the room, I saw her. You gotta be further ahead than that."

"I'm sure *she* is, but we aren't yet. I'll keep you informed."

"You better. Or I'll tell Taz that you're furious she doesn't want a third child."

"But I don't. We agreed we wanted two and—"

"God. You're so fun to tease."

Jeremy groaned. "Got me. I'm gone."

And he was.

Heidi stared at the phone but couldn't think of who else to call.

"What's next?" She called out to Harry.

"NRO." It struck her with a major flash of heat. If he was down to the National Reconnaissance Office, that meant he'd already cracked a whole lot of databases wide open. Her man was so good.

"On it." She considered calling General Elizabeth Gray-Nason directly. They'd never actually met, but she'd place a fair bet on the result of playing a friends-of-Jeremy card. Though maybe not as she'd probably be crazy busy at the moment, what with the President and...oh shit, her husband going down on the plane.

She glanced over at Harry. Maybe sooner rather than later on the kid thing. A piece of him, for her...just, you know, in case. She finally got it—damn Jeremy!

Not wanting to dump more on General Gray-Nason's plate, Heidi decided to forego the phone call and hack the NRO instead. She didn't need much—flight tracking, satellite imagery, and any secure comms—and the general must have other priorities. Besides, this would be more fun.

19

THE MOSCOW WINTER EVENING SEEMED TO BLOW BITTER COLD through the very walls as Inessa Turgeneva sat on the couch in her private parlor on the fourth floor of their luxurious central Moscow townhouse. This was her private space, one her husband would never dare to trespass. She'd carefully chosen a mix of contemporary Russian and Western pieces to furnish the room. None too new, and only a few truly old. She wanted her guests to feel Inessa's importance, yet also to feel comfortable. The showpiece, which she'd selected strictly for herself, sat off to the side. Her rolltop desk in the same French Rococo style as Catherine the Great's famous desk. It also stated that a woman of great power sat there.

She didn't furnish the room for herself, but rather for the wives, mistresses, and other female confidants of Russia's oligarchs. It communicated a clear message—femininity and security. She gathered them here to discuss culture, fashion, and news. And—most especially—to gossip. Inessa collected all their rumors and sent them to where she hoped they would do the greatest good for her country. Not the Russia that existed in the minds of the modern breed of *oligarkhi,* but of the

Mother Russia she increasingly feared existed only in her imagination.

The powers that ruled had not found or stopped her yet any more than they'd stopped Miranda's mother thirty years before when the Chases had swept her under their wing. It had taken until long years after their deaths to understand that they'd been CIA agents, not merely the most beneficent force of her entire life.

As a result of her women's salon, greedy Russian capitalists were consumed and ruined by what they'd whispered between sweaty sheets. Avaricious social climbers often climbed the ladder of their wife's woes only to be plunged straight into hell. Slowly, man-by-man, rumor-by-innuendo, Inessa removed the overtly powerful. The right word in the right ear, sometimes delivered by these very women while rumpling other sheets, would cause the rabid dogs to turn and consume another of their own. Someday the great *oligarkhiya* would find that they stood upon nothing but air—and then they would fall.

Or so she'd dreamt. With each passing year and each new travesty against justice and basic humanity, her achievement of those dreams faded like last year's fashions.

Today Inessa sat alone and watched the American announcement on television. Because of her husband's high status in the FSB—the latest and perhaps worst version of the KGB—she had access to all the Western news. She silently watched the captions on the BBC, Al Jazeera, and DD News in India. She didn't bother with the Chinese as it would be even more skewed than Russia's state-run TASS.

No one knew more than she did. In fact, most knew less—significantly less.

How fascinating that dear Miranda and her companion Andi were the ones to swear in the President. Inessa was very pleased they were still together as she'd liked both women upon their brief meeting. She hadn't missed the kiss or the significance of the matching gold bands. There must be some safe way to send her congratulations.

If any other person had sworn in the new President, Inessa would assume that it was a planned conspiracy. Had it been in Russia, she would *know* it was a conspiracy. And Miranda would be the perfect person to plan an undetectable crash of their magnificent airplane.

She would also be the last person to ever do so.

Yet someone had.

Who would have a reason to remove President Cole despite so few days remaining in his leadership?

Had he survived, he would have been a formidable statesman-at-large. Especially with the changes she'd seen in him this last year since the lovely redhead had begun appearing at his side. Like recognized like. Inessa had researched Rose Cole and wished there had been some way for them to meet. She would have liked to know if the woman ran a spy network of her own and, if so, on whose behalf. It would have been a very interesting conversation.

Now Rose Cole was dead, and Inessa would never know.

Might they have faked their deaths?

If they had, they'd kept it from the overly serious President Feldman and from Miranda, as she would never assist in swearing in someone who didn't belong. With her autism, she would never understand the need for such a subterfuge.

Subterfuge.

It raised two key questions, which Inessa only now understood had been plaguing her for quite some time.

How much longer should she continue her struggle to free her country from the dictatorial yoke it seemed to wear so comfortably?

And how much longer could she trust her husband?

She had been instrumental in elevating him from major, past lieutenant colonel, and on to colonel. She could claim some credit for his becoming a major general, though events of those few critical days had seemed to take on a life of their own. Or had someone else also been manipulating events from behind the scenes?

His recent and abrupt elevation to lieutenant general, and the two bright stars he now wore so proudly, spoke of an ambitious climber she had *not* thought existed in him. What, or more importantly *who,* was he feeding into the vicious maw of the FSB that the President's right-hand man Murov would elevate him so quickly?

She couldn't look away from the screen and its scrolling banners of the American President's death. They were reporting that over five hundred people had already claimed responsibility, but none of them were considered as potentially valid. The streets of Iran, North Korea, and Venezuela appeared to be throwing massive block parties.

Had her husband been the one to give Murov the American President's death? It was too horrid to contemplate...and too possible to ignore.

Artemy Turgenev, a decade her junior, was young enough to be positioning himself as a future leader, perhaps *the* future leader. He merely had to outlive the last few survivors of the KGB-era oligarchy—or wait for them to be disappeared by Murov's men. There were fewer than twenty of them left.

Would Artemy overreach and cause the both of them to be quietly removed?

Or might Murov's men become Artemy's?

No, his mind simply didn't work that way; she was sure of it. Nor would Murov tolerate it.

But if Murov, the puppet master behind the President, wanted a man with less ego and more pliable strings to pull, Artemy would make a fine choice.

And if that happened, would she be the next one to be disappeared?

Would Murov or even Artemy arrange some accident for *her* so that her general-husband would be free to marry the President's powerful second daughter? The woman had already divorced one billionaire; might she be enticed into a liaison with a fast-rising FSB general next? She was *not* part of Inessa's social circle despite several carefully couched attempts. Few of the daughters were. The wives and mistresses, yes, but not the daughters.

Inessa shivered at the thought that her opportunity to fix Russia had slipped out of reach forever. She should have been able to shrug it aside as mere foolishness—but couldn't.

When the speech and swearing-in of President Sarah Feldman was repeated on the television, she turned up the volume once more and studied it carefully. If there were any hidden meanings in the words of their forthright new President, Inessa could not find them.

After she muted the sound again, she dispassionately considered her own and her country's status. Her conclusions were also distressingly forthright and lacking in subtlety.

20

Lieutenant General Artemy Turgenev stood at the foot of the stairs to the top floor of their Moscow townhouse. He hung onto the banister to keep from falling to the carpet. The gateway to his wife's private social salon; he hadn't crossed its threshold since they'd bought the house and she had declared the top floor hers. The security guard, who'd helped his driver get him out of the car and up to the front door, had informed him that Inessa was home. And that she was alone—upstairs. She only ever used that private suite when she had guests.

Unsure of how he'd arrived here, he stood at her stairs, holding on like it was a pitching ship.

Normally when he returned from his Lubyanka office, she would be in the living room, reading or writing letters. Of course, he wasn't returning from the office today, hadn't been back there since before lunch, but she never needed to know that.

Inessa was one of the last people he knew who still used the post. Her letters had been checked, of course, and he'd seen the reports. No more than friendly notes between women of society, mostly relationship advice and encouragement.

She was from a world gone by: a classic beauty, a gentle spirit, and so charmingly old-fashioned. He'd witnessed her effect on himself and others since their very first meeting; every room she entered seemed to slip back to a previous era: not of the Soviets but of the tsar and tsarina. The sensation was slow to fade when she departed. One of the few self-made billionaires of Russia with no obvious political connections or graft, she was unique. There wasn't a fashion trend set in Russia that didn't start with Inessa and end with her interconnected corporations of importers, designers, manufacturers, and shops.

She had trained him in how to speak, behave, and respond like the others of her class. Now, others sought *his* praise, *his* advice, and feared *his* retribution. But she couldn't change the way he thought—the way he felt inside.

The higher his banner flew, the more he missed his days as a pilot. Though with the failing state of the nation's aircraft and the wicked, pointless war to the west, he was glad to be clear of the fray. But every place she took him to see and be seen, he'd much prefer to have been kicked back in a run-down *kabak* reeking of wheel grease and kerosene fuel slopped on clothes. Sitting with a group of pilots swilling Green Mark, cheapest-on-the-shelf vodka, and peeling strings of salty Chechil cheese to at least suggest the harsh spirit had a flavor. Telling stories of close calls and hot women.

He knew that FSB Director General Mikhail Murov favored him because he'd been a pilot for years before his wife had turned him into a political animal. Yet she was the one who'd also taught him to always be military-first with Murov; *the politics will take care of themselves if you take care of him.* And she'd been right—as always. He would never have dreamed of reaching such heights. And now that he had, he wondered why it had all looked so desirable. One misstep, perhaps like today, and he'd—

Except it wasn't a misstep.

He rubbed at his forehead as he faced those stairs, *her* stairs, but nothing became the least bit clearer. General Murov had *suggested* the lunch. Not with him, of course, as he rarely left his desk. Rather lunch with the commander-in-chief of the entire Russian Aerospace Forces—space and air forces combined. He'd flown for the latter, back before the former existed.

His afternoon had started with a three-martini lunch.

Just like a Western businessman, one for each star! three-star General Sokolov had toasted him in Moscow's most-exclusive Club Cloud 99.

Even with Sokolov as a dining companion—too powerful to keep out—the door wardens had hesitated over his own admission. Neither Sokolov nor being a two-star general in the FSB had tipped the balance. His wife's name, Inessa, had opened the door wide.

Her. Again! He was a lieutenant general, yet she was the one who opened the door to the most elite club in Moscow. Not even her married name, his name, simply Inessa—as if he was nothing! That she'd probably never been there didn't matter.

Artemy crossed into the master bedroom and made it to the small bar they kept for when they wanted a nightcap without going downstairs. Gin, scotch whisky, sherry, aperitifs. He poured three fingers out of a bottle of Beluga vodka into a crystal tumbler and knocked it back.

Sokolov, twenty years his senior, had been the oldest in the whole club. Turgenev himself was perhaps the next oldest. Inessa might be powerful, but even being on the young side of her generation wouldn't let her fit there. Artemy was on the old side of the club's members, but not beyond it.

Unlike Inessa's quiet restaurants where she commanded the best table without asking and was greeted in careful whispers, Club Cloud 99—ironically hidden in a deep subbasement—

vibrated. All of her fancy places with elegant materials were nowhere. They had black-leather-and-brass booth seating. Indirect lighting became hard-edged down-spots over tables so that one could lean in and out of the shadows as the conversations flowed.

And they flowed.

After Sokolov had departed on a pretext that sounded like an assignation with his mistress, people he'd never met joined his booth uninvited. They leapt into conversations without hesitation. Smart people—many Western-educated far beyond his training at the Gagarin Air Force Academy. Inspired people—driven by ideas, not fears.

Beautiful people.

Many of the women wore Inessa's fashions, but so altered he barely recognized them. The way a half-shredded blouse slid from strap-free shoulders and offered creamy skin and unsupported cleavages made a whole different statement than his wife, the ever-so-lauded designer, probably ever intended. American jeans were a hot item. Some were so tight they showed every single curve. Some, cutoff shorts frayed right past the starting curve of their butts despite the chill January weather outside, were impossible to look away from.

And they were fit, athletic women. There were men too, but he didn't notice them one way or the other.

Inessa's body was a work of art. She had placed second in the last-ever Miss USSR beauty pageant and had allowed her figure to shift only as befit a mature woman. She still often modeled the top items of her fashion lines at the shows. And everyone applauded like it was still thirty-five years ago.

The women who gathered about his and the departed Sokolov's table had figures that kept his head spinning with where to look. Party animals, athletes, the children of Inessa's privileged class. *These* were the elite in every way imaginable: status, wealth, and body.

Gods above and below, it made him hard all over again remembering them.

He poured two more fingers of Beluga and turned to stare at their bed.

Sex with Inessa was always a gentle wonder. Sex with Tania—Fairy Queen fit her perfectly—up against the black marble wall of the women's bathroom had been hard, fast, and left them both laughing for how good it felt to acknowledge the animal inside without hold or bar. He'd forgotten what that felt like from back in his pilot days. Except then it had been a whore in a pilot's bar, not the eldest daughter of one of the twenty great oligarchs.

His wild Fairy Queen radiated power. A top track-and-field athlete because she had the vision, the drive, and the body—Gods but she had the body, all sleek muscle and blonde hair down to her perfect ass. The last double handful of that lovely hair was a wide stripe of silver and above it a slender line of the richest blue he'd ever seen as a pilot flying beneath a clear Arctic sky. It wove and rippled and she wrapped it around his throat like a great thick scarf while he took her against that wall. They didn't stop once during the long afternoon. They drank and laughed and danced and screwed again before dancing and drinking even more.

He'd been drunk enough to make the mistake of asking for her number. She waved a hand at the club as if the answer was obvious. If he wanted to forget the outside world for an afternoon, he might find her here.

Drunk enough to ask for her number but sober enough, barely, to stop at the barrier of Inessa's private stairs.

To hell with that.

He'd thought to shower off any hint of his afternoon tryst.

To hell with that, too. Women said they could always tell, but that was just some rumor they spread about like cow manure to keep husbands in line.

To hell with Inessa's limitless power.

And Inessa's perfect refinement.

And her gentle ways in bed.

And—

Just thinking about Tania's bucking body and clawing sun-gold-glitter fingernails aroused him all over again. He thumped down the empty crystal tumbler, returned to the hall, climbed Inessa's stairs—his stairs, by God, it was his home too—and shoved open the door.

He slowed only enough to note that it was a room for women. It was all pretty and refined and smelled of roses in the middle of winter and—

Artemy Turgenev was an FSB two-star general, by God, who had just fucked a wild Fairy Queen a decade his junior twice in an afternoon.

Inessa sat with her back to him, alone on a velvet sofa. The cashmere sweater made her look soft; the linen slacks made her sleek as he stopped behind her and looked down the front of her blouse to where he could see a hint of black satin. Tania wore no such restraints, needed none to keep her figure in perfect form.

"Good evening, Artemy. How was your day?" She asked without turning from the silent TV showing who cared what. The same greeting in one way or another, every day. Always glad to listen, to suggest, to—

He didn't give a shit.

Right now? All he cared about was what *he* wanted. He buried his face where her thick hair swirled around the side of her neck, grabbing a breast through the cashmere. It wasn't enough! He plunged his other hand over her opposite shoulder, down inside the sweater, the silk blouse, which lost several buttons, and under that satin bra to grasp the other of those award-winning breasts. He knew that many of his peers lusted after Inessa—how many called him a lucky bastard or said he didn't deserve her—but she was his to have.

"Well," she huffed out a breath, "That's a change of pace."

He'd show her a change of pace. He yanked his hands free, grabbed onto the couch, and flopped it backward. Inessa tumbled with the couch to lie before him. Not bothering with button or zipper, he tore open Inessa's pants. The button shot aside and the zipper cried out as he jerked it apart. He yanked her slacks off one leg, in too much of a hurry to bother with the other. He drove his hands upward, scooping the sweater aside and destroying the rest of the blouse. He freed one breast and fell on it while he clawed at the bra until it tore between strap and wire to expose the other.

When he fumbled with his own pants, she helped him. The ever-so-proper Inessa let him spread her in her shredded clothes. When he wanted to feed on a breast, she drew him tightly against it. When his taste went lower, she dug her fingers into his hair and arched to meet him.

And when he drove into her, she wrapped her legs around him.

He took and he took and he took. The more he did, the tighter she held him as if she'd never let him go. He took all that he could manage from Inessa until he left her tousled, disheveled, dressed in tattered remnants, and lying half on the back of a tipped couch and half on the Persian carpet in her ever-so-feminine boudoir.

Even so, her perfection remained intact.

Not once did she complain.

But neither did she moan when the release slammed out of him.

Nor did she laugh for the sheer glory of being alive as his Wild Fairy Queen had—*Wild Fairy Fucking Queen* Tania had whispered when he'd told her his name for her, just before her body had spasmed in a massive release.

Afterward, Inessa made no move to push him away or cover herself.

He buried his face against her chest, his nose against the tattered remains of her bra, to hide from what he'd done to her. As she cradled his head and stroked his shoulders, he wished that the soft breasts pressing against either side of his face belonged to his Wild Fairy Fucking Queen's taut physique—and felt even worse.

Had he seen Inessa's expression, he wouldn't have understood it.

Thoughtful and sad, perhaps even the frisson of fear, he might have recognized. But he'd never understand the resignation to an unstoppable future or the silent tears for all that was lost no matter how she tried to hold on.

The commentator on the television had still found nothing useful to add to the new American President's speech.

21

———

WANG DAIYU EASED OUT OF HER BED AND MOVED TO THE LIVING
room shutting the door quietly behind her. She could never
sleep after sex, especially good sex. Tonight she felt
supercharged as the sex had been particularly excellent.

Over these last months she had developed a simple routine.
Once he slept, she would turn on the world news in the other
room and do her yoga. Eleven at night in Beijing was ten a.m. in
Washington, DC, and midday in Europe, so the news was rarely
dull.

Daiyu could have been a world-class athlete in a different
culture. But she'd had a bad cold on the one day the scout had
come to their village and tested all the children. Her four-year-
old underperformance that single day had relegated her to a
life on a floundering collective farm fifty kilometers from the
bitterly cold northern city of Yichun.

Refusing to accept such a fate, she began training herself
for the military the next day and joined the Red Scarves of the
Young Pioneers of China on her sixth birthday. On her
fourteenth birthday she signed up for the Communist Youth

League of China and at eighteen the PLA. Once away from Yichun, she'd never gone back.

After joining the People's Liberation Army, she'd fought for every step up that ladder as well. She'd excelled by being smart about when to pretend stupidity. And she'd never neglected her body. It was the latter, as a title-winning ultra-marathoner for the PLA, that won her promotions by her commanders. It was the former that brought her to the attention of Liú Zuocheng, the vice-chairman of the Central Military Commission and the second most powerful man in China.

She'd been striving for a position in the CMC's Falcon Commandos. They were the elite, direct-action team who answered to the CMC—and no one else. She'd outcompeted the few women and many of the men physically, but all her training would not have been enough—had she not placed first in every intelligence test.

Daiyu was sent through the full training course and only learned afterward that she was not to join Falcon but rather become the vice chairman's personal operative. He sent her into ever more challenging situations until he trusted her independent decisions to consistently serve his goals.

Only once had the assignment been a hardship. Her infiltration into General Zhang Ru's household as a spy through the expedience of an arranged marriage had been hell—useful, but awful. In recompense, Zuocheng had allowed her to administer the *coup de grâce* and literally burn out the man's black soul. With his death, she'd set that time firmly behind her.

Very tall for a Chinese woman at a hundred and sixty-two centimeters, she was precisely average for a Western woman: five-foot-four. The few times she had traveled to the West, she'd felt strangely small, as she normally towered over most other Chinese women and many of the men. Thankfully, her Manchu features were not as sharp as some, allowing her to pass as Han. No Manchu would be trusted by a Han—not after the tiny Manchu minority had ruled them for the three centuries before Mao's revolution. No one would tolerate her rising to power, except for another outsider like Chairman Liú—Han but from as desperately a remote origin as hers. He alone knew her true heritage.

Here, in her apartment, she felt tall as she rose on her toes and reached for the sky to start her first Sun Salutation. Having left the warm bed, her bare skin prickled slightly in the cool apartment. She liked it that way and her lover seemed to enjoy the reminder of his own hardscrabble youth, never touching the thermostat or covering himself. On the rare occasions General Zuocheng didn't fall asleep afterward, he would follow her from the bedroom to sit in the armchair and watch her exercise. He never interrupted, but he did enjoy watching. Always a very private person, she didn't mind it from him. Not with the way their relationship had begun.

She smiled as she thought over how they had come to be more than master and field operative.

Their first real conversation had been a simple sharing of tea and discussing her eclectic collection of books upon her return from a particularly trying yet remarkably successful mission to investigate a plane crash in Antarctica. They discovered a shared passion for unearthing possible modern applications of traditional political and military wisdom.

From that day, they'd approached it together with the care and attention to detail of archeologists. Lao Tzu, Sun Tzu, Confucius, Mo Di, and others fell to their debates over successive quiet teas on stolen afternoons. Soon he was encouraging her to refute his own policy decisions—not to change them as they rarely disagreed—but to hone them until sharper than a Mongol horseman's spear. When one or the other of them hadn't read a particular text, the other gifted it to them so that they could study it together.

One day he had gifted her a book they had not previously discussed. Also unusually, he had wrapped it. *Open it after I leave, consider it, and let me know if you wish to discuss it.*

It was a very old copy of *Su Nü Jing–Classic of the White Goddess*. A brief manuscript written nearly two thousand years ago, perhaps during the dynasty of the Three Kingdoms. It promised the teachings of three goddesses on the purpose and methods of Taoist sex. She didn't open the text to read it, instead she waited.

Upon his next visit, after they had sat over tea dissecting a particular paragraph the Confucian philosopher Mencius had scribed three hundred years BCE, she opened the *Classic of the White Goddess* and read the first of the flirting movements aloud. Then she closed the book. They discussed the section at length and in tantalizing detail. Over the next months, they worked through the twenty paragraphs on flirting. As world events shifted, their primary focus remained on political discussions. But when she felt they had strayed too long afield, she would open the White Goddess's book and read aloud the next section for consideration.

Each of the twenty-four *tricks* of intimacy they studied much more carefully and at quite some length before moving to the next.

After the seven *Losses* and upon reaching the second *Benefit,* an afternoon, even a long one, proved insufficient for their mutual study. Zuocheng's wife, who had never been much of a factor, was returned to the distant countryside from which she and Zuocheng had both come. After that, their mutual explorations often continued long into the night. His large home felt too expansive, as if filled with ghosts. Enjoying her place in his bed, she'd been reluctant to mention the sensation. But when they reached the peculiar section of cautions about having sex with ghosts, she included her response to his home in the discussion. When she had, he hadn't questioned or doubted. They had simply returned to spending their nights together in her small one-bedroom apartment whenever he could manage a visit and she was not off on an assignment.

Her body hummed as she shifted into Tree Pose, one heel placed high on her opposite thigh and both arms stretched to the sky. She could balance on her flat foot for five, even ten minutes. Zuocheng had initially observed that pose while looking at his watch. She had considered it a yogic triumph when he had finally set the watch aside and simply enjoyed the form her long body created. The time she slowly rose to her toes and managed to hold balance there, he had stood and applauded.

Tonight, they had combined the Third Method described by Xuannü the Black Woman with Daiyu's yogic *Setu Bandhasana* Bridge Pose. The results had been revelatory. In honor, she again rose to her toes and held her Tree Pose far longer than ever before, maintaining her center well past when her leg trembled from the strain. Zuocheng would be very sorry to have missed his chance to witness that from his comfortable armchair, but he had earned his rest most thoroughly this night.

As she settled to a flat foot before switching to raise the other, the bright red flash on the screen drew her attention.

Breaking News.

22

———

Liú Zuocheng woke from a dream of glory only to discover it was real.

Wang Daiyu leaned over him, her fine, high breasts such a perfect balance above her trim waist and ribs. Even the accent of her strong shoulders enhanced their ideal shape and balance. The slightest mismatch only emphasized their beauty. She kept her black hair at chin length so that its slight Manchu curliness remained hidden. Personally, he deeply appreciated her keeping it short so that he might always see the curve of her neck and her unusually high cheekbones. Tonight it shadowed her face as she leaned over him, lit only by the flickering light of the television from the other room. He slid his hand out from under the blanket to run it up her warm thigh.

"You've been exercising without me."

"There is something you need to see."

Zuocheng sighed; he assumed it was not one of her exotic poses that could rouse the jade stem of a dead man. He wished he could rise from bed with the effortless grace Daiyu exhibited so thoughtlessly, but his age and his attempts to match her exceptional prowess in the night made him move more slowly than he ever wished her to see.

However, her expression was not that of a lover but rather of one of the most skilled field operatives he'd ever found. He allowed her to offer a helping hand but no more. Half his age, but she never showed any signs of complaint or distaste for his body. When they reached the limits of his abilities, she accepted without comment. He was pleased that those limits were expanding with their practice.

In the living room, she didn't need to point. On the television was one of the forbidden American channels that he had made sure she could access. Her mind, as incisive as her body, needed accurate data to make the leaps of logic so familiar from his youth but becoming more of a reach in his seventieth year.

He saw the banner of *American President killed.*

"Sound."

She turned it up. "I only saw the initial announcement before coming to wake you."

They stood side-by-side as the station replayed the new President's speech. His English, only a little behind Daiyu's, was more than sufficient to the task. Roy Cole had often used curiously complex sentence structures, making it difficult to keep track of all the nuances of his speeches. At least this once, Sarah Feldman made every word as simple and sharp as the tip of a spear.

They both gasped, then laughed when Miranda Chase came on screen to swear in the new President. They had discussed the peculiar woman at length as they'd each had an opportunity to work with her, though under very different circumstances. And the curious Chinese-American warrior who always stood by her side. Though a hand-width shorter, he had personally witnessed that she was a fighter to compare favorably with Daiyu.

It made him think of the single-line comment in an alternate translation of the *Su Nü Jing* spoken by Su Nü, the White Goddess, herself: *There are women who pick women and they are wonderful.* His favorite granddaughter had made that choice. But two years out of graduate college in the US, Mui and Mei-Li's stars were already rising in fascinating ways he looked forward to leveraging in the near future.

He'd discussed the implications with Daiyu as dispassionately as they analyzed every other topic in the short work. She'd been absolutely frank regarding her own thoughts and unexpectedly varied experiences—her discretion ran deep indeed—but neither of them were yet willing to expand their current circle of one yang and one yin. Still, it was an interesting thought to be with two warrior women together. Perhaps they would discuss it again at a later time.

An unexpectedly abrupt regime change in the world's most powerful country—no matter what foolishness their own President boasted of China now being the supreme global power—was always a time for great care.

After the new American President finished, Daiyu muted the sound and asked, "Was that us?"

Zuocheng turned to Daiyu. There! There was the mental agility he could feel slipping from his grasp. He'd have asked the same question...soon. She asked it now. He pulled her head down enough to kiss her forehead, for he stood no taller than she did.

"Have I mentioned how thankful I am for you, my dear Daiyu?" He tapped a finger where he'd placed the kiss so that she wouldn't mistake his meaning, though she never did. He didn't await her response. "Not to my knowledge. Let us make some strong tea."

Once she had, they moved to sit as they had that very first afternoon together, in two chairs separated by a tea service beside a bookcase that had expanded to two over these last three years. He wore the forest green silk wrap embroidered with white cranes that she had gifted him. They reminded him of his birthplace in the high mountains, where only she had ever visited.

She wore the wrap commissioned especially for her. The silk was black, as her name meant Black Jade—rare and highly prized—and embroidered with an elaborate green jade dragon, the ultimate symbol of strength and wisdom. She was Daiyu when they were discussing history, politics, or world events. But he'd taken to calling her the precious Black Jade stone itself, *Hēi Yù,* when they were studying the intricacies of Su Nü.

Neither of the short coverings were about modesty or warmth but rather formality of serious discussion. The cool air caressing his skin through the fine silk made him feel the energy of his youth when he'd been the sole hunter for his family in their remote wilderness cabin. He wished for a fireplace, more for the light that seemed to eventually reveal all secrets than for the heat, but Daiyu's inner Beijing apartment didn't have one.

"Was that us?" Zuocheng repeated her question. "If so, it either came from above or below. I did not order it."

They discussed the President of China only briefly. If he had wanted to do such a thing, he would have come directly to Zuocheng to make it happen. There'd been no hint of his own sidelining prior to a removal; the President depended on Zuocheng as co-chairman of the Central Military Commission far too much to purge him. Their leader's often chaotic responses were due to poor information and poorer self-control, but he was smart enough to leave Zuocheng maneuvering room to compensate when required.

But was there another rogue general somewhere in the over-inflated command structures below or even within the CMC? Perhaps a devil like Zhang Ru, seeking to drive his own agenda at any cost—even risking a possible war with the Americans?

Again, the President of China seemed an unlikely source of support for such an action. He had so buffered himself from reality—with yes-men and sycophants afraid to report less than perfection—that only chance ever aligned his decisions with facts. Even Zuocheng himself had to be careful how he addressed the President, though he was trusted to do what must be done—and he did so, without necessarily informing the man. That would cause their leader to lose face. Such a loss he would never tolerate in public or private.

Perhaps the biggest surprise was that he was effective at all on any front.

The current political landscape created immense opportunity for those below to act with little compunction as long as they steered clear of the overly zealous, yet highly corrupt, anti-corruption committees.

Zuocheng and Daiyu discussed each possible scenario and potential bad actor long into the night.

At the hour when late night became early morning, the time of a summer sunrise—though outside it remained a howling night of *bīngyuè,* Ice Month on the old calendar—he waited. They had made many plans to discover the truth of China's possible involvement in the downing of the American's *Air Force One* jet. They would approach it separately from very different angles but with a shared goal.

They had also discussed ways in which China might use this as an opportunity while winding a circular path around the new American President's direct warnings.

Then he fell silent and waited. He'd had the next thought. Yet it was so extreme that he was unsure whether he dared give it a voice.

But would she?

He saw Daiyu judging his silence with the great delicacy she had proven on previous uncertain topics. Zuocheng did his best to hide his thoughts. No face had ever been more familiar than they were with each other's—their perfect intimacy since he'd introduced her to the teachings of Su Nü made that a given. But he tried.

She finally nodded her acceptance that she must speak first. Once decided, she didn't hesitate. "What can we learn from this to use upon our own Supreme Leader?"

Wang Daiyu's bravery overwhelmed him, She could be tortured and executed for such a statement, and yet she spoke it for him so that he didn't have to. Then he noted that she didn't even add, *should the need arise.* Like the warrior she was, she had no tolerance for waste—at any level.

He considered...and agreed with her assessment. Thankfully, Zuocheng was too old to be tempted into grasping for power himself. Regrettably, China had only ever accepted a single female ruler, which had been thirteen centuries ago as an aberration in the midst of the Tang Dynasty. Besides, he would never wish such a burden on Wang Daiyu. She was too competent and too much the warrior. Not a political player, she would never be more than the fearsome weapon she had honed herself into.

But what a weapon she'd made. That she'd gifted it to him to wield was beyond price.

"*Hēi Yù,*" he whispered and held out his hand to her over the twice-renewed tea service.

His Black Jade took his old hand in her strong one and rose from her chair. Once she stood between his feet, she turned away and lowered herself ever so slowly. The black silk of her green dragon cover slid above her hips until she sat upon his lap so that together they might enjoy the Black Woman's Seventh Method combined with Daiyu's *Utkatasana* chair pose

—the first advanced variation they had created and perfected themselves.

Yes, there must be some way to use this unique moment in history—unless it had been China's doing. If it had, Zuocheng would take the American President's advice; he and Daiyu would run fast and hide deep. None would look for them at the abandoned hunting cabin high in the central mountains.

23

SARAH FELDMAN'S SPEECH AND SWEARING IN WENT INTO FULL-ON Fourth Estate replay. Every journo in the world had a theory and insisted on airing it as much as possible between replays of that thirty-second speech she'd made after becoming President.

"Well that sure as shit didn't go as planned." There was no one to respond because there was no one to hear.

It was going to make the next move a hundred times harder.

But, as those Navy SEALs kept saying on TV and in books, *The only easy day was yesterday.*

24

Miranda discovered that it was nearly as hard to get out of a crashed White House as it had been to get in. Again, the Secret Service had to escort them, except this time the various guards didn't want to open doors at all. It didn't matter that the other side of each door reported all was quiet.

Andi had whispered that they were still in shock from the President's death.

"Are you in shock? Am I supposed to be in shock? I don't feel like I am."

Andi paused, causing a ripple of upset in their escort. They hurried along together. "I'm trained to deal with shock. When my copilot Ken was killed in mid-flight, I finished the flight first before allowing myself to feel the horror. That's what I'm doing now, I suppose. It will catch up with me later. There's only so long that suppressing something like this works."

"What about me? Will it catch up with me?"

"Uh, when I was reading up on autistics... You know I did that, right?"

Miranda shook her head. "I didn't, but it makes sense that you would if you're dating one."

"Married to one." Andi held up her beringed hand.

"Oh, right." Miranda held up her own hand and then nodded. "Why is it that the biggest changes are the hardest to remember?"

"Let's take that question up later. My reading said that there's no way to predict how you will handle loss. Grief or not. Gently when the time allows or a catastrophic blast to your psyche. No way to really know, though I'd like to place a strong vote against the latter option."

Miranda nodded. She'd second that vote. "Actually, the way I dealt with my parents' loss was to study airplanes."

"Sure, the first time, when they died. But when you found out about who they really were and how they really died?" Andi made an explosion noise and moved her fingers up past her head like...like...the top of her head blowing off.

"Oh, I got that one!"

"Well done you!" They traded high-fives.

"You're right. Let's not do that one either."

Finally, they escaped onto the South Lawn, and the world seemed normal again. It was still unseasonably warm for January. The weather driven north by the Georgia hurricane that had spread high cirrus horsetail clouds across the early morning sky, presaging a change, had delivered though it wasn't even noon yet. Now an overcast of high-level altostratus was moving in. Rain was predicted, but nothing nasty. At least not by onshore standards.

But a sunken plane at sea—one that reached high enough to experience wave action—could quickly turn problematic. They must hurry.

Freed from the crashed White House, the grounds team was setting out the three two-meter aluminum disks to support the Marine Corps HMX-1 aircraft that President Feldman had authorized for Miranda's use.

Holly, Mike, and Jeremy reached the South Lawn at about the same time she did.

Jeremy jumped right in. "That was crazy getting through security but we're here."

"Would have been sooner," Holly shoved against Jeremy's shoulder, "Except Padawan here brought his usual lock, stock, and kitchen sink."

Miranda didn't see a kitchen sink anywhere, and those were too big to hide, even a small one. She had an NTSB field vest of tools useful during an air-crash investigation; Jeremy carried a field pack of them. Still, it wasn't big enough for a kitchen sink and she didn't think Jeremy carried any locks in there. Stock she was less sure about, so she didn't ask.

"Taz isn't here because our usual babysitter is at her kid brother's school concert. Once she shows up, Taz is going straight to the Pentagon in case we need help from there. She'll also go after any communications and work logs. It works out okay because first she has to pump some milk for Davito anyway. And then she—" He slapped a hand over his mouth and mumbled, "Sorry. TMI."

"Seriously, Padawan." Holly aimed a punch at Jeremy's arm.

Miranda noted he'd become nimbler on his feet and managed to dodge behind Mike despite his heavy pack.

"So what's the plan, Boss? Let's start by getting out of this cold. Why are we meeting here?"

Miranda pulled a thermometer out of her crash-site investigation vest and took a reading. "It's sixty-seven right now. That's unusually warm for this time of year. While not record breaking, weather patterns suggest that temperature may well reach record levels today and tomorrow. To your second question..." Andi was always encouraging her to stretch against her perceived boundaries. Miranda decided to try completing a verbal statement with nonverbal communication and pointed at the dot of a helicopter that was approaching over the National Mall.

Holly looked up and shaded her eyes. "Goodonya!"

Her mixed-media communication had succeeded. She would have to try that again sometime. Perhaps next time she'd see if a text or other electronics might be substituted for the physical action—though opening a large red arrow on her phone to point it toward the sky didn't strike her as terribly practical.

A Sikorsky VH-60N White Hawk helicopter, the Presidential lift version of a Black Hawk, slowed to hover over the three disks laid out by the grounds crew. Despite the heavy down-blast of air blowing past her from the helo's rotor as it settled onto the lawn, Miranda could feel the attention from all the reporters in the Press Room driving toward her. Now, instead of having to fight through the White House security, she felt thankful for it. All the windows in the Press area faced north. There was a door to the south permitting access to the Rose Garden and the South Lawn, but it would remain shut due to the lockdown. At least it would delay them hunting her down.

Still, despite her autism, she could guess that they were all speculating about the helicopter they could easily hear landing on the lawn, even if they couldn't see it. *Who was coming? Or who was leaving?*

No one! She wanted to shout over the heavy beat of the big rotors. *No one!*

After the President's broadcast, they had all watched the television news to gauge initial reactions. And the first question every newscaster had asked wasn't about the new President. Nor about how had *Air Force One* crashed after such a long, flawless record. Not even how had so many died. No, it had been about who had just sworn in the new President. It had all been about her until she wanted to scream at them to stop.

Sarah had made several unkind remarks about the press, proving that she was indeed comfortable with expletives.

The rotors didn't stop. There was no ceremonial Marine opening the door and saluting them. Instead of formal blues, the crew chief who swung open the door wore a battledress uniform, complete with helmet and an M27 Infantry Automatic Rifle. He waved them aboard.

"I'd take it back if I could," she shouted to Andi as she ducked low to clear the rotors. It wasn't really necessary. The lowest point of a Black Hawk's rotor blade sweep was directly ahead of the helo. If the pilots were applying full downward force on the collective, which she could see they weren't, the lowest tip point would be seven-foot-seven high. That would be twenty-seven inches over her head and twenty-one inches above Holly's tall five-ten. Approaching as they were from the side, it would be ten-foot-six minimum clearance, over twice Andi's height, yet she found herself to be instinctively ducking.

"Take what back?" Andi, who knew more about helicopters than anyone here, perhaps including the Marine Corps pilots, put her hand on the top of Miranda's head and kept it down despite the high clearance as they scuttled unceremoniously aboard.

Miranda reconsidered her calculations of their clearance from the blades but found no errors. But Andi would know best, so she ducked further until she felt as if she was playing a child's game, *Be an elephant, now be a monkey.* She felt as if she should be dragging her knuckles on the green grass. At least it made it easier to scoop up Meg and hug the dog to her chest. "I'd take back being on television. I don't like people looking at me."

The ceiling inside the White Hawk was only four-foot-eight, so now they really did have to duck. Perhaps that was what Andi had been preparing her for. Holly and Mike sat on the forward bench seat, which faced back into the cabin.

Jeremy banged his head hard on the low ceiling and collapsed into one of the two side-facing armchairs on the opposite side of the reconfigured cargo bay. When Miranda went to sit in the forward-facing armchair by the door, Andi grabbed her arm and pushed her into the back-facing one before sitting beside Jeremy.

Once the crew chief closed the door, she saw why. The forward-facing armchair bore the Presidential Seal woven into the seatback. She was very glad to not be sitting there. It wouldn't make her feel the least bit Presidential. Only more obvious than she already was.

"But you did great!" Andi assured her.

"I don't care!" With the door closed, enveloping them in Presidential-level sound insulation, her complaint turned into a unintentional shout. "I'm fine," she said before Andi could ask. "See?" She pointed at Meg already settling in her lap with no signs of alarm about Miranda having an episode. Next time she'd keep her thoughts to herself—and she'd run away if she saw a television camera.

As they lifted off the lawn and Andi turned to talk to Jeremy, Miranda pulled out her personal notebook. She made the first-ever entry in the things-that-she-didn't-appreciate-about-Andi column. She felt bad about doing it, but it was true: *Hiding behind A. is an ineffective strategy for avoiding national TV.*

The crew chief leaned close; Miranda would have backed away, but she was seat-belted into the armchair. "Where to, ma'am?"

She'd thought that was obvious. "US Coast Guard Cutter *Bear*."

He squinted at her. "We're supposed to know where the puddle navy is keeping their boats?"

"It's where *Air Force One* crashed."

At that his eyes shot wide, which she was pretty sure meant surprise. "Excuse me?"

"Where have you been, Sergeant?"

"We were on a training run when we were told to redirect to make an emergency civilian pickup at the South Lawn."

"Oh. The President, Roy that is, is dead. Sarah's just fine. The *Bear* is fifteen kilometers off the Delaware coast. We need to go there. Would you like the coordinates?"

She didn't need her reference chart to understand his expression; Miranda had seen it too many times over the years.

"I'm not crazy. I'm autistic."

The phrase was her only defense, though it rarely seemed to help. It was like…like being autistic was the same as being infected with a highly communicable plague. Pointing out she wasn't infectious never helped either.

He leaned back in his seat and swung his microphone into place. After a short back-and-forth, his mouth shifted—it became tight and formed a straight line. For that she had to check her emoji page and was pretty sure it matched *grim.* It might also be *angry,* but she couldn't tolerate looking at his eyes to see if they'd narrowed.

Whatever his expression meant, the White Hawk tilted strongly nose down and they raced eastward.

25

———

"WE'RE NOT AUTHORIZED TO LAND ON A US COAST GUARD SHIP."

"But you know how?"

"We're Marines, ma'am."

Holly took that as an affirmative. "So how about if I open the door and throw your Marine ass down onto that boat? Then they'll have to come and get you, right? Of course, you might get a little broken along the way, as we're still thirty feet up, so I'll apologize for that up front because that's the kind of considerate gal I am."

He grabbed her wrist and applied pressure that would make any civilian collapse. She knife-handed him in the solar plexus, not very hard, just enough to get his attention.

In answer, he reached for his sidearm. *Unbelievable.*

Holly didn't break his wrist—quite. She did take his Sig Sauer M18 and jam the nose of it up under his chin. "Please tell me you aren't this stupid in your personal life." She turned to Andi. "Hit the intercom, Army, do your thing."

Andi didn't hesitate in picking the handset from beside the President's chair that connected her to the cockpit. "Marine, proceed with landing on that ship. Your authorization is that there's a dead President here and the new President has sent our team in to find out why. Once there, you will remain on deck until *we* give you permission to depart. Are we clear, Marine?"

She listened for a few seconds, nodded to herself, and hung up.

Holly gave her a thumbs up and Andi stuck out her tongue.

The Marine crew chief gurgled something.

"Whups! Sorry." She safetied his weapon and slammed it back into his holster. His glare as he rubbed at his chin made her mutter to Andi, though loudly enough for him to overhear. "No pleasing a Marine."

"Never was." Andi smiled this time.

The helo did the strange hover and side-slip that was indicative of a helo landing on a moving ship. Holly tipped her head at Jeremy and Miranda, then shared a nod with Andi. In a lively sea, it was an incredibly dangerous and precise helo technique that made landing a jet on an aircraft carrier not look so tricky. Andi would have flown this trick probably hundreds of times during her service, and Holly had certainly ridden through it often enough during her years in Aussie Special Operations Forces. The two civilians, not so much.

She glanced over at the helo's crew chief, but he still looked some kinda pissed. Not really in a sharing-the-joke mood. Then she remembered why they were here and decided that she wasn't in much of one either.

There was no way to brace for the landing; all she could do was stay loose and let it happen. Miranda and Jeremy were catching up on married life or some such shit. She, Andi, and the crew chief all waited for the landing.

It would come abruptly once the ship's landing officer had guided the helo as low as he dared above the rising and falling stern of the ship. Then, as a wave lifted it toward its highest point, he'd signal the helo down hard. If all went well, the descent would close the last few feet of gap before whapping down on the deck at the top of its arc; then ship and helo would descend together. Then the deck crew would scramble into place to chain down the helo by the wheels, hopefully before the ship rolled unexpectedly or a rogue wave lifted the cutter abruptly. If it did, the stern of the eighteen-hundred-ton ship would swat the ten-ton helo like an annoying fly.

Holly heard the landing happen by the sudden load change on the rotors from hover to hard descent. But she never felt the contact.

Her stomach said they were riding down. Were they about to join the passengers of *Air Force One?* Escaping from a flooding helo in a winter ocean was not a high-probability-of-success sort of challenge.

They finally bottomed out and rode back up—in a gentle rising-ship way, not in an oh-God-we're-all-gonna-die way. The landing had been dead smooth.

"Well, shit," she turned to the crew chief, "At least your *pilots* are real Marines."

He looked ready to spit on the deck at her feet but probably didn't want to muss the President's bird. *Ah, the simple joys.*

26

WHEN THE CREW CHIEF OPENED THE CARGO BAY DOOR, HOLLY surveyed the situation.

Sea State 4 meant that diving was going to be possible, just annoying as hell. The altostratus clouds over DC were thickening into a heavy marine layer here off the Delaware coast.

She pointed up at them and Miranda nodded—then she typed something on her phone before turning it to Holly.

Yes.

"Yes, what?"

Miranda just sighed and shook her head before tucking her phone away. Whatever she'd meant, time was definitely of the essence.

Checking the surface of the sea, Holly saw that the three big white USCG cutters with the wide orange slash across their bows were anchored in a triangle about a kilometer on a side. In the center, a small fleet of the 47-foot MLBs were shuttling back and forth across the waves. One slowed to pick up something from the water—briefcase-size, not body-size. That was a relief. Though there'd be plenty of bodies soon.

Holly couldn't tell if their escort to the ship's bridge was a guide or a guard. She braced herself to keep fighting the battles against knotheads who should be left deep in the Never-Never with an empty canteen and no knickers.

"You certainly arrived quickly." A man wearing the three bars and a star of a Coast Guard commander greeted them without rising from his chair on the bridge. He was one of the only two present—three, counting their escort. The other stood close by the helm. "We only dropped our hook a few minutes ago."

"The VH-6oN can travel at two hundred and eighty-two kph," Miranda informed him. "As your ship is presently anchored two hundred and thirty-four kilometers from the South Lawn of the White House, that gave us a transit time of forty-nine minutes. Steaming at your flank speed from your normal berth, seventy-two kilometers southwest of here, you had a transit time of approximately a hundred and twenty-two minutes. It is more by coincidence than planning that we arrived so closely in time."

"Who the hell are you, lady?"

"I'm Miranda Chase, the Investigator-in-Charge for the NTSB."

The commander stared at her long enough to make Holly shift up on her toes.

"Huh. Ms. Chase, since you arrived on a Presidential-lift helicopter, I'm assuming you can tell me what the hell is going on. Is that..." he waved a hand helplessly toward the triangle formed by the three anchored cutters "...really *Air Force One?*"

"Yes."

Holly barely managed to suppress her laugh. It was inappropriate in such a moment, but she was kinda an inappropriate gal.

"Well...shit!" the commander finally concluded.

Her burst of laughter came out—a little more on edge than

she liked, so she killed it quickly...but not fast enough. The Coastie guys turned to look at her and then turned away. Even Mike and Jeremy looked at her askance.

"Sue me!" she told them all. She hadn't lost someone she cared about in a long time. It was something she'd achieved, ever since losing her SASR team in an unnamable jungle, by the decision to care about as few people as possible. But she respected the hell out of Drake and rather liked President Cole. If these people didn't like that their loss made her jittery, screw 'em.

Miranda hadn't reacted at all. "Have we now dispensed with the pleasantries traditional for a new meeting of people? If so, I'm ready to start my investigation."

The commander pushed out of his chair and stepped over. "Well, if you're high enough up to co-opt one of the President's Marine helos, that's good enough for me." He held out a hand. "Commander Randy Davidson. How can I help, Ms. Chase?"

Miranda cringed.

Holly stepped in and shook his hand for her. "Nothing personal, Commander. She's not big on touching anyone, other than her new spouse—the short one." She nodded toward Andi.

Andi's punch landed fast and hard on the nerve in the radial groove of her upper biceps. A spike of pain shot up into her shoulder joint and down to her hand, where it hung out until her fingers felt thick and numb.

Duh! Don't piss off the little Chinese woman. By her previous standard of Andi teases, it seemed rather an overreaction. She squinted her question at Andi as she rubbed her arm back to life.

"Sorry," Andi actually did look sorry...and seriously sad. "The last person to tease me about my love life is..." she swallowed hard and nodded toward the center of the triangle "...down there."

Now Holly was the one who felt like shit. "Uh, can we get this show on the road?"

"I thought I already asked that question," Miranda looked puzzled.

"You did," Commander Randy Davidson assured her. "And the answer is yes. I'm not much of an expert on jet planes but I'm guessing we don't want this one just sitting in the water. I'm thinking we need to tow it out of here before that weather moves in."

This time it was Jeremy who started laughing, which saved Holly the trouble. Except his wasn't some nervous mess like her laugh had been...and her gut was. Two hours ago, she'd been watching Mike sleep with a baby girl in his arms and now she was at the site of a watery mass grave.

"I'm sorry, Commander, for what is about to happen." Holly could tell that Jeremy was gearing up and nodded for him to go for it.

"Your ship weighs eighteen hundred long tons, that's about eighteen-three in standard measure tons. A Boeing 747-200B, before conversion into the VC-25A, has an empty weight of a hundred and seventy-six tons. The upgrades are classified, but let's toss in twenty tons as a working number. And that's Operating Empty Weight, OEW. To fly to Africa, it would have carried—" Jeremy stared at the metal ceiling of the bridge.

"Twenty-eight thousand, five hundred gallons," Miranda said.

Jeremy nodded, "Right. About that. We'll round that off to another ninety-seven tons. And now the fuselage is filled with ocean water. Water is a non-compressible fluid weighing eight-point-three-four pounds per gallon."

"This is seawater," Miranda corrected.

"Oh right, make that eight-point-five-five. The volume of the 200B's fuselage is approximately seventy-three thousand cubic feet—"

"You forgot the tapered nose and tail. I'd estimated fifty-two thousand."

"No, that would be sixty-one—oh wait. The non-water-permeable fittings take up some volume. And the people who are primarily water, so they aren't going to compress much except for their lungs and stomach. So, yeah, a fifteen percent reduction of volume works, which equals fifty-two thousand cubic feet."

"Fifty-two thousand seven hundred."

"Right. Replace that with seawater. That's another sixteen hundred and eighty-five tons."

"That's actually about four hundred-and-twenty pounds light, but it is sufficient for a first-order approximation."

Jeremy nodded his agreement. "So the plane a) won't float for towing, and b) it presently outweighs your ship by approximately—"

"Enough already!" The commander rubbed his face.

"I warned you." Holly was feeling at least a little better. But maybe letting the comedy-duo of Chase and Trahn loose was kinda inappropriate to the moment. Even by her own low-humor standards.

Davidson nodded. "So we have a hellaciously heavy waterlogged aircraft—"

Miranda held up a hand to stop him. "Don't forget that its nose is stuck in the mud."

"How do you know that the nose isn't crushed?"

"The plane hasn't fallen over to the seabed, so something is holding it up. I expect that it is stuck like a lawn dart into the seabed."

This time Andi had the inappropriate laugh—one that definitely leaned over into the edge of hysteria. She covered her mouth and pulled it back. "Sorry. *Lawn darter* is Army slang for Air Force pilots, especially of the F-16 that was known for doing a lot of high-speed nose plants during development."

"Helmsman," Miranda asked, "What's the sea depth here, from the wave troughs?"

"Uh," the man's voice cracked at being called upon. He consulted his instruments, watching them through three waves. "It's a hundred and ninety...three feet, ma'am."

"So," Miranda nodded. "Assuming minimal crushing of the nose, *Air Force One* is stuck thirty-eight feet into the mud. Applying mudhole parallels in a deep-water environment for strength of adhesion between differing materials isn't well studied. There have been studies of bogs that—"

"Miranda," Mike finally stopped playing observer. "How about we table that calculation for now and work out how to fix the immediate problem?"

Holly could see the gears clashing in Miranda's head. Mike could too and sent her a desperate look. Maybe messing with the commander's brain by letting Jeremy and Miranda run hadn't been the best idea. Holly had forgotten what it was like when the two of them geeked-out together; Miranda had screwed herself deeper into the ground than *Air Force One* had into the seabed.

Andi didn't say a word. She simply stepped so close to Miranda that she almost knocked her over.

Miranda said a small, "Oh." Then she hugged Andi.

Andi hugged her back.

After about fifteen seconds, Miranda let go and started speaking as if she hadn't stopped—or been sidetracked by Jeremy in the first place. "First, we need to recover the black boxes. We must determine cause first and worry about recovery later. That was President Feldman's orders. Mr. Helmsman, I see by the ping-back on your sonar that we're missing the Number Four Engine. Commander, could you please have someone find it? It will lie somewhere east of here."

"That's a heck of a big area."

"You may limit your search to the closest two hundred

kilometers along a line from here back to the turn I had General Owen initiate at," Miranda rattled off a latitude and longitude. "He didn't mention losing the engine, so it is likely between here and that turn, since the final time I spoke to him."

"That's still a lot of ocean. Can't you call the general again?"

"I could, but I doubt that he'd answer. His cockpit is approximately two hundred and fifty-seven feet below the surface right now."

The commander looked a bit sick.

Holly leaned over to Andi, after covering her upper arm with her other hand—it still throbbed—and whispered. "How did you do that?"

"Automatic hug threshold," Andi whispered back.

"Christ, Wu. You're talking like she is now."

"Really?" Her face lit up. "Neat."

Just what she needed, another Miranda.

27

—————

Glad of a mandate, Commander Randy Davidson leaned into the task. He was the senior skipper of the three cutters—by seven whole months. He'd also been lead ship out of the port and decided that was good enough to put him in operational command.

It was a make-or-break assignment. If he screwed up, it could well be the end of his career—which would sure as hell end his marriage. If he pulled it off, he just might be the golden boy in both worlds. Did it make him a shit for thinking that? Probably. Didn't matter; he was in it now.

In minutes he had each ship deploy their RHIB to join the MLBs. The Zodiac rigid-hull-inflatable boats made a better diving platform. The motor life boats were designed to support rescue swimmers, not guys wearing deep-dive SCUBA gear.

He let Miranda brief their most technical guy, Petty Officer 2 Stanik. While she instructed him and they found a diving kit for the blonde Aussie—he'd caved on including a civilian when she showed him her qualifications—he pulled his chief diver aside while all that happened.

"Look, Eastman, we need to show the US Navy, and more

importantly the new commander-in-chief, how essential the US Coast Guard is. It's our first demonstration to power, maybe our biggest ever. I want bodies coming up to the surface fast. There's a storm coming and I have no idea how we're going to move that plane. Second priority is to assess the condition of the hull. A lot of secure equipment aboard, maybe we'll have to demo it in place, so third task is do an assessment on what kind of charges would smithereen that thing. But first and foremost, I need a hundred percent personnel recovery before this storm kicks our ass. Go in through whatever emergency exit you can and get them moving to the surface. Start one team at the top, so we can show action fast."

"Remember, Skipper, at these depths, the deepest dive has to be the first in a dive series."

"Roger that. Lead a second team yourself as deep as you can get. Get those, uh, occupants of the foremost cabins," Randy swallowed hard, "out of there personally. We don't know the conditions at the nose, so be damned careful."

"But get them," Chief Petty Officer Eastman nodded. "Request permission to—"

"Take everyone and anything you need from all three boats except for Stanik. Full gear. Full safety. If we need to send you goddamn hot meals while you decompress on the way up, we'll find a way to do it. By the book, Chief, because nothing you've ever done will be so thoroughly raked over the coals afterward —but shave that dime as close as you dare."

Eastman nodded and hurried off.

When Davidson finally worked his way down the list far enough to order an ROV into the water to assess the plane's condition, that had sidetracked Miranda along with her Chinese and four-footed shadows—the Vietnamese kid followed tight on their heels. Heading to the nerd shack, where the science team ran their gear to watch the feed, got them out of his hair. Next, he cut an MLB loose, had it rigged with a magnetometer and a towed side-scan radar, and sent it off to go searching for that Number Four engine. That made his bridge much emptier.

"You're making me feel pretty useless, Commander." The quiet guy with dark hair and an easy smile who'd come off the helo with the others spoke for only the second time since boarding.

"Call me Randy. Why useless?" He eased down into his chair, watching the RHIBs converge on the tail of *Air Force One* with a full load of divers perched on the rubber gunwales. He hated this part of being a captain: order your people out, then sit on your ass and watch.

"Mike Munroe. Because my specialty is human operations and making sure things run smoothly for Miranda."

"That woman is some strange piece of work."

Rather than taking umbrage, Mike didn't hesitate to nod. "More than you can possibly imagine. She's also better at her job than probably anyone in the world. That's not personal bias; that's bankable."

Randy knew he was good, but the best? What would that be like? Would he have to be as odd as her to achieve that?

"One suggestion, if I may?"

"Fire away."

"Get a tanker out here that can swallow however much fuel she and Jeremy said. With long hoses and a big supply of high-pressure nitrogen. It will drive the fuel out and fill the tanks with an atmosphere that won't flash over."

Randy surveyed the water. No oil slick. The fuel tanks were still intact. That was some equipment he didn't have aboard; the USCG *Bear* was only so big for storing contingency items. The ability to pump tens of thousands of gallons of highly combustible fuel wasn't among them. Also, he didn't have any spare tanks for thirty thousand gallons of fuel. He carried five times that, but in diesel tanks for his ship. His jet fuel load for servicing his lone helo was a tenth that, and it was still half full. No help there. He called out a fueler.

"What was all that about loads anyway? She and that young guy on your team got very strange on the topic."

Mike didn't pretend to misunderstand him. "Holly was yanking your chain a bit, but it got away from her. Her competence isn't people."

"What is then?"

Mike's soft smile told Randy plenty about the man's feelings. "She's a survivor. You wouldn't believe what she's been through, even if I was authorized to tell you, yet she's walked out the far side each time."

"So far."

"Yeah," his sigh was long suffering, "Yeah, so far."

Randy laid a hand on his shoulder like he was one of the ship's crew. "Well, this may be urgent, but it shouldn't be all that dangerous."

Mike didn't look any happier before he answered softly, "Not yet. These things have a habit of going sideways."

Randy looked out at the small boats gathering around the tail section of *Air Force One*. Mike made it sound as if it hadn't merely been some stupid mistake or bird strike or something rational.

Zeb, his XO, had tracked down a replay of the President's speech. Randy hadn't had time to watch it yet, but Zeb had told him about Feldman's threat. Somewhere there was going to be hell to pay. He just hoped that it wasn't by him.

The first news helicopter hove into view thirty seconds later.

Shit!

28

––––––

Inessa managed to get Artemy to bed. She then showered and scrubbed but felt no cleaner. He was now one of the *elite*. Enough so to have a mistress who was important in her own right rather than merely some whore or naïve girl. If it was the latter, she wouldn't worry—she'd simply squash them like a bug. But now he'd feel powerful enough to believe he could get away with anything. That was much harder to deal with.

How did the wives who were cast aside tolerate it? Her first husband, she'd known what he was when she'd married him, and he'd been very useful—until he accidentally killed himself in Antarctica. His tastes had run far more to the slut category. She hadn't minded being shut of him, but she'd thought Artemy was cut from a better cloth.

Apparently not.

Returning to her third-floor sanctuary, she didn't sit. The television now showed a view from above the crash site through a long telephoto lens. A cluster of ships and small boats all circling an area where something washed in and out among the waves. She didn't have the background to make sense of the odd shape that appeared stuck there. A graphic came on the silent screen of a plane nose down in the ocean bed with its tail sticking up through the water. That explained it.

Some ghoul had created a counter that tallied bodies as they were brought to the surface; thirty-two and counting.

She surveyed the room. The tasteful balance of gentle colors. The subtle accent pieces in the white, blue, and red of the Russian flag. A vase here, the trim of a curtain there, a cushion on a pale lavender couch. Too subtle to connect unless one studied the space. It had worked. Her social salon of women felt comfortable and safe enough here to share freely.

So many stories had happened in this place. The warning of pending international sanctions from the commerce secretary's wife had allowed her and others to reposition several key business assets, mostly cash, overseas—without enriching the Chinese after all other international banking routes were severed.

The authorization to launch military operations against Ukraine that General Sokolov's mistress had shared in such an excited whisper. It had allowed Inessa to send the crucial twelve hours' warning to Kyiv of the coming invasion. Her warning had stopped the immediate takeover and stymied the Russian President's plans to expand his brutal dreams of empire. Every decision had its consequences though. She hadn't expected that he would bleed his own country of its young men as no one since Hitler had—a quarter million dead and a million wounded, almost all men. Not the twenty-four million of World War II...yet.

Worse, it wasn't to stave off an invader, but rather to feed his own dreams of a perfect dictatorship. Would Russia again require that a man take multiple mates to repopulate the country as the Soviets had quietly mandated after Hitler's demise?

Inessa ignored the irony that it was the same General

Sokolov who a friend of the same mistress had spotted leading Artemy into Club Cloud 99 earlier this afternoon. At least she'd been unsurprised by Artemy's state on his return home, no matter how depressing it was. Her attempt to hide from the consequences in her private space had been naïve—not a mistake she'd repeat.

No longer a sanctuary for women, it had been violated far more by Artemy's entrance than the sex he had demanded. She could have defused that easily—in retrospect. But some part of her had chosen not to think of how. Perhaps it had been a final chance to believe that she could preserve her own small slice of the world if she held him close enough.

Such illusions were for dreamers, not realists. Definitely not for survivors.

There was only one solution, and her inner pragmatist knew it had to happen very soon. Artemy, or whoever had arranged for Sokolov to escort him to Cloud 99, would quietly arrange her removal.

Why *had* Sokolov taken Artemy there? It had certainly surprised his mistress. *He's never been there,* his young mistress had been desperately upset, *but several friends confirmed it was him.* Sokolov's mistress was of the proper age for that young-persons-of-power gathering place; he was not. Artemy still was, though she was unsure why they'd let him in.

That was why Sokolov had gone, to take Artemy.

That meant—oh God! Inessa had to brace herself with both hands on the back of the couch. Her hands landed where Artemy had grabbed hold to dump the couch over but she couldn't ease her grip.

Who wielded sufficient power to instruct three-star General Sokolov to take an underling like Artemy to Cloud 99? Who had been controlling his every move these last three years since the fiasco in Antarctica?

Murov! Four-star bloody General Murov. After decades as

the Russian President's right-hand man, Murov had lost control of him. So he was grooming Artemy to replace him—with Murov's fist tight about Artemy's strings. And Murov had to do it fast before the current regime drove all of Russia into the grave. If allowed to continue, the President would fracture the country worse than any time since Rurik of the Rus peoples had first conquered and unified the Eastern Slavic states in 862.

Artemy hadn't merely been taken to Club Cloud 99. She'd wager that Murov had made it clear to the young women that he was *the* future of Russia—the banner they wanted to attach themselves to. Murov would have made sure that only the women who were powerful enough to serve Artemy's elevation would know that he was the Golden Child—the Chosen One. He'd probably been mobbed by the most eligible and elite. And, knowing Artemy, he'd never caught on to what was happening.

Fast. That was the key. Murov would make this happen as fast as politically possible.

His first step? Elevate Artemy sufficiently to be interesting to these young women of connection. That explained Artemy's abrupt promotion to a two-star general in the FSB. No one of the necessary class would pay the least attention to a one-star. But his *rapid* elevation to two-stars marked him as a favored son of the Federation.

Next was making sure it had worked. This afternoon proved that done as well. He hadn't screwed one of the President's daughters, but with the death of Murov's own daughter, he'd certainly nailed—or been nailed by—the third most powerful daughter of the current age. In fact, a brilliant choice for the future, as she had all the political savvy and connections that she knew Artemy lacked.

His next step? Inessa Turgeneva needed to have an accident to open the way for the girl to Artemy's side.

Very soon!

Her normal channels would take time—too much time.

Inessa focused on breathing as she clutched the back of the couch with all her strength. In. Out. In. That was all she could manage.

There must be a way, a path, a channel, an escape that she hadn't set up previously because she'd been naïve and stupid. There should have been more time. There should have been a chance to turn her country's future onto a survivable path. Neither with the current dictator-in-all-but-title nor with Murov pulling the Artemy-puppet strings would the country recover.

She groaned as she rested her forehead between her hands. She felt the roughness of the cracked wood beneath the fabric where her weight had broken the antique as Artemy had flipped it over.

Inessa looked up and stared at the room that had been her sanctuary in a world that favored chaos. And at the television news of the crashed airplane. Crashed, that was the key.

She'd met a woman from Miranda Chase's team who had made a promise two years ago. Then months later, there had been a phone call. An impossible call. An incredibly secure impossible call.

Would it work the other way? If it did, would it be secure?

If not, she would be removed the moment the FSB monitored it. Artemy's path to becoming Murov's puppet would be cleared just that much faster.

But if it did work and was secure, did the promise still hold?

29

———

Heidi Geller slouched low enough in her chair to stare hard at their office ceiling. Not that there was a whole lot to see on the ceiling of the basement of the CIA's New Headquarters Building, but she'd count it as a vast improvement over what they'd been finding on the screens.

Harry was still at it, but the whole damn thing was a dry hole.

They'd found the Air Force's conversation with the senior pilot, General Owen, which provided little insight beyond a lot of technical questions about engines and computer systems. Neither of them had ever tried to hack *Air Force One*—there'd been no reason before this. Now one was gone and the other remained powered down, so there was no access until they started it up, not that they'd learn much that way.

Then Heidi had stumbled on Miranda's call. They'd both stopped working to listen to that conversation.

"Man, she is one chill technical lady."

Heidi could only nod in agreement with Harry's assessment. She hadn't understood half of what Miranda had told the pilot, but she'd really tried to save them. Too bad none of that had worked either.

The patch through for her to say goodbye to the President had Heidi reaching for tissues. She knew Harry was equally touched by how hard he pounded on his keyboard as soon as the playback of the call ended. He even left his half slice of pepperoni-and-mushroom pizza on the plate by his station. Harry never left unfinished pizza.

"You asleep on the job, Geller?"

"Can't you go fuck with someone else, Reese? Anyone else?"

Clarissa didn't snarl. Didn't even complain. Where was the fun in that?

Instead, she grabbed a paper plate and a slice of pizza before plummeting into the chair Heidi often used as a footstool. Clarissa said that she only ate junk food when she decided to hang out down here in Cyber Division.

Heidi wished she'd thought to walk through mud this morning so her footprints would be walking all over the D/CIA's perfectly toned ass. She'd never grown past lean. And while Harry definitely appreciated it, she wouldn't mind having an ass that good.

"I've got no one else to fuck with." It didn't sound like her normal level of acid.

"You checked your pH level lately?"

Still no response.

Heidi looked sideways at her without lifting her head from the chair back. Reese looked as tired and frustrated as she sounded. Some of the sheen had come off the woman. She was still perfectly dressed in that power-sexy-executive mode that Heidi couldn't emulate even if the success of her next hack depended on it. Reese might not be Superwoman but she was definitely the Woman of Steel.

"What dented your adamantine carapace?"

Clarissa took a bite of her pizza and slouched down until her position matched Heidi's. CIA Director Clarissa Reese *never* slouched, not with that steel rod up that well-toned ass.

"You okay?"

Clarissa closed her eye and shook her head as she chewed.

Heidi knew that she'd lost Kurt Grice last year. She'd thought they were actually a good match—Woman of Steel and the uber-creepy head of the Special Operations Group, the CIA's black ops and assassination squad. Both utterly ruthless. Reese had been thrown badly when the man went down hard in North Korea. Harry had dug the footage of his execution out of DPRK's systems. It was an ugly piece of work, though they'd told Reese they'd only found the barest details—certainly not giving her the high-def video.

But she hadn't been thrown like this.

Heidi stared at the newsfeed on one of her side screens. The death scroll continued, with a section for new bodies recovered and identified—no names, that would come after next of kin notifications, but they kept the count. With no explosion or fiery crash, the bodies were surprisingly intact. Every ten minutes or so, a news anchor re-explained that maneuvering body bags underwater was next to impossible, and drastically slowed the recovery process. Instead, each victim had a bight of rope looped under the armpits. A big, rope-conveyor loop reached to the surface from a pulley anchored deep down inside the plane somewhere. It hauled people to the surface to be extracted before the simple one-rope harness went back under.

It was a gruesome show, so, of course it had crazy-level viewership here in the US. Probably elsewhere, though Heidi hadn't bothered checking. One of the anchors with too-perfect looks explained that most corpses still wore their security ID badges. Few were disfigured. *They also write each person's seating location on the individual's palm with an underwater pen. Those will be cross checked with the seating rosters.*

"Oh, shit!" Heidi finally connected the pieces.

Reese nodded without opening her eyes. Her piece of pizza still had only the one bite out of it.

Rose Cole, the President's wife...widow...fellow deceased, had chosen Clarissa as her Maid of Honor at her own wedding and as her one guest to Miranda's. They'd actually been friends, as hard as it was to imagine Clarissa having one. DC leading social queen—who had the reputation for being the quintessential definition of old-world manners and kindness—and her Woman of Steel utter-bitch boss. They'd been BFFs. How weird was that?

Heidi pushed up in her chair and really looked at Clarissa. Worn. Almost haggard? "Is there anything I can do for you, Clarissa?"

Clarissa opened one eye. "Did you find the bastards who did this yet?" Her tone was mild, almost...friendly. She must be crazy stressed.

Heidi shook her head and Clarissa closed the eye. "Do *that* for me."

Heidi looked at Harry. As he wasn't pretending to be busy or deep in a hack, he sensed her attention and looked up. A slight shake of his head said that he'd learned nothing new.

"We've dug into all the likely suspects and a lot of the unlikely ones. Nobody is claiming it except the usual whack-jobs. Nobody, prior to the crash itself, was talking about it."

"How *unusual* did you get so far?"

"Russia, China, Korea, every Middle East player. India just for the hell of it, Pakis...everyone we could think of."

Harry never wanted to antagonize Clarissa, so he spoke little louder than the cooling fans on their jacked-up machines. "I've also run through most of the allies: Canada, Mexico, Europe, and Australia. I'm working my way through the

Africans, going from most advanced to least. Still not a peep." Then, like a turtle withdrawing back into his shell, he hit his keyboard again, but not with the harsh buzz of avoidance—or being hot on someone's trail.

Clarissa had nodded once, taken a second bite of pizza, and might be sleeping if not for her slow chewing.

Heidi slouched down to once again study the ceiling. White. Lots of white inside the CIA. She should paint a night sky up there so that she could pretend she was looking at the stars and not locked away in some ultra-secure basement hideaway. About the only place more secure than the Cyber Division was the Director's Personal Archive, handed down from one director to the next. Heidi still hadn't found a way in on that. First, it was physical, actual printed stuff; neither her nor Harry's forte. Second, it was rabidly guarded by the CIA librarian, and she was a woman no one wanted to mess with.

"That's weird."

"What's weird?"

Harry pointed at his screen.

"Not being helpful there, Wizard Boy."

He glanced over at Clarissa, but it was too late. She'd already opened her eyes and turned to look at him.

He sighed and tried to delay by getting another slice of pizza. Heidi knew his ways and saw his plan die as he discovered the half still sitting on the plate by his station. "I, uh, set up this ultra-secure phone call a couple years back. Single use. At least I thought so. I never erased it. It, uh, just rang through, but in the other direction."

"Who does it connect?"

"I don't know who is calling."

That had both Heidi and Clarissa sitting up, though Heidi managed to get the first word in. "How can you not know?"

"Hello, ultra-secure. My instructions were to make it so that even I couldn't crack the call."

"And you actually built that?"

"I did."

Heidi smacked her forehead. Any decent hacker knew that information was power. Clarrisa had taught her that it was a weapon as well. Harry hadn't learned that yet.

"Can you stop it?"

He shook his head. "A single text message by the duration. Already done and disconnected."

"Who had you set it up?" Clarissa had now turned her full attention on Harry. A slice of pepperoni teetered on the tip of Clarissa's pizza slice, but it refused to fall and blemish her clothing perfection. Heidi resisted the urge to reach out and give it a little nudge. If she did it just right, it might tumble down into Clarissa's impressive cleavage. Not that she was one of those women who flashed it about, but the top of her blouse was open as if she'd yanked it wide. It was the only part of her that looked disheveled.

"Uh..." Harry did his best to disappear behind his screen. But his glance up at the news gave him away.

"Someone on the plane?"

Harry shook his head.

"Someone..." Then she remembered the swearing-in ceremony. "...Miranda?"

He shook his head.

"Stop with the damned twenty questions already. *Who?*" Clarissa's sudden outburst and the slight jerk of her hand was enough to break the pepperoni's adhesion to the tomato sauce. It plopped down—on her sleeve. It would leave a stain, but it was hardly worth a laugh.

Besides, Heidi knew. "Holly Harper."

"No fucking way." Clarissa turned on her like a rabid rottweiler. Okay, maybe a rabid poodle that had just missed out on being named Best in Show. But she still had kick-ass blonde hair to the middle of her back instead of Heidi's curly brunette disaster—in other words, still plenty dangerous.

Relieved to be out from under the gun, Harry nodded from behind Clarissa.

Because she loved him, and he hadn't given in to Jeremy's pressure about wanting to have a kid right away, she took the hit for him and told Clarissa, "Way."

30

———

HOLLY DRAGGED HERSELF UP THE USCG *BEAR'S* SWIM LADDER
with every intention of collapsing prostrate on the deck. Except
when she got there, every available spot was filled with a body
bag. The way she felt, it was tempting to shove one aside and lie
down beside them anyway. They could even bag her if they
wanted. At this point she wouldn't care—or probably notice.

Sea State 4 had become Sea State 5. Waves taller than the
roof peak of the one-story shithole she'd lived in for her first
sixteen years had pumped constantly over the tail. Working
close below the water, the pressure built and died, built and
died. She'd had to clear her ears so many times that it was a
wonder she'd gotten to use her hands at all.

The bright-orange Black Box recorders had been perched in
an utterly impossible place to access. She and Stanik had
entered *Air Force One* through the flooded rear stairs, dodging
the bodies going up the rope system. As they passed, each one
insisted on pressing its face against hers as if trying to suck face
or steal her air straight through the mask. Young, old, male,
female. All in inner-DC-fine clothes—they'd been traveling
with the President on *Air Force One* after all. Suits, dresses,

uniforms with a lot of rank on them. Hair cropped short or hair streaming behind them as the rope conveyor hauled them up and out. Eyes open. Eyes shut.

They weren't shot up by drug lords, then blown to shit before falling a dozen stories, the way her team had been in the gorge underneath that bridge she'd destroyed. But most heads of the *Air Force One* dead lolled at impossible angles from necks broken by the severity of the impact.

It was a wonder she and Stanik didn't both barf in their respirators.

Once inside they'd climbed vertically upward into the rear tail cone, which held the final air bubble aboard the aircraft. With each pumping wave outside, the water sloshed and the air pressure jolted inside. She wanted to drill a hole and let the air out, but maybe it was the only thing keeping the plane upright.

The FDR and CVR—Flight Data and Cockpit Voice Recorders—were mounted in a handy cabinet. Handy if you were standing on the deck or even lying on the ceiling. Bobbing up and down in the wash of a cabin gone vertical, with too many sharp corners and nowhere to grab for leverage, made it a cast-iron bitch. Their floor, the aft bulkhead between the cabin and the rear service space, was too far down to stand and reach the rack.

Petty Officer Stanik didn't hesitate. He squatted spreadeagled over the horizontally submerged access hatch and signaled her to perch on his shoulders. He was alternately underwater and in the air, but hadn't complained once. Holly had worked as fast as she could in the sloshing chaos lit only by the headlamps they'd both donned. Two wing nuts to free each recorder—if only it had been so simple. Last one had been jammed tighter than a virgin's...well, yeah, tighter than that.

But they did it.

They'd unmounted the damn things. Hadn't dropped them where they'd probably fall through the access hatch and disappear to somewhere in the labyrinthine depths of the tortured plane. And hadn't died in the process. *Three for the win!*

Except the plane was getting restive, and it wasn't only the increasing wave heights battering against the two-and-a-half-story-tall vertical stabilizer. While they'd been battling the recorders, a fuel tanker had arrived and begun pumping out the wing tanks. The nitrogen gas they were pumping in, so that no explosive air-fuel mixture formed, was lightening the plane. Not enough to float it, but it might be enough to unstick it from the bottom. If it did, odds-on were *Air Force One* would finally complete its failed landing—horizontal on the seabed. If they were still inside, they'd be dragged down with it to a depth of sixty meters. Bad news in any diving manual she'd ever read. And that was assuming they and the others working aboard weren't trapped in the fall.

They finally got out of the tail cone space—alive. She sent Stanik to the surface with the recorders. Once he surfaced, that would set his deepest dive point for the day. He knew it too. Unable to go deeper on his next dive to help his teammates clear the bodies was gonna rankle deep.

But she'd had an idea as they washed in and out of the stupid air bubble in the tail cone and wanted to check it out. Letting her hand-light lead the way, she swam down past the body-conveyor rope. Every minute or so, another body drifted by and mournfully looked at her mask so nicely full of air.

At first, she swam into the starboard rear cabin. The bodies had been cleared but the piles of equipment that remained— cameras, video gear, and a flurry of good-old notebooks—said it was the press area. She had to bat knapsacks and camera cases aside, but couldn't find any hole big enough that a body could have slipped out. The body conveyor, once she was past the worst of the horror, had reminded her of Miranda's comment in the PEOC that one body had surfaced, and Holly wanted to find where it had come from. She'd been very careful to not look at the screen once it was obvious there were no survivors.

She hit pay dirt in the port-side rear cabin. The failure point was the second window from the aft bulkhead. Everything else looked alarmingly intact, except for the various firearms that had collected against the forward, now lower bulkhead. Aboard *Air Force One* only the Secret Service would have been armed, making this their seating area. The weapons should have remained in the individuals' holsters—though maybe not.

Miranda had said that the worst-case scenario was an eight-g impact force. The condition of the passing bodies' necks proved that no matter how extreme the prediction, Miranda was rarely wrong. At eight-gs, a two-pound weapon would briefly weigh sixteen—twice the rating of even the most secure holsters, four times a normal one.

Again, a rolling nausea swam through her, but she managed to choke it down. These were, had been, her kind of people.

She swam down into the staff and guest passenger area but didn't probe any deeper. She kept an eye on her gauges and was hitting her air-time-depth limit. Also, the corridor narrowed off to one side and bodies had started coming up from the deeper reaches of the plane.

A whole line of men and women in white shirts and military jackets. The upper deck watch crew. In their midst, a body bag that someone had taken the time to wrestle with at depth. General Drake Nason, it had to be. Because he would be nowhere else than on the command deck when the worst was coming.

Though his body bag was head up and she floated head down, Holly offered him her best salute until he disappeared up the rear stairs.

After the command deck crew, a pair of body bags came up

farther apart. The way they floated and twisted, whoever was inside was no longer intact.

Yeah, she was done. She grabbed onto the rope in the gap after the second body bag and let herself follow them to the surface.

It was a mistake.

The rope ran close by the horizontal stabilizers. When a couple tons of water in a four-meter-high wave slammed a dead body against the aluminum skin, they didn't care so much. When it did the same to Holly, it blew all the air out of her lungs, blasting her regulator out of her mouth. She was lucky to have hit flat and back first, but she was going to be black-and-blue from her heels to her shoulders. Her vision tunneled as she groped about blindly for her regulator in the next crashing wave.

The only thing that saved her was that her instincts hadn't released the rope. She was hauled clear and dragged onto a Zodiac like a dying fish—with a lungful of burning seawater that she had to choke out. One of the seamen removed her tank and mask, then helped her vomit over the side. By the time she was done and could breathe again, the Zodiac was already headed back to the ship with a load of ten dead and one living —at least technically, though it sure didn't feel that way.

Looking aft, she could see that another RHIB had slid into place to gather more bodies.

She'd waited until the bodies were transported aboard. How she'd managed to climb the swim ladder to stand among the dead on the *Bear's* afterdeck would have to remain a mystery.

"You look like shit."

Holly had never been so happy to see anyone in her life. She wrapped her arms around Mike.

"You're all wet." But his arms came around her.

She buried her face against his shoulder and breathed him

in. The life and warmth in him wrapped around her as they stood on a deck of death.

Alone. Under that long-ago blown-up bridge, there had been only her and the dead.

Here? Not alone. Mike held her tighter and tighter. The pain across her back and shoulders didn't diminish, but it was far less important.

She wanted to ask why he held her so tightly. Why he clung to such a royal mess of a person. The first sob wracked through her worse than being wave-slammed against that stupid stabilizer.

Not alone. She held onto Mike as hard as he held her—and wept.

31

———

JEREMY AND THE FLIGHT RECORDERS WERE HEADED BACK TO THE NTSB aboard the Marine's HMX-1 White-top helo. He had a black box reader with him, but that wasn't strictly protocol and Mike had told Miranda to insist that this time everything must be done a hundred percent by the books.

She didn't really understand why, but she knew better than to question Mike on those kinds of questions.

They'd all gathered on the helo deck and seen Jeremy and the recorders depart and head for shore.

Mike had been keeping an eye on the afterdeck where the bodies were being brought aboard. Without warning, he sprinted away, rushing down the ladder from the helicopter platform so fast that Miranda feared he'd fallen. Then she saw him dodging body bags across the rear sea deck and grab a hold of Holly, so everything was okay. She'd been worried when Holly hadn't returned with the recorders. Now she could stop worrying.

"Okay, what's next?" Andi asked.

"I…" Miranda didn't have an answer. Not because there weren't actions to take, but because she didn't know which ones took priority. "...don't know. There isn't..." She looked around at the hundred disconnected pieces. Three ships, the fuel tender pumping out the plane's wings, rescue boats in many sizes, Jeremy was now headed to NTSB headquarters in Washington, bodies kept coming aboard the ship, news helicopters circling. They weren't allowed to fly over the wreck, but they did circle.

"Do they have cameras?"

"Sure."

"Television cameras?"

Andi nodded.

Miranda checked her notebook to be sure: *Hiding behind A. is an ineffective strategy for avoiding national TV.* She'd remembered it correctly. She always did, but she liked having the written reminder to be certain. "*National* television cameras?"

"What's wrong?"

She showed the note to Andi—who laughed. "Well, if they're going to look anyway, let's give them something to look at." And she stepped so close that Miranda could hug her or fall over backward. She hugged her. Maybe the cameras weren't so awful.

"Forget about them. All right, I know you can't do that, but they aren't important. What's next?"

"I really don't know."

Andi stepped back and studied her face. Even with Andi, Miranda couldn't look at her eyes when she did that. "Why not?"

Miranda flapped her hands helplessly. There were so many pieces. So many different bits moving about. Hundreds of Coast Guard men and women hurrying about their tasks. It was so important. President Feldman had been very insistent about the importance of this investigation. It was a plane crash. What could be more important than that? There were too many—

Somewhere, sounding very far away, a dog whined. Something butted hard against her calf.

Andi looked down and away. Then she swore vehemently.

Miranda didn't know why. Couldn't see anything but the thousand decision threads tracing away from her in dark light like an impossible labyrinthine...labyrinth!

Andi twisted to face Miranda so abruptly she nearly stumbled backward down the stairs Mike had descended.

"I'm so sorry, Miranda." Andi clamped strong hands on each of Miranda's biceps and pulled her close. Her voice suddenly shifted to very steady. Very soothing. "Miranda. Take a breath. Take a breath. Good. Now another. That's it. When you feel ready, we'll look at your crash notebook together and figure out what to do."

Miranda gasped. Then she leaned in and kissed Andi. Then she pet Meg for being such a smart dog.

"What was that for?"

She made a quick note in her personal notebook and showed it to Andi.

"*Remember to ask Andi for help.* Well, duh!" They smiled together. "Why this time?"

"I never started my notebook for this crash." She pulled out a fresh one and carefully labeled it *Air Force One.* Then she extracted her weather gauge from her vest pocket to measure the temperature, wind speed, and direction. "I wish I'd measured it when we first arrived." She noted the readings.

"The Terrain is next." Andi knew Miranda's system of investigation almost as well as she did. The nested spheres of: weather, terrain, debris extent, debris, the crash itself, and human factors—in that order. She must not forget the outer meta-sphere to which she could attach temporary hypotheses for further consideration. In this case, there was only one and it was a fact because General Owen had told her himself before he died. She wrote *Four-engine failure (actual)* in the meta-sphere category. Then she crossed it out and added another, new sphere, *Known Facts* and re-added the entry. It wasn't the whole answer, but it was nonetheless true. And it was a whole new sphere that she'd added without prompting.

When she showed the innovation to Andi, it had earned her a smile, hug, and kiss, reinforcing that she'd done something right. Besides, it felt far better than merely patting herself on the back. She made a note to consider the implications of self-based versus other-provided positive reinforcements...when she had more time.

Under Terrain she noted down: *Ocean - Continental Shelf.* The latter seemed relevant as the nose was stuck down into its mud.

Debris extent was trickier.

"They already collected all the surface debris before we got here," Andi pointed to the small pile on the lower deck. It was beside the first body bag that had been the only one when they arrived. "I went through it. Just what you'd expect, various personal effects. Nothing from the plane itself. That ROV we sent down didn't spot anything on the ocean floor. So that's the extent of your debris field."

"No, that isn't correct. Engine Number Four is still missing."

Andi nodded. "You're absolutely right. We'll inspect that when it's found."

Miranda made a note of that. "What's next?"

"The crash itself."

"Should we suit up and go see it?"

"No," Holly's voice was rough as she came up to them. "You really don't want to do that." She leaned heavily against Mike as if she might collapse to the deck without his support. Her wet suit covered her from the waist down. A towel peeked out either end of the heavy USCG coat that someone had wrapped around her. Her eyes were bloodshot and her fair skin looked even paler than usual. Holly's hood was up, making her look like a military street thug who was half human and half neoprene mermaid.

Miranda patted herself on the back. She wasn't sure if it was a good metaphor, but it was certainly one of the most complex she'd ever managed to assemble.

"The plane isn't embedded as hard into the mud as you might expect; it's definitely reacting to the wing tanks being pumped dry. I swam down, only one window is out, at least in the aft two-thirds. Probably the one for the seat that first body had been in. Once we have the bodies out, we could close the rear stairs and have the Coasties fabricate a window patch—second from the rear on the port side. Then we could try pumping in air. She might refloat on her own if there are no bad surprises farther forward. Though towing her through this shit might take some serious doing." She looked up at the sky.

Miranda did too. It didn't take a degree in meteorology—Miranda had only taken it as a minor in college but she'd stayed abreast of innovations since then—to see how fast the weather was shifting. As much as she hated to remove a plane from its crash site, it would be far easier to inspect on land. That's what they'd done with TWA 800. They'd spent months collecting parts from the ocean floor and then spent years reassembling it in a land-based hangar.

She and Andi exchanged looks. Without speaking, she could see that they agreed that was the right next step. "Let's go talk to the captain."

"Uh," Mike glanced at Holly. "You two go ahead. We need to talk about something."

Glad to once again have some understanding of the situation, Miranda tugged on Andi's hand and they hurried inside and up the many stairs leading to the bridge.

32

______

Holly leaned her head against Mike's shoulder. "Thanks. I still need a minute."

"I wish I could give you that." He pulled her phone out of his pocket. "You got a voice message while you were under. One of those voice-message-as-a-text things."

"*We have a great job offer. No previous experience required?*" If it promised she could work from home, she didn't care if it was a scam or not.

Having a place to really call home for the first time in decades had been Andi's doing. After Miranda's home had burned down on Spieden Island, along with half the trees, Miranda had been rootless. She'd never been happy in the team's shared house in Gig Harbor. They were based in Washington State and it had been very convenient to a local airport, which had been their home base for several years. But as Miranda's discomfort grew with the temporary setup, Andi had switched into some frantic new-home-search mode—in her utterly chill US Army / Chinese-Zen sort of way.

She'd come up with a pair of old missile silos on three hundred acres that backed up against thirteen-thousand acres of Tiger Mountain State Forest wilderness. Each had a surface house and a tunnel to their personal silos. The lower levels were flooded with groundwater but had been sealed off by the previous owner leaving two generous floors of living space. With other renovations and the addition of a hangar for Miranda's planes and helicopter, they were surprisingly comfortable. The old command-and-control bunker between their two silos had been converted into the team office.

And right now she could empathize with Miranda's joy of being able to shut herself underground behind a great big blast door. Closing out a world where people like Drake, Roy, Rose, and all the other innocents on that plane were murdered, sounded damned good at the moment.

"Sorry, no. A woman left it. Had one of those seriously lovely, deepish voices like Rose Cole's...uh...did."

"A call from the dead?" She wouldn't be surprised by anything at this point.

Though Mike was. "How did you know?"

"Know what?"

"Her message was: *Tell the woman with the Taser that I most urgently must die. And I wish to again meet my Little Sister.* What does Taz have to do with this?"

Holly wanted to bury her face once more against Mike's shoulder. "Nothing. Not a single...God...damn...thing."

33

MIKE AND HOLLY TRACKED THEM DOWN IN THE SHIP'S MACHINE shop. Miranda was overseeing the construction of the necessary window plug to fill in the missing one. A simple steel sandwich held together with long bolts. Inside they had placed thick rubber gaskets and a fitting for an air hose run through both plates. The seal needed to be effective, not perfect.

Holly watched as the machinist used a bending press to apply a slight curve to each plate under Miranda's direction. Once done, she recognized that the curve would precisely match the hull. Overkill, really, as the gaskets were more than thick enough to compensate, but that was Miranda.

"They have all but the last of the bodies," Andi reported, "And they're trying to suction out the last of the fuel that accumulated at the front of the tanks where there's no drain."

Holly figured that was a good trick at thirty meters down. "Good engineers."

Andi nodded.

Holly tipped her head toward Miranda's back in question.

"We're just waiting on the fabrication. Actually, not even that. The dive team is going overboard with it in a few minutes.

Once they start pumping, we'll back everyone away for safety. Nothing much for us to do until we see if she refloats or not."

Holly tipped her head the other way, indicating a quiet corner of the shop—or as quiet as could be while the machinist was drilling a one-inch hole for the air fitting through a pair of thick aluminum plates.

"I'm standing right here, you know." Miranda hadn't turned, but Holly could see their reflection in the screen of the milling machine. So much for being subtle.

"You are, sorry." Holly nodded toward the corner. "I have a question for you. Can we go talk somewhere quieter?"

Miranda simply turned and walked away from the machinist. "He's very good. I am confident he'll complete that task satisfactorily."

When Holly tried to follow, her brief immobility had allowed her body to seize up from the battering it had taken. She wished for the old days. As a Spec Ops operator, she'd have had a pouch of emergency meds. Chewing on a couple of Vicodin might taste worse than dingo droppings, but it pumped the painkiller into the body plenty fast that way. Here in civilian-world, it was a Schedule-II narcotic, and she'd never thought to stock any. Maybe after this, she'd hit the infirmary and see how stiff-necked Coasties turned out their medics. She could use a handful.

Last moving, last to arrive, but she made it across the shop without begging for a stretcher.

"I've got a problem, Miranda, and I need your help to solve it. I need to kill someone."

"The person who crashed *Air Force One?* But I haven't determined the how. Do you already know the who and the why? And you can't be judge, jury, and executioner. We're bound by the same laws as—"

Holly shook her head and her neck wished she hadn't. "No, nothing to do with all this."

Mike was watching her. She should have explained the message to him first, but she felt the clock inside her head ticking away far too fast.

Andi's eyes had gone even narrower than usual.

"Seriously, nothing like that. I have a friend who needs to *appear* to have died. Very convincingly and very soon. At the same time, I have to get her out of the country."

"What country?" Andi managed to get to the question first.

Holly closed her eyes, trying to picture a harder scenario, and she couldn't. "She's in Moscow."

"Moscow isn't a country."

Holly managed a smile at Miranda. "Not the one in Maine or Idaho or wherever else they are. She's in Moscow, Russia. I need to figure out how to create a plane crash without, you know, creating a plane crash."

Miranda backpedaled into a rack of assorted pipes and tubing. Thankfully, they were secured against the ship's motion at sea, but it made a loud enough racket to have the machinist twist around to see what they were up to.

Andi rolled her eyes. Holly mouthed, *What?* But Andi just shook her head sadly before turning to Miranda and taking both of her hands.

"It's *not* like your parents, Miranda."

Holly was such an idiot. She should go to the machinist and have him drill a couple holes in her head so that maybe some intelligence could leak in. Even a little would be better than what she had.

Miranda's parents had been murdered by crashing a plane in 1996—a Russian plane. Then, to cover that up and hide that they were CIA agents deeply embedded in Russia, their bodies had been inserted into the near simultaneous wreckage of TWA 800 that had exploded off the Long Island coast in a completely unrelated event.

And she'd just thrown all that in Miranda's face.

"It's not—"

But she could see there was no point. Miranda had slid down the pipe rack until she sat on the floor with her knees hugged against her chest and her breathing rapid. Meg had rushed over from watching the machinist and dove into Miranda's lap. She didn't even reach out to hug the furry little beast.

"I—" She tried to squat, but couldn't without a major muscle transplant.

Andi blocked her view of Miranda. She looked as livid as Holly had ever seen her. "Get the fuck out of here." Andi never swore.

"I didn't mean to—"

Andi didn't strike out. She merely pointed at the ladder up to the deck.

Holly had just crashed Miranda's brain through her own ineptitude. Bowing her head, as much as her stiff neck allowed, she went.

34

"Well that didn't go so great."

The fulminating look that Holly sent his way told Mike that his own skills weren't holding up very well at the moment. Holly had only cried a few times in his experience, but she'd never wept like her heart had been ripped out. Instead of feeling strong for being able to offer her comfort, he'd felt utterly helpless in the face of her pain.

He tried again. "Look, I know it's against your nature, but tell me what's going on. Maybe between us we can figure it out. You need to *kill* someone without really killing them, right? Who?"

They'd come up out of the cutter's depths to wind up on the bow. He'd thought they'd been going the other way, but the ship's inner spaces seemed to twist and turn with a mind of their own. Large military ships weren't big in his repertoire. Maybe he'd use that as the excuse for why he was missing so many cues.

Anchored directly downwind of *Air Force One,* the bow pointed at the wreck like a compass needle. The waves weren't big enough to kick spray over the bow, though they soon would be. The RHIBs were having more and more trouble fighting the waves. Not that the twenty-four-foot boats weren't built to take it, but holding their positions in the ten- to fifteen-foot waves was another matter.

Holly winced as she leaned slowly back against the white steel of the big deck-gun turret.

"Are you hurt?" He moved forward to inspect her for injuries.

She stopped him with a raised palm. "Nothing that some Vicodin and a week sleeping on my stomach wouldn't fix. Too bad that's not an option." She closed her eyes and simply lay there for a minute or more.

Mike couldn't stand it anymore. "Holly—"

She shook her head. "Not what's important. Do you remember—"

"You stupid bitch!" Andi pushed between them. "Don't you *ever* think first?"

"No, that's your and Mike's job. You know that about me. Is she okay?"

"You dare ask after throwing her parents' deaths in her face with that stupid-ass question?"

"Do you remember Inessa Turgeneva?"

Mike didn't recognize the name, but clearly Andi did. For some reason, that brought her rage to a screeching halt.

"If I don't go save her now, she's dead. You want that?"

Andi shook her head.

"Who?"

Holly glanced at Mike. "Remember Kaliningrad?" Then she turned to Andi, "I'm sure that your short ass definitely does."

Mike had aged a hundred years during that mission. Holly had parachuted alone into the Russian exclave sandwiched between Poland and Lithuania to rescue Miranda and Andi from kidnappers. He'd never gotten the whole story, but Holly had ejected Andi from the team immediately afterward without consulting anyone. For almost a year, Miranda had staggered along worse than a malfunctioning automaton without her. But he'd never heard of—"Inessa who?"

Holly sighed. "She, more than anyone else, stopped the US and Russia from going to war that day. Between them, she and Miranda had the keys to the downing of that Osprey over the North Sea off Scotland. Way back when, she was mentored by Miranda's parents when they were undercover CIA. Inessa is also a very smart lady."

"What was the line about the Taser?"

"I shot her husband with one while I was there. Only the two of them and this one," she nodded toward Andi, "Know that. Proof of identity."

"Oh." Mike didn't know whether to be amused or furious that Holly hadn't shared this story with him. Of course, she'd been crap about doing that until it had almost broken their relationship and nearly destroyed Miranda. Neither of them had been willing to rehash anything from that hard year. "Does he play into this?"

"No. He's just some two-star general in the FSB."

He snorted out a laugh. "Oh, is that all? That's their secret police, FBI, and CIA all rolled into one, right?"

"Pretty much." Holly hadn't looked away from Andi. "I need to make everyone think she's dead *and* get her out of Russia. Probably in the next twenty-four hours. You know I'm not the big thinker, Andi. Not at the level of Miranda. It's got to be a hundred percent bulletproof—so to speak."

Andi...shifted. Her stance was that of any landlubber standing on a pitching boat. To Holly it might have been dead calm. His years as a downhill skier let him compensate for each wave's passage with some modicum of stability. Andi's skills were the delicate control necessary to pilot a military helicopter. She staggered a step one way and then two the other under the gross motion of the Coast Guard cutter. But no...she was more unstable than that.

Slow, Mike! When did he get so damn *slow?* Andi had followed them with the clear intent of inflicting serious harm on Holly. Then she'd become as cowed as Mike had seen her since the day he'd given her permission to try to heal the breach with Miranda. Now she looked thoughtful.

"You want to save this Inessa?" Mike asked.

"I promised."

"Her husband—"

"Kidnapped Miranda, I know. Inessa set her free."

"Inessa hurt her like hell!" Andi shouted, now shifting straight through furious and back into dangerous.

"How?" Mike asked before the two women could go at each other.

Holly didn't answer, instead meeting Andi gaze for gaze. He'd been shocked that Andi had gotten that earlier punch past Holly's defenses. And that was before the battering she'd taken aboard *Air Force One.* For once, his bets might not be on Holly in a fight though she towered eight inches over Andi.

Andi finally answered. "Miranda's parents treated her like shit her whole life. Like she was a failed component and a burden. If not for her therapist and governess, they'd probably have rammed her into an institution. But they treated Inessa like their beloved daughter."

"That explains it," Mike nodded.

"Explains what?"

"The message said that Inessa wanted to meet her *Little Sister.* I'm assuming that's Miranda."

Andi closed her eyes. And when the next wave caught the ship's bow a little sideways, it almost tumbled her to the deck. She stumbled a few steps away before recovering. "Yeah...that's Miranda. Inessa said that, the day I betrayed—"

Holly reached out and grabbed her shoulder.

Mike knew he'd screwed up. Her stagger had placed him three steps too far away to intervene in time.

But rather than attacking, Holly simply shook her. "That's done now, Wu. Yeah, we never had our talk and I'm guessing that now we don't need to. Miranda loves you with all her heart is capable of and she married you. And, yes, you finally pounded it through my thick skull. I want to spend the rest of my life with Mike, and I'll figure out how to tell him sometime soon without freaking both of us out."

Mike wanted to respond, he really did. It wasn't that he was freaking out. No. The big surprise that had stolen his breath away? That he was *not* already overboard and swimming for shore. He looked at her and knew it was true; he wanted to spend every day he could with Holly. But she wasn't looking at him. Instead, she was watching Andi.

Andi in turn studied the deck intently. Did it until she finally managed a nod. Then she faced Holly as if nothing had happened. "Miranda can't help you with this, what can *I* do?"

35

<hr>

Miranda had let Meg and Andi's double hug bring her back. That and her simple statement, "You take care of *Air Force One*. I'll take care of Holly."

They were a team of two and Miranda knew to her very core that Andi always spoke truth. So not having to worry about what Holly said anymore, she'd pushed away the darkness and returned to watch the machinist as Andi went on deck. Though she did keep Meg clasped tight in her arms. Meg had calmed enough to rest her head on Miranda's left shoulder as usual when everything was okay.

After a careful inspection, she made a few suggestions. The man had agreed and implemented them quickly.

She felt the heft of the finished two-plated window seal. The chief petty officer had done a fine job and done it quickly. This seal would hold against fifty atmospheres of pressure, five times the necessary maximum.

"Do not let them bleed the air in too quickly, Chief, or they will risk blowing the hull of the fuselage. It is in balancing the internal and external pressures that will provide a chance of success. If this does work and the plane does rise, you will have to rapidly release the pressure back to one atmosphere or it may rupture and sink again."

He held up a box with four switches. "Petty Officer 2 Stanik will be holding this. We've rejiggered some steam relief valves to add a remote control. We shoved 'em through the top and bottom of the fuselage as we don't know which way she'll come up. Put 'em fore and aft, so as to balance her if we have to."

Miranda nodded. She enjoyed working with competent people.

He took her nod as approval and hurried toward the ladderway leading to the deck. They'd used a single media, non-verbal communication. Yes, that worked nicely too.

Competent people.

She stood alone in the now-silent shop. She enjoyed working with her NTSB team because they were all competent people. All different, but skilled at what they did.

Andi Wu was good with helicopters and Miranda herself when she became flustered.

Mike Munroe was good with people.

Holly Harper was—

Mike was good with people!

"Mike, is Holly right about *planning* a plane crash?" Except he wasn't here to ask.

However, Mike had come with Holly when she'd asked that horrid question. Why would anyone crash a plane that had done nothing bad to anyone? But Mike hadn't turned Holly aside before asking her question.

"You understand people. I don't." She continued her one-sided conversation with Mike.

She pretended that Mike stood there with that patient smile of his, waiting for her to find the answer.

"But..." Miranda stopped. With no idea regarding what came next, she knew that she *never* would understand people.

"What are you thinking so hard about?" Andi came back down the ladder.

"I don't understand how to decide if Holly's question was more important than the life of an airplane."

Andi came up and took her hand. "Miranda, I think you may be the most thoughtful woman ever born."

"But I don't understand my own thoughts."

"That's okay. You wouldn't be who you are otherwise. And do you want to know a little secret?"

Miranda unlocked her phone. *Yes* still showed as the final screen she'd had open.

Andi understood. She nodded and smiled.

"I wouldn't worry too much. We neurotypicals don't understand our own thoughts and reactions a lot of the time either."

"But that's..." Miranda searched for a word but *ridiculous* didn't quite fit.

"Nonsensical?" Andi suggested. "It is."

It was. "Should I go and try to help Holly?"

Andi gazed up at the shop's ceiling.

Miranda didn't see anything there except the overhead cables and service pipes that traced through so much of the ship's structure. Despite being deep inside the ship, she did hear the sound of a departing helicopter.

Andi nodded upward, apparently indicating the departing helicopter. "I'd say that she's past where either of us can help her. But don't worry, Mike went with her."

Miranda slipped out her notebook to check. But once she did, Miranda couldn't bring herself to point out that Andi's expression exactly matched the worried emoji on her emotional reference page.

36
____

Liú Zuocheng knew in the first five seconds that the President of China had not set up the American President's death. But it had taken him an hour to pacify the man before he could get away. He'd barraged Zuocheng with questions.

Does this change our trade relations?

It wasn't relevant, because the woman would have become President in two weeks anyway if Roy Cole had lived. His own leader had clearly not thought anything through ahead of time. And the longer they spoke, the clearer it became that he wasn't evading or pretending; he was deeply concerned about things he didn't understand at all.

Zuocheng went from there to his office for the emergency meeting of the Central Military Commission that he'd called. Their concerns were better formulated but equally lacking in premeditation of consequences. Anyone who had planned this would have answered several of his many questions themselves or at least couched them differently.

By the time he'd convinced himself of his fellow commission members' innocence, Wang Daiyu was waiting outside his office. It gave him pause—which he was careful not to reveal even to her. What kind of connections had Wang Daiyu developed that she could be sufficiently certain so quickly? Or had she found the guilty? No, he could see that much revealed in her carefully schooled expression.

She waited until he'd closed his office door and swept the room for bugs. Neither of them fully trusted the other CMC members. Each was the best man he'd been able to place in the role—past the President's whims. But that very competence made them much more dangerous and harder to trust.

"They're stunned," she waved a hand outward as she stood before his desk as an underling delivering a report properly would. "I thought it would require a long and careful quest, but they are like mythological Taoties, eating themselves for lack of anything else to feed upon. Every finger is pointed elsewhere, and none appear to have given any thought to leveraging the opportunity, even now."

He let his smile tell her that he'd found much the same.

"Does no one think anymore?" She rarely showed anger; her gentle voice went deeper and grew a harsh edge. She stalked about his office as if fighting a cage, circling again and again around the conference table. He loved watching the way she, even when furious, moved with such grace and stealth. Zuocheng turned away to stare at the photograph of the mountain woodland cabin he'd grown up in.

He tried to picture the two of them there, an old man and his Black Jade. It wasn't difficult. She had so loved the few times they'd managed to get away there together, hunting together for their dinner and making love together under the starlit heavens.

Then the slight shiver of nerves that had kept him alive and let him climb to the second most powerful position in China slid along his spine. Had Wang Daiyu become too dangerous to be his *Hēi Yù* in such a dream? And if that was true, how much longer would the leash of loyalty keep control of her? For a while, he assured himself. For long enough. But then he would have to think hard about some of his choices.

He could still hear her circling the room like a falcon not yet freed from a long jess he kept tied to her ankle. He knew what being trained as a Falcon Commando meant; he'd simply never fully attributed those skills to his Black Jade. A dangerous mistake he wouldn't make again.

"Those who can think, are afraid to..." he murmured.

"...and those who can't, pretend." She sighed, then stopped her circling and returned to stand before his desk. "We must make our innocence clear to the Americans."

Zuocheng's thoughts took longer to catch up with hers. When they did, he turned to face her—she was right. But how to convince them of China's noninvolvement in their President's death? His one back-channel contact into the US government was even now being extracted from the crashed airplane. The television screen showed that only two people's remains had yet to be recovered.

"In person," Daiyu pronounced. "Nothing less would be sufficient."

Again, she was right. In this, Americans were practically Chinese—the power of face-to-face obeisance was not to be underestimated. He certainly couldn't make the trip. The President had made it clear that he would *wait and see,* thus officially closing all diplomatic channels on this topic.

He could send Daiyu, but how would she reach so high, without being seen by Chinese operatives in the embassy— ones he might not trust the loyalty of? It would have to be done without her saying, *I am the emissary of General Liú Zuocheng, co-chairman of the Chinese Military Commission.*

"I have a way, if I may have permission to contact your granddaughter."

Startled, he had to sit with that thought for many heartbeats. He didn't see how, though he had no reason to doubt her assessment. That was not the main consequence. He had not anticipated using Chang Mui for some years to come, not until she and her lover had burrowed far deeper into the American systems. Activating an asset of such potential too soon might damage its future utility. Yet the situation was sufficiently urgent that he must grasp at any chance.

Reading his decision, she rose to her feet. She opened her phone and tapped something—sending a message she must have already composed. She had known it would come to this exact decision. Wang Daiyu, a weapon more dangerous than he'd ever have guessed. It still didn't make her wrong. That's when he noticed the small pack she'd brought with her.

He raised a single eyebrow.

"My plane departs from Beijing Capital International in precisely one hour."

Zuocheng nodded and escorted her to the door.

Before he could open it, she stopped him with her fingertips on his chest. "No one knows of...us?" Her meaning was clear.

"My security guard. My administrative assistant knows only that you work for me. There are no others."

She rested her palm against the center of his heart chakra. He recognized the gesture from her explanations of her yoga practices. "None of the committee or other guards?"

"None."

Daiyu rested their foreheads together, touched noses, then shifted against him chakra by chakra down their bodies until their root chakras too were pressed together. They had never touched even a fingertip outside her apartment except for the brief period in his own bedroom. The arousal that raged through him at her pressing the entire length of her body to his here in his office at the very heart of the Eight-One Building at the Ministry of National Defense, was among the most powerful of his life.

For nine times nine heartbeats, just as Su Nü said of the

first and most essential method of joining yin and yang, they remained pressed together down the length of their chakras. When Daiyu stepped back, he opened the door and held it for her.

She left with no words and no looking back.

37

There were presently five US companies with a market cap over two trillion dollars, all of them in the tech sector.

Though there were five of them, Chen Mei-Li thought of them as the Three Big Giants in the universe. A chip maker at the top made no sense and they were bound to crash, or at least diminish, when their stock prices equalized with reality. And at some point, everyone's love for an overpriced smartphone was going to go away.

That left three giants in the ring—an operating system provider, a retail monster, an overly invasive search engine. They bore clear parallels to China's mythological giants Pangu, Kuafu, and Xingtian. Pangu created the world. Kuafu chased the sun to capture it, dying in the pursuit. Xingtian was the unyielding fighter, battling on after he was slain. To her, Microsoft embodied the creator, Amazon the overly ambitious pursuit of shiny objects, and Google the unyielding determination to control all the world's user data. More importantly, all three modern giants delved deep, deep, deep into creating cutting-edge AI.

She and Mui agreed that's where the ultimate power of the

future lay. They had started their American journey in Seattle, Washington, so it was only logical to merely shift across Lake Washington. They joined Microsoft, the biggest of the three, as the best platform to launch their future plans from.

We can't be seen going straight to the jugular vein, Mui had counseled. She was always the thoughtful one. Given the chance, Mei-Li was far more likely to tear down the front door. So they'd found her a different path, one that fit her better anyway. She was no coder, but with her independent study master's degree at the intersection of psychology, political theory, and economic game theory, she'd already proven herself to be a virtuoso strategist in their gaming division. In only her second year aboard, she'd been brought in on the development side of their next big showpiece.

Chang Mui, sweet Mui, with a gentle smile that could melt even Mei-Li's hardened heart, had applied her incisive mind and MBA to becoming one of the assistants to the Director of the AI division.

The Friday let's-get-next-week-preplanned meeting had run long and been atypically contentious. Senior management's unexpected presence meant that Mei-Li hadn't ripped everyone a new one for indulging in large doses of ego and raw stupidity as she'd wanted to. At the moment Mei-Li hated the world at large and far too many others to list. Senior management was worse than an infestation of weasels. She didn't want to go home to Mui in such a mood, but she'd promised the exact opposite—when she was in such a mood, she *must* go to Chang Mui.

"I'm here!" It took all her will not to hammer the door of their townhouse shut. Between their salaries, they could have easily afforded more. There had also been the startling amount that had appeared in their American bank accounts with no explanation. It hadn't taken long to form a hypothesis.

General Zhang Ru had owned Mei-Li for years, giving her

body to whomever he needed favors from. He'd used her to scrabble his way onto the Central Military Commission, then, two years ago, he'd abruptly disappeared and never been heard from again. He must have crossed General Liú, but they hadn't been able to confirm that. Mei-Li still had nightmares of Zhang Ru suddenly appearing at the door of their Redmond, Washington, condo and demanding what little shreds he'd left of her soul. Someone had stripped him of his fortunes and sent a portion of it to Mei-Li—perhaps Mui's grandfather General Liú.

However the small fortune had arrived, they had both lived in China for their first two decades. Neither of them would ever be comfortable with the crass consumerism of the massive homes that fellow Softies purchased up on the plateau to the west of town. A townhouse with kitchen, living room, and two bedrooms—one for them and one for their home computers—was all they needed.

Mui must have seen Mei-Li's schedule and anticipated her mood. She was already in the kitchen cooking Mu Shu Pork—Mei-Li's favorite. She wrapped her arms around Mui's waist from behind and rested her chin on Mui's shoulder to watch her cook.

"Remember the proverb."

She sighed and, stepping away, boosted herself up to sit on an unused section of counter. "Before setting out on revenge, dig two graves."

Mui nodded without turning.

"I survived Zhang Ru, thank the gods he's probably dead." The general had enslaved her after she'd aged out of the national gymnastics program. Aged out or been cast out for *only* winning a silver at the Olympics? She'd transcended being ripped from her family at the age of three to enter the program —or liked to pretend to herself that she had. But by nine she'd become the coach's personal pet in all the worst ways. Then—

She buried her face in her hands and tried to peel off the black shadow and cast it aside. The action helped only a little.

"And how did you survive Zhang Ru?" Mui tossed the thin-sliced pork in the soy-hoisin-wine marinade and began chopping vegetables. She made it look like artwork. Mei-Li's efforts tended to look like someone had run a lawnmower through the produce.

"By letting events take their natural course." Someone else had silenced Ru for her. If she ever found out who, she'd kiss their feet.

"Precisely. You have sworn vengeance on the entire Central Military Commission. We are in no position to bring this about. So what is the best way to damage their power?"

It was a discussion they'd had so many times that she'd had dreams about it. Mei-Li dampened a finger with her tongue and dipped it into the small bowl of toasted sesame seeds. Licking them off, she crunched on them while fighting to convince herself that Mui's plan was the right one. Worse, she knew it was, but her fourteen years embedded in China's gymnastics training had taught her to drive for perfection at every moment. This slow slog grated against everything she was.

"Well?"

"By helping America advance until China becomes irrelevant. And we are best served by doing our part of keeping America in the lead until those bastards all wither under corruption, demographic collapse, climate change, and everything else that could possibly curse their shriveled souls."

Mui poured the whisked eggs into the hot wok that responded with a sharp sizzle and snap. She ignored Mei-Li's singsong delivery. "Precisely."

Mei-Li crunched on another fingertip's worth of sesame seeds. She did like the way that sounded. Besides... "We *are* young."

"We are," Mui slid the slab of scrambled egg onto the cutting board, tossed in the meat, then made quick work of slicing the eggs into long strips. "The old men of the CMC are all many decades older than us. Grandfather Liú Zuocheng by fifty years and he is not the eldest."

"They will be dead for decades before we are their ages." That cheered her up as well.

"And we're beautiful. They aren't."

Despite her mood, Mei-Li couldn't help herself and giggled. Mui was a great beauty, a generational one. Mei-Li knew her own best feature was an athlete's body, something she'd maintained as well as possible since winning the silver medal that Mui had insisted on hanging as the sole ornament on their bedroom wall. "We *are* young and we *are* beautiful."

Mui added the vegetables as she nodded.

Mei-Li hopped down from the counter to re-warm the Mandarin pancakes briefly in the bamboo steamer. As always, Mui had broken her dark mood. At first, there had been inescapable nightmares—every night. But over their four years in America, those had become rarer and easier to escape.

She opened her mouth to tell Mui how much she loved her, but Mui beat her to it by simply saying, "I know."

Mei-Li laughed properly this time as she flipped the pancakes.

Her phone pinged, and Mui had a pained look. Dinner was ready.

"If it's work, I won't answer." She pulled it out and looked at the screen. "It's—"

"What?"

Mei-Li tapped in. "It's...airplane tickets. For both of us."

Mui stopped moving with dinner half transferred into the serving bowl. "It's what?"

"In six hours. To Washington, DC. Not China." That had

been a terrifying possibility. If forced back there, even their American citizenship might never again set them free.

"Scam or a prank," Mui finished scraping the wok clean, tossed in a cup of water that flashed to steam as she gave it a quick scrub with a steel brush. Then she spilled that into the sink, ran a swirl of oil over the hot steel, and turned off the burner to let the metal season and cool.

"Our names and traveler information. Prepaid."

Then she found the proof that it was real and turned it to Mui.

Mui read it twice, then turned very slowly to gather up the serving implements. "It seems," she took a slow and careful breath that worried Mei-Li even more, "we're going to DC tonight."

38

"Let's go somewhere new."

Tech Sergeant Jeffrey Wilson didn't want to go anywhere, except maybe to curl up and die. But he couldn't show it, not here, not today. Especially not with Major Nelson asking. The man had taken him under his wing as their parents were friends. Not many folks left their small city of Liberal, Kansas. Most stayed for the meat packing plant or the oil field work. Those few who left inevitably went military.

"Sure, you name it."

At Momma's suggestion, he'd gone Air Force just as Nelson had. Over a decade younger, he'd had only fleeting memories of Nelson back home in Liberal. What he hadn't expected was for Nelson to reach down through the ranks to give him a hand. A hand he now wished he could cut off.

"Been to Eddie's Pizza? Heard good things about it."

Jeffrey had always been good at writing code. And people in Liberal who were good at code didn't turn into hackers, they turned into office workers.

"I could use a couple slices."

Which was what he'd done. Except his *office* was in the secure hangar at Andrews Air Force Base. The one that had been purpose-built to contain the two 747s that served as *Air Force One.*

"Out the Virginia Gate, left on Old Alexandria Ferry Road, and it's just before Woodyard Road on the left. See you in ten."

No one had gotten any work done today. Everyone had been mesmerized by the unfolding disaster and recovery efforts on the screen. Thankfully he wasn't the only one who'd had to go barf his guts out. Their job was making sure that *Air Force One* remained one hundred percent available at all times. And they'd just killed the President.

"Sure."

Except he alone knew that *he* was the one who'd killed the President. He'd put the code in place. Not being part of the flight planning or preparation team, he hadn't known about the changed assignment for President Roy Cole's tour until they were rolling the plane out of the hangar. Nothing he could ever do would make it right again.

He managed to get into the old Dodge Ram 1500 pickup his parents had passed on to him when he graduated high school. It felt as if he was in an unreal video game, controlling his own body from some remote, faraway place.

Rolling down the window to let in the strange spring-warm air in the depths of winter, he headed south out the Virginia Gate. At the moment he couldn't even recall *why* he'd done it. Everything was a blur. Alone for the first time today, the tears came. He kept blinking them away enough to see, but they wouldn't stop.

Left on Old Alexandria.

The first drops of rain spattered the windshield. But he couldn't roll up the window. Couldn't turn on the windshield wipers. He *had* to tell someone. They'd lock him away forever.

His parents would disown him. He couldn't, but he must. Jeffrey knew he'd never be able to live with what he'd done.

Thankfully, he didn't have to.

He wasn't looking to his left where the Andrews Air Force Base East Golf Course ran through the maple and poplar trees just the other side of the security fence. So he never saw what hit him.

The golf ball was traveling at two hundred and seventeen miles per hour—just twenty-three miles per hour slower than the acknowledged world record fastest drive—when it struck Tech Sergeant Jeffrey Wilson in the side of the head. At that speed, it would have easily passed through the driver's window and probably killed him. Because his window was down, the variable of the glass didn't enter into what happened. The ball entered close above his left ear, smashed through the temporal bone and the midbrain—effectively cutting his spinal cord— and departed out his right. It had sufficient remaining momentum to punch out through the passenger window.

With his body cut off from his brain functions, his hands and feet went lax. He'd already been driving slowly. His foot slid off the gas pedal. With no additional fuel, the engine dropped to an idle and the truck slowed further. It stopped when it bumped into the end of a low guardrail. A road crew would later determine that there was insufficient damage to bother fixing the small dent.

The investigating officer was never able to identify who hit the ball that had left a round hole in the window and a messy one in Jeffrey's head. He figured that no serious player would want to admit to hitting such a bad slice. The golf ball itself was never found and the case was closed as an accidental death.

No one *had* hit the golf ball; it had been fired from a custom-built slingshot rifle. After passing through Tech Sergeant Jeffrey Wilson and the truck window, the ball had bounced once on the pavement and landed in the back of a passing pickup where the incoming rain would wash it clean long before it was discovered.

Jeffrey Wilson wouldn't be telling anyone about anything he'd done. He'd just been executed by a Titleist golf ball.

39

AIR FORCE ONE HAD NOT GONE QUIETLY TO HER GRAVE. NOR DID she resurrect gently either.

The storm had stabilized at Sea State 6. With the deep swell triggered by the storm continuing to travel north, the waves around the crash site were forming up in great, long rollers up to two stories high. Most of them were whitecapped and some were blowing spray.

Initial delays in raising the plane occurred when two fresh dive teams were sent down to the very nose of the 747 to attempt recovery of the last two bodies. Neither team was successful.

Colonel Vic Franklin had spent innumerable hours over the last year waiting outside of various Presidential locations, both on land and in the air. Whenever the President left the White House, a rotating staff of colonels from each of the services made their best effort to keep the briefcase known as the nuclear football (properly the Presidential Emergency Satchel) within fifty meters of the President.

During those hours, he'd developed quite the crush on Tabitha Ray, one of President Cole's secretaries—the one who typically traveled with him. Rumor said she'd gotten a divorce six months ago, and he hoped this trip would give him the chance to ask her out.

He was mid-forties and knew he'd topped out; he wasn't general material and wasn't going to let himself become a useless lump of ROAD—retired on active duty—colonel for another twenty years. He'd be out as soon as he figured out what came next.

And there was Tabitha, the walking, breathing proof that fifty was the new fantastic. Besides, she was one of those genuinely nice people; it just radiated off her. They were both part of a truly rare breed, born-and-raised DC natives. That too had given them a connection to rest his hopes upon. As always, their seats were side by side on *Air Force One* along the left side of the plane facing the President's office.

It had been going well...until the engines had started winding down. After General Drake Nason had come out, shutting the President's door so firmly that the Do Not Disturb signal was clear, Tabitha had reached out and taken his hand. They hadn't let go even during the final impact.

Vic had struggled and failed to keep ahold of both Tabitha's hand and the nuclear football when the initial surge of the water struck. It had rushed aboard, ripping their seats free from the fifty-year-old floor supports. The three of them—Vic and Tabitha still belted into the business class seats, and the forty-five pound briefcase—tumbled together. The pressure wave had driven them down into the President's personal apartment at the very nose of the aircraft—landing them in the President's bed at the very front of the cabin.

The nose of the plane had survived generally intact, except for the massive radar assembly that had driven the forward bulkhead of the cabin into the compartment like the engine into a car's passenger compartment during a head-on collision. They were dead when they landed, then crushed by the radar assembly, but they'd finally gotten into bed together.

After the failure of the two dive teams to recover Vic and Tabitha's bodies, though they had recovered the nuclear football, it was decided to proceed with the attempt to refloat the plane. Once the storm broke off the tail, the recovery would become far more difficult. It would also drastically delay the analysis of what had caused the crash.

The final dive team had entered every space as they slowly ascended, to make sure that no one other than Vic and Tabitha had been left behind—there wasn't. But the diver also noted that the blown-out copilot's window was packed solid with mud.

On surfacing he asked to see the commander. The two small women wearing NTSB vests were with him.

"I understand that the concept is to blow air into the plane, using its pressure to drive the water out the missing window in the bottom. But that window is below the level of the mud. The water will be hard to drive out."

This had caused the next delay as another team mounted a jet pump deep in the fuselage. Somewhat counterintuitively, a jet pump removes water by pumping more in. A small amount of water is driven down a high-pressure line. At the bottom, the stream is turned upward and fired into an uptake pipe with a narrowed throat. Just before the narrowing, a pickup pipe is open to the ocean. When the high-pressure stream enters the narrow tube, the resulting Venturi effect accelerates the stream further, creating a very low-pressure zone in the pipe. This sucks the water in from the pickup pipe.

They would need to create a balance between air pressure pumped into the airplane and the jet pump ejecting water from inside the plane to out on the surface. Getting them out of balance could explode or crush the fuselage.

To monitor that, successive pressure gauges, both water and air, were placed at intervals down the length of the fuselage. By the time everything was ready, the RHIBs had to be pulled from the water because they could either handle the waves or be useful, but they couldn't do both.

The five motor life boats had become ten, and those could ride out a hurricane. Commander Davidson ordered those to pull back as well.

The sun had set hours before and the searchlights of the three cutters made the sea look even worse than he knew it was.

Commander Davidson inspected the situation carefully from his command bridge. Air, water, and power lines ran from the USCG *Bear* out to *Air Force One*.

The *Northland* and *Harriet Lane* had upped anchor to ease the brutal ride rather than constantly jerking against their anchor chains.

"Station keeping," he ordered the helmsman to keep them exactly where they were, then raised the *Bear's* anchor. When everything was squared away, he gave the command.

"Let's do it. Start the pumps."

He'd thought that the crisis of his command would be the rescue and body recovery. Now he glanced aloft at the blinking lights of the few news helos braving the storm and wondered what they'd say if he got *Air Force One* to the surface and then lost her to the depths.

40

ALREADY LIGHTENED BY THE REMOVAL OF THE FUEL, *AIR FORCE One* was shifting several degrees each way as the waves washed by her tail.

"Two meters, holding." Miranda announced.

Randy Davidson would rather have one of his own men monitoring the gauges, but his senior chief told him no. "She's..." Senior chief petty officers were the backbone of the enlisted Coast Guard and were never at a loss for words. "Shit, Skipper, pardon my language, but I know when I'm outclassed. You want *her* on those controls."

So he'd set the senior to watch over her, literally. Taller by a foot, he watched over the shorter woman's shoulders but didn't say a word. Maybe she really was that good. He sure hoped so. He checked on her dog, asleep at her feet. Mike Munroe had tipped him off about keeping an eye on the dog to help judge Miranda Chase's mental state. So far so good.

"Four meters of air evacuated, pressure holding. No increased motion." Miranda announced.

"Keep pumping." He left her to the job and twisted around to watch the scene. Big roller. Glimpse of the plane's tail in the trough. Big roller—this time spewing enough spray to block any view of the tail.

How the hell was he supposed to tow this thing if it did surface? He'd called in a pair of deep-sea salvage tugs and hoped they had a better idea than he did. Miranda had suggested attaching a line to the front landing gear—except it was several meters below the surface of the mud. Not wanting to lose the plane if it did surface, he'd lassoed the tail with a single run of two-inch hawser and attached a couple floats to it. He also had two able-bodied seamen standing by where the line came aboard with axes if they had to cut it fast.

"Six meters, holding."

"Now it gets interesting," he mumbled to his XO. Zeb nodded but didn't have anything to add.

They both knew that the first twenty feet had been clearing the rear electronics area and past the fold-down stairs. The plane was still very narrow back there and the water pressure would only be two atmospheres. Now, as they pushed deeper and had to increase the air pressure, they would be working their way past lines and lines of windows, lavatories, and a hundred other possible failure spots. Miranda had enumerated these at length.

The only solution they could implement rapidly was to send a diver all the way down to close the window shutters on every single window to add that bit more strength. Another diver had gone down with a couple large tubes of epoxy and plugged each toilet. Any more deep work and they'd have to fly in fresh divers. All three ships had limited-out all their divers at depth over the last ten hours.

"Eight and holding. Increased swing with wave motion."

"Physical or structural?" Another thing she'd explained was that the whole plane might start to move as a single physical piece—or their actions might blow the tail off.

"Indeterminate," Miranda said as if she was sitting in a deli discussing which mustard she preferred rather than overseeing the highest profile plane crash in history.

"Great, just great." He didn't know if he died a little or hoped a little more with each meter they gained, filling the fuselage with air instead of water without shattering the plane.

The damn thing was only seventy meters long from tip to tail and they had blown out past fifty before anything notable happened.

Then it all happened at once.

41

THE NOSE OF *AIR FORCE ONE* HAD CREATED SIGNIFICANT adhesion with the muddy ocean floor by the simple expedient of hitting it hard. The nose's initial impact had occurred with sufficient force to compact the soil. Underwater, this was achieved by driving the water out of the sediments. At sixty meters depth, the six tons per square foot pressure actually compressed the ocean floor and resisted water reentering the soils.

With the lightening of the plane, it began to work back and forth. This created a pumping action within the mud, making it expand and compress, rebalancing the degree of water saturation. The water forcing its way in began acting as a lubricant, allowing a tiny amount more motion with each shift.

The wave that broke *Air Force One* free from the bottom wasn't notable in any way. First, its leading trough washed across the tail at a sixty-degree angle to the wide flat planes of the twenty-meter-wide horizontal stabilizer. *Air Force One* swung steeply toward lying belly up. But it didn't release from the bottom. Next the wave caught the stabilizer and swung the plane in the opposite direction. At depth, the plane finally ripped free from the ocean bed.

It shot to the surface tail first. The tail and forty meters of the fuselage broke clear of the waves before slamming down to plant the tail much as General Owen had first intended to attempt his landing—with a hard smack and a huge cloud of spray.

The three US Coast Guard cutters had been holding station at the points of their kilometer-a-side triangle. This placed them each five hundred and seventy meters from the plane.

When *Air Force One* shot to the surface, it accelerated rapidly until it was traveling backward at thirty knots atop the waves moving at twenty themselves. It now had sufficient buoyancy that it didn't wallow in the waves but rather skidded over the wave crests as if hydroplaning along a highway.

The *Bear's* chosen station lay directly downwind from *Air Force One.*

Commander Randy Davidson had trained his entire career to act quickly when something threatened his ship.

"All back full! All back full!" In hindsight, he should have had the stern facing the airplane. Fat lot of good that did him now. A Famous-class cutter was not an RHIB speed boat, especially not backward.

They'd been half a kilometer from the sinking site. Forty meters of plane had shot out above the surface and finally impacted the water a hundred and fifty meters from the sinking site—a third of the way to his ship and closing fast.

"Sound general alarm!" He had to wait out the seven short ringing tones and one long one before he could continue. "Evacuate bow and all compartments forward of Frame Three. Seal all hatches throughout the ship."

Bear began crawling backward away from the fast-approaching plane.

"It will not impact us, Commander."

He spared a glance at Miranda.

"As it slows, the water we were unable to evacuate will slosh toward the forward end—that would be the forward end of motion, which is the stern of the aircraft. This will cause the tail section to dig in. That would imply a different course for best action than the one you have chosen at this momen—"

"Get to the point, woman."

"Stop engines and reel in on your tow line as quickly as possible. Otherwise the tail will dig into the waves and the plane will likely sink, this time to the bottom of the sea."

That felt even worse than being rammed by *Air Force One*.

"Winch full," he commanded, though he wasn't about to stop his retreat. He prayed to God that she was right. That tail section was as tall as the top of his ship's mast. It was a damn big piece of metal to watch coming his way.

42

"Oh dear," Miranda whispered to Andi.

"*What?*" The senior chief petty officer who'd been looming over her shoulder for the last hour spoke for the first time. That and his abrupt tone were such a surprise that Miranda jolted away, except there was nowhere to go. The hastily rigged panel of controls and readouts trapped her. Meg woke up and growled at the senior.

"Why's that, Miranda?" Andi asked the same question, an unnecessary repetition but her tone was calm and curious, rather than demanding.

Miranda swallowed hard and pointed at the nightmare scene out the bridge windows. "You'll see when *Air Force One* catches the next wave. Though I shouldn't call it that as *Air Force One* is no longer technically *Air Force One*. With the successful removal of the President's body, it is once more *SAM 29000*. I'm sorry for that mistake."

That this was foolish in comparison to the error in her calculations and what happened next, didn't make her feel any better.

Because of the initial slack that the skipper had left in his line wrapped around *Air Force One's* tail section and the fast approach of the 747 itself, the winch built for power rather than speed couldn't haul in the line fast enough to make a difference.

As she'd initially feared, the tail did indeed dig into the next wave. This caused the water remaining in the cabin to slosh toward the stern and drive it downward. The plug they had added to Allyson Liddel's rear window functioned perfectly.

What Miranda had failed to account for was that the high pressure air that had been pumped into the fuselage would have expanded as the aircraft surfaced. Once the missing copilot's window was clear of the mud, excess pressure wasn't merely released. The rapid expansion of the air with the aircraft's decreasing depth acted more like a water-driven rocket engine.

She saw her mistake by how much of the plane rose so rapidly out of the water. Her conclusion was supported by how lightly *SAM 29000* was surfing across the waves.

The plane dug its tail into a big wave.

"I am sorry."

The commander twisted in his chair to look at her. Miranda didn't look away fast enough and saw his eyes had gone wide.

Very wide.

She tried it herself and it made her eyes hurt.

43

AIR FORCE ONE'S TAIL PLOWED INTO THE WAVE, WHICH DROVE THE tail downward. The small volume of remaining water also did indeed slosh into the tail section and pull it downward. But the weight was no longer sufficient to drag the plane once more into the depths.

Instead, it acted like a pole vaulter jamming his pole into the box. Because the plane had been skimming on the wavetops, there was little adhesion between the aircraft's aluminum skin and the water. And the momentum of two hundred tons of airplane and water moving at thirty knots had to go somewhere.

The front of the 747 flung upward as if trying to stand on its submerged tail. It balanced there in the brilliant work lights shining from above the bridge of USCG *Bear.* The long white fuselage tipped with sky-blue accents towered fifty meters above the cutter. The metallic-silver wings made it look like an angel of doom as it balanced above them.

Neither the wave that slapped against the underside of the tail nor the thirty-mile-per-hour wind were enough to tip the 747 all the way over—the combination of the two was.

Though it only took three-point-four seconds, it seemed to take forever to fall, slowly gaining momentum like a mighty hammer from heaven. The people aboard the US Coast Guard Cutter *Bear* were helpless to do more than watch as it accelerated toward them.

Commander Randy Davidson's order to continue reversing altered the scenario. Instead of smashing into the bridge and destroying the forward half of the ship, the nose of *Air Force One* merely clipped the bow of the cutter.

Now emptied of fuel, passengers, and the bulk of the water, the 747 weighed just two hundred and eighteen tons compared with the *Bear's* eighteen hundred. After falling from a height over fifty meters, the nose was moving at thirty-four meters per second—a hundred and fifteen kilometers per hour.

In just clipping the bow, everything that lay forward of the *Bear's* 76 mm deck gun was twisted past recognition. Despite the sudden shortening of the *Bear* by ten meters, the Frame Two hatches only leaked and the ones at Frame Three held strong. The worst injury was the Coast Guard machinist who had been thrown face first against the pipe rack in his shop— he would be wearing an eye patch for the rest of his life. Once over the injury, he rather liked being the Pirate King of the shop.

The damage to *Air Force One* was surprisingly minor in comparison. The stout deck gun caught on the plane's mangled forward radar assembly and ripped it free like a surgeon's scalpel.

The plane came to rest in the waves on its back, with its three remaining engines sticking up above the waves. It floated nose-to-nose with the *Bear*. It floated high enough in the water that the damaged nose section remained clear of the waves. Perched on the remains of the cutter's twisted bow, in addition to the shattered radar, were the contents of the President's private suite. Colonel Vic Franklin and the

President's secretary Tabitha Ray were both now aboard the *Bear*.

No one, living or dead, remained aboard *Air Force One*.

Commander Randy Davidson managed his first breath since the fall of the plane began, but it was that NTSB woman, Miranda Chase, who managed the first words.

"Well, that didn't go quite the way I anticipated."

44

———

Neither of them had slept on the red-eye flight from Seattle to DC. Worse, there'd been a connection and a flight delay. It didn't matter. Mui and Mei-Li had discussed the possible implications of the tickets throughout the flight. Knowing the who had offered no clues as to the why.

Logging onto the plane's Wi-Fi, they'd been able to watch the curious entourage off the Delaware coast. Two deep-sea salvage tugs towing an upside-down *Air Force One* through the heavy waves. It was hard to know whether to laugh or scream at the hundreds of gawkers' boats that had come out to meet the plane. The Coast Guard had to launch more and more assets into the storm to rescue them as they swamped, capsized, collided, and every other variation imaginable.

After them all, a lone cutter continued to drive backward. News reporters said that it was to keep pressure off the damaged bow. They were backing their way to Norfolk.

At first, she and Mui conjectured that they were going to meet the *Air Force One* plane when it reached land. At the slow towing speed, the 747 would have covered the eighty kilometers to Norfolk, Virginia, at about the same time they themselves would be landing in Dulles airport. It was ridiculous, yet their arrival must be related somehow. Knowing that their questions wouldn't be answered until they landed didn't help; they couldn't stop discussing the possibilities.

And for the long hours in between, when all new ideas eluded them, they watched mesmerized by the slow towing of *Air Force One* back from its ocean grave. The commentary was all about how could the plane have crashed and who could they blame and how the entire Air Force should be fired for incompetence and… But other than various bits of archive footage, it was the action shot they had.

There were also hastily assembled obituaries tracing the life and times of Roy and Rose Cole and Drake Nason. Roy and Drake had signed the card welcoming her and Mui to US citizenship after expediting passports for them. They had offered her and Mui a citizen's safety at a moment when they'd expected their lives were over. They'd given her hope.

Mei-Li had never killed anyone, though there were many she had wished she could. Curiously, almost every one of them was now dead—by others' hands or events, but dead nonetheless. She still had the card signed by Drake, Roy, and Lizzy welcoming her and Mui to the US. It had been included in a simple mailer with two US passports—the best gift of her life excepting only finding Mui. If she found out who had killed Drake and Roy, she wouldn't wait for anyone else to kill them. She'd find a way to do it herself and damn the consequences.

"No instructions," Mui noted for the tenth time as they cleared through the security exit.

They'd traveled light, carry-on only. Mei-Li had considered checking a small bag so that she could bring some weapons with her, but that had never been her strength. And the person who'd bought their tickets and they were probably meeting was beyond expert. For lack of anything better to do, they headed to the baggage claim conveyor for their flight.

And there she was.

Mui stood close before Wang Daiyu and bowed in greeting.

Mei-Li remained far more cautious. Yes, she was the assistant of Mui's grandfather, Liú Zuocheng. But he was the powerful head of the CMC, which she despised beyond breathing. If she could figure out how to reach them all together, she'd gladly have sacrificed herself just to remove them from the face of the Earth. Wang was also Zhang Ru's wife—the man who had *owned* Mei-Li for years, giving her body as favors to the rich, the powerful, and the thoughtlessly cruel—until she managed her escape. She wished them both slow and painful deaths.

Daiyu's careful bow showed that she read Mei-Li's distrust.

"You bought us tickets, and we came. So why are we here?" No pleasantries. No gentle greeting. No inquiries about her and General Liú's health—she threw the words in Daiyu's face. And she refused to feel ashamed by her own rudeness.

"You have adopted many Western ways already."

Daiyu might as well have slapped her. Shame's heat rushed to her cheeks despite her orders not to.

"I have been in the air for eighteen hours." Without another word Daiyu turned and led the way through the travel-battered people gathered at the various conveyor belts. Daiyu led them into the Café Americana at the end of baggage claim.

At Mui's easy shrug, Mei-Li followed along, though she didn't like it. But she did notice that Wang Daiyu's pack was no bigger than either of theirs, little more than a daypack. She too carried no suitcase or luggage. Which meant no weapons—or at least no obvious ones.

Mei-Li ordered a Reuben sandwich—she'd grown a real weakness for them since coming to America. Daiyu and Mui split a Buffalo Chicken pizza that also smelled great. She and Mui invariably cooked Chinese food at home but, when eating out, it was always American fare.

"Why are we here?" she asked again after taking the time to savor the first bite.

"Two reasons. First, I must speak to the President."

"He's in China."

"The American one."

Mei-Li shrugged, "So speak to her. Call the embassy or whatever. I'm guessing she's kind of busy today."

Mui rolled her eyes, but Mei-Li ignored her and took another bite of her sandwich.

"It is forbidden. It must be without their knowledge." That, at least, was interesting. "This information can *not* ever be traced back to me."

Before Mei-Li could jab at Daiyu again, Mui spoke softly. "Which means it must not be traceable back to Grandfather Zuocheng. I don't understand how we can help. Our best connection was to their general who died aboard *Air Force One* yesterday."

"I met his wife, the one to be the new Chairman of their Joint Chiefs of Staff." Mei-Li shrugged. "But it was very brief; we were at an airshow. I doubt if she'd remember me. We never actually spoke."

"She is not the only one you met at that airshow. Zhang Ru told me."

She could never trust a woman who had been with that... that...monster! Especially not by choice.

Daiyu obviously read her expression but her own remained unchanged. "A small fact that may interest you: I had the pleasure of ending his existence. Then we left his body for the wolves to feed on so that his spirit would never know rest."

Mei-Li was slow to recover. She'd *assumed* his death or imprisonment but not dared to truly hope—the death of Central Military Commission members wasn't exactly public news. Slow, deep breaths didn't help make it any more real; but there was no doubting Daiyu's statement. Mei-Li managed a nod for her to continue, the best she could manage at the moment.

"You met others." Daiyu picked up her pizza and took a bite to signal it was Mei-Li's turn to provide some useful information.

"There were the two women who swore in the US President yesterday. I can—"

"Not Miranda. I had the opportunity to work with them a few years ago. I would trust her discretion only if hard pressed. She has certain..."

"...challenges." Mei-Li recalled hearing about those. Hearing about those from Taz and Jeremy. Taz. Colonel Vicki Taz *The Taser* Cortez. Maybe she would know how to make such a meeting happen.

She pulled out her phone and found the number. They hadn't spoken in four years, but just maybe...

45

"Now what?" Commander Davidson had come to terms with Mike Munroe's assessment—maybe Miranda Chase was the *best* there was at what she did. Against all probability, they had raised the President's 747 within twelve hours of the crash. A task he'd have declared impossible a dozen times today. The commander of the entire US Coast Guard had already called in his congratulations for a job well done.

Once he'd convinced Miranda to stop apologizing for the sole error in her calculations and planning that had led to damaging his boat—and that had taken some serious doing—she'd turned into a whirlwind that even her companion said was unusual. She'd identified best towing points without any use of a calculator. It had been her advice to steam to harbor in reverse. Coast Guard cutters weren't designed to reverse gracefully, especially not for long distances in rough seas. She'd arranged for a pair of the motor life boats to tie up just aft of the ruined bow. From there, they acted like bow thrusters to keep him on course. Even Zeb—his XO was generally the most creative guy on ship operations—had been impressed as hell by that move.

They were finally out of the heavy seas. The Hampton Roads Bridge Tunnels and Rip Raps Island lay behind them. The big waves were dissipating as they spread out over the broad inner bay of the Entrance Reach.

Command was kicking out plan after plan of what was supposed to happen next, and none of them agreed. He'd finally made his own command decision and called Miranda and Andi to the bridge.

"We need to stop here." Miranda, typically he now understood, hadn't explained. To her it was simply so obvious.

Not a single message sent by the various tiers of commanders trying to horn in on the glory had suggested such a thing—he called for an All Stop. This was much easier said than done. The two big tugs had to slow, but not too fast. Stopping the *Bear* wasn't enough, they had to stop the MLBs that were acting as his bow thrusters. The massive small-boat entourage that had gathered around them surged ahead, then doubled back, causing a wide variety of collisions—mostly curses and scratched paint. There were more boats than water in the six kilometers from the Naval Yard's Vista Point out to all the craft run aground on the Hampton Flats Hard Clam Harvest Area. Thankfully, that was now more the local police's problem than the Coast Guard's.

Once he had them stopped, she called for a floating crane.

"Not a rig in these yards can lift her."

"They won't need to."

An hour later, he could only watch in amazement. She had the crane sling a cradle around each engine. Then, despite the passage of the storm dropping the air temperature back to a more typical five degrees above freezing, she personally went out to walk on the inverted wing with the Boeing technicians and studied each engine before she'd let them be unmounted. Somehow, for reasons he didn't quite understand, he'd ended up as the dogsitter while she did this. Neither he nor Meg were particularly happy with the arrangement, but they managed.

Next came the unmounting of the wings. It was a much bigger operation; another task she watched closely. Then she rode over on the crane's hook and meticulously cataloged each item snagged on the *Bear's* bow before they were lifted clear and set on the barges with the engines and wings. She paid the same attention to the two bodies and the large radar array as she did to a pillow that must have graced the President's bed.

While she'd been doing that, she'd left him with a long list of instructions.

First, Petty Officer Stanik led a crew out to seal up the passage between the ruined Presidential Suite and the rest of the plane. He also fully secured the quick patch they'd managed to slap over the copilot's missing window while fighting the rough seas. Then they finished pumping the interior dry—or at least relatively dry.

Stanik reported that the interior was now a gloomy cavern lit by hundreds of windows, with water dripping from every surface to splash and pool on the ceiling of the inverted aircraft.

Next on his list had been to secure a long loop of line around the base of one wing stub—as she'd already removed that wing—and over the top of the fuselage. Once she had the other wing cleared, Stanik swam under the plane to tie another hawser over the other wing stub.

Back aboard, she arrived on his bridge still wearing the wet suit and tools that she'd been working with. "Now have the two tugs pull the two lines tied to the root of the wings directly away from the airplane, perpendicular to the sides. Very slowly."

He passed on the command and wished he had a video camera with a long lens as he'd hung well clear. Damaging his boat twice in one day wouldn't go over well. Who was he kidding? The news helos had all been grounded—because of all the drones aloft. For every ten they knocked into the sea with lasers, rifle fire, and signal jamming, twenty took their place. There'd be a thousand feeds of this on every social media channel any time he wanted to watch one.

As the two tugs, on opposite sides of the plane, tightened up their lines, the plane lazily spun on its long axis. As it rotated, one of the giant horizontal stabilizers on the tail rose from the water. When the fuselage had rolled onto its side, the tower of the vertical stabilizer surfaced and, after some initial resistance, it too swung aloft.

Finally, *Air Force One* rolled onto its belly. Unlike that plane that landed on the Hudson River, no panicked passenger had opened the rear passenger door to the sea, making the tail fill with water, partially sinking the plane. Because they'd pumped *Air Force One* dry, it rode high in the water as if nothing was more amiss than a damaged nose and missing wings.

"There. Now, if you'd be so kind as to tell them to tow it to Dry Dock 8 in the Norfolk Naval Shipyard, I can finally start working on what happened. Did you find Engine Four yet?"

He'd forgotten about that and had to call in his question.

He could only laugh at the answer. Miranda didn't laugh when he told her, but at least Andi Wu seemed to think it was funny.

The reason for the damage to *Air Force One's* nose was that it had landed directly on Engine Four. It must have been ripped off the wing during the landing and raced the plane to the bottom. The engine had stopped the plane in place before ripping free. The broad nose of the 747 had landed on it like a pile driver.

46

Taz didn't know President Feldman, but she knew General Elizabeth Gray-Nason. The catch was that Elizabeth also knew her. During her final year of working for General JJ Martinez, their relationship had been largely adversarial.

Jeremy was friends with her, but he was still in the NTSB lab going through every scrap of data in the Black Box recorders. Miranda never should have told him to go by the book, even if Taz knew why she'd said it. The command had unleashed Jeremy's inner nerd. He wasn't releasing any information until every single word had been crosschecked by a panel in the voice lab and every data point extracted, verified, charted, indexed, and who knew what all.

Mostly it meant that neither she nor the kids had seen him in the last twenty-six hours and might not for as long again.

That also meant that this was up to her.

Much to her surprise, a quick phone call had gotten her an appointment with Elizabeth. Conveniently, she'd been at the White House. Taz left the three Chinese drinking sodas at the Old Ebbitt Grill because it was directly across the street from the Treasury Building and went in alone.

Elizabeth met her in The Situation Room. This was Jeremy's spot. He'd been in here a number of times advising President Cole. Miranda, Holly, and Mike had as well. She'd been in here *once*. Or was it twice? She couldn't remember, and telling her Air Force colonel nerves to get their shit together wasn't happening. Once, during which she'd done her best to speak as little as possible. Now she was—

"Hello, Taz." They traded salutes. "Take a seat. What is so important? Do you have news from Jeremy or Miranda yet?"

Instead of sitting, Taz snapped to attention. "Oh God, General. I seem to be here under false pretenses. I'm so sorry. I have no news regarding what happened to your husband or *Air Force One.*"

She could see the pain slash into Elizabeth.

"I'm here on another matter entirely. No wonder you agreed to see me. Again, my apologies. I'll go now." She saluted again but couldn't force herself to leave. This was too important.

"Colonel Cortez. Come. Sit. Tell me why you're here."

Taz hesitated and Elizabeth waved her toward a seat. "I'm really sorry about that, ma'am."

Elizabeth shrugged uncomfortably. "None of it has been easy. As you're already here, what's on your mind?"

Taz finally managed to sit, perched on the edge of the seat with her spine absolutely straight. "It's about China, ma'am."

Elizabeth waited without comment.

She swallowed hard and continued. "I have two Chinese-US citizens and a Chinese national of unofficial standing waiting at the Old Ebbitt Grill across the street. They wish to speak with the President."

The general had the decency to only laugh at her a little.

"Chen Mei-Li, the former, uh, servant of General Zhang Ru. Chang Mui, the granddaughter of General Liú Zuocheng, co-chairman of the CMC. And Wang Daiyu. She asked to be remembered to you as the Chinese operative during the

Antarctica disaster and as the personal operative of Liú Zuocheng."

Elizabeth inspected her. "You make very interesting friends, Taz."

"Yes ma'am."

"Do you know what they want to speak to the President about?"

Taz waved at the monitor. They were replaying something Taz had missed, the rolling over of *Air Force One* to sit upright in the water. Miranda, it had to be, because no one else would think that up.

Then they showed tugboats nudging it into a massive dry dock. "They didn't say. But by the timing? That's a fair guess."

Elizabeth too watched the monitor as it showed the USCG cutter being nudged into another dry dock. Its rear deck was clearly still covered with neat rows of body bags. The weather and all the drones cluttering the airspace had been deemed too rough to safely fly them back to land. That would include Drake.

Taz didn't know what to say, so she kept her mouth shut.

Finally, Elizabeth picked up the phone. "Felicia. Could you ask the President for five minutes of her time? And could you send Kali and a team to escort three civilians from the Old Ebbitt Grill's bar to the Situation Room? I expect three Chinese women together will be fairly easy to spot. They're unofficial, so make it very low profile and bring them in through the Treasury Building."

Then Elizabeth turned her back on the monitor and faced Taz. "Tell me a funny Miranda story. I need *something* to smile about today."

There were so many, the trouble was choosing one. "Well...I remember this time that Drake told Miranda to search to the ends of the Earth if needed to solve a crash. *But the Earth doesn't have ends, Drake.* And she led him round and round in circles of logic including the history of mapmaking back to the flat-Earth days and possible interpretations of the saying perhaps being rooted in the fact that the Earth isn't a sphere but rather an oblate spheroid. None of us could believe it was happening as they went on and on. But I swear the general was having a great time discussing geopolitical history, geomorphology, and whether or not an idiomatic saying was *required* to be inherently foolish or merely must possess internally illogical reasoning."

Elizabeth smiled, she didn't laugh, but she smiled. Under the circumstances, Taz counted it as one of the best things she'd done since giving birth to Davito. Elizabeth then told her how the first time she and Drake had slept together had been largely Miranda's fault for almost crash-landing her jet on the National Mall in front of the White House.

47

____

"Sorry for keeping you waiting. It's been a busy morning." It was Sarah's first trip to the Situation Room as President. It would have been nice if it hadn't been needed for, oh, another four years. No such luck.

"It's afternoon." Elizabeth smiled after they'd all jolted to their feet at her entry. She wasn't used to that either.

Kali, as head of her protection detail, had refused to let Sarah meet with three unknowns without a guard. She positioned herself just off Sarah's right shoulder.

"Right," Sarah headed for the seat at the right of the table, but Kali was in the way. Kali pointed her to the chair at the head of the table. Deep breath. *I am the President.* And she sat in Roy Cole's Situation Room chair for the first time. He was right, not comfortable at all despite the nice padding. It was also set for someone with much longer legs and she had to lower it.

She waved everyone else to sit. "And I know it's afternoon because I had a long, leisurely lunch during which nothing happened anywhere in the world for, oh, at least thirty-five seconds. Oh wait, that never happened." She tapped the intercom. "Could you have someone get me a sandwich, I don't care what, and a coke on ice, no sugar, no caffeine. Thanks." The exchange also gave her a moment to assess. If anyone had tried to prep her on the meeting, she'd missed it. She'd been President for about thirty hours and was sure she'd eaten, slept, and had bodily functions—though she couldn't recall any of the above. The small Latina in the Air Force colonel's uniform looked familiar but she couldn't place her.

She must have read Sarah's look. "Right here in this room, ma'am. Three years ago while you were still the National Security Advisor. I'm Colonel Vicki *Taz* Cortez. We met during a..." she glanced at the room's three unknown occupants, "...not wholly dissimilar situation. I'm also a part of Miranda Chase's team. Or perhaps an offshoot of her team now."

"I remember. Thank you. And I assume that I'm here to meet your companions." *Not wholly dissimilar.* Trouble with the Chinese—no, with China's Central Military Commission. *Shit!* The last time it had cost a half-billion dollars to repair an aircraft carrier and only narrowly averted a war. This was only her second day on the job. And Roy had worried about her getting too comfortable in his chair? She was calling bullshit on that one.

Taz introduced them.

"I know of Ms. Wang." There was one of those thin files on her. Her years as National Security Advisor had taught her how to read those. Some were thin because the person was barely of sufficient interest to justify a file at all. And others were thin because so little was known of them. Wang Daiyu's file read like someone who lived in the shadows but always seemed to be nearby when something major happened. The near disaster in Antarctica for one. Oh, and Colonel Cortez's tangential reminder—perhaps the aircraft carrier as well.

"We," Mei-Li, the smaller of the two young women, indicated herself and Mui, "Um, have worked with Taz once before. And Jeremy. President Cole and the two General Drakes were nice enough to expedite our citizenship for, uh, services rendered."

A glance at Elizabeth verified this. "It would have been before your time, ma'am."

"Then you'll have to explain it to me, at some other less-pressing time. So why am I here?"

There was a discreet knock. Kali let someone in. A sandwich, chips, a side salad, a brownie, and her Coke were all delivered. All she wanted was a sandwich and a soda, but they hadn't learned that about her yet. Or perhaps some rogue dietician was lurking about the White House watching for crimes against healthy fare. Pastrami on caraway seed rye with stone ground mustard. At least they'd let that through.

Once Kali closed the door, both of the younger Chinese looked at Wang Daiyu. Now they were getting somewhere past the groundwork. Elizabeth to Taz to two young naturalized Chinese women and finally on to...whatever Ms. Wang was.

Daiyu nodded before turning to face her directly. "I am here for three reasons, ma'am. The last may lose meaning after answers coming to the second."

"Then let's get Number One out of the way."

She nodded. "The President, the President of the People's Republic of China that is, has chosen a wait-and-see approach to discussing possible Chinese involvement in recent events." Daiyu waved her hand toward the monitor, which kept showing new angles of the slow process happening at Norfolk Dry Dock 8. "He has forbidden use of any diplomatic channels for messaging at this time."

Sarah wished she was eating the damn salad. At least that wouldn't go so sour in her stomach.

"General Liú Zuocheng and I have investigated this matter at every level we could do so in the time available. I am here personally to assure you that we can find no evidence of China's participation in these tragic events."

That stopped her. "How sure can you be?"

"General Liú has no thoughts that I do not know. I have made myself as his closest confidant for the last three years."

That earned her a startled expression from the other two, which said that simple statement meant far more than it sounded.

"Continue."

"He has investigated the President and the CMC members to the limits of his abilities—which are not insubstantial—and deemed them innocent of collusion in this event. As General Liú's personal Falcon Commando operative..."

That, in turn, elicited a big reaction from Elizabeth and verified her analysis of that *too-thin* file on Wang Daiyu. It also brought Kali's hand onto her weapon as she rose up on her toes. That she revealed being one of CMC's personal elite warriors had interesting implications. Did she say it to distract or to provide a very convincing level of honesty?

"...I myself maintained access to a moderately extensive network of, uh, willing informants. These include most of those able to envision and execute such an act. There is nothing from any of them either."

Sarah looked at Elizabeth.

"It fits. The chatter we've been seeing does nothing to contradict what Ms. Wang is saying. It also explains the odd caginess of the PRC's ambassador this morning; he'd been muzzled and didn't know why."

Sarah took a second bite of her sandwich to buy herself some time to think. The pieces fit well enough—until she found something new. "Okay, let's consider that answered for the moment. My thanks to you and your general for going to so much trouble to inform me directly. What's your Number Two item?"

Daiyu didn't speak right away. Instead, after taking a

steadying breath, she spoke briefly in Chinese, which earned her questioning looks from her two companions.

"What was that?"

"She asked us for forgiveness for what she has just done." But Chang Mui's voice was tentative, asking a question even as she answered. Whatever her secret, Wang Daiyu held it alone.

48

———————

Inessa had nearly leapt out of her skin when her phone rang last night. For three long hours she'd paced her broken top-floor refuge. Should she make a run for the border? Would they let her escape? Would anyone on the other side of any border accept her arrival?

For the first hour after risking the message, she'd awaited the arrival of an FSB kidnap squad to assist her in suffering a fatal accident to release Artemy into Murov's plans.

For the next hour, she'd slowly shifted to hope that the message she'd dared send just *might* have arrived safely and securely.

And by the third hour, Inessa had recovered enough sanity to start thinking about how she might save herself if she never received an answer—though she'd found no solution yet.

Any attempt to leave on a commercial flight would fail. She must assume that her name was already on every database. Murov couldn't afford to have Artemy's wife alive and out of the country. If she remained in Russia, that would give him the necessary time to arrange her accident. Escaping abroad or being *disappeared* would only taint Artemy's political future—she had to die very publicly.

To escape, she'd need her own pilot and plane. But would she be shot down for trying to fly over a closed border, even if she could find a pilot willing to do so rather than betray her? She simply didn't know.

But it was guaranteed that she knew too much to be left alive. Not only had she counseled Artemy, but General Murov had often asked her advice of late. If she ran, they would hunt her down. Her fate would become that of the Skripals and Gebrev in England, and Navalny when he'd refused to die any other way—killed by poison.

And how could she—

The phone call was all that saved her from madness. It came from that same odd number as before, with a single ring. As before, she'd swung the phone in a slow circle about the room. Two years ago someone had hacked her phone's camera and not actually called until she'd proved she was alone. Once she had shown her empty room, it rang again.

Holly Harper's voice was such a gift, she'd had to stop her after twenty seconds and ask her to start over. She hadn't heard a word through the intense wave of relief.

"Do you ever travel to remote places for your business?"

"All the time. I try to cultivate universal appeal by resourcing designs from—"

"Is one of those places Nalchik?"

It wasn't.

"I want you to pick a series of small cities you've never been to. Hire a private jet and go on an...I don't know what."

"A fashion scouting tour?"

"Sure, yeah, whatever that is."

Under other circumstances, Inessa might have smiled. She would probably never find a person who cared less for her life's work in fashion.

"In twenty-four hours, I want you in Nalchik. Make it your second stop and the next stop should be to the west from there."

"It's midnight here. And most of what lies to the west is the Black Sea and the Ukraine War."

"By dawn then. Thirty hours from now. Figure out something. We're out of time for the security of this call. All I can promise is that we'll try. If we aren't at Nalchik, you can send flowers to our funeral. Dress warmly."

Inessa managed a laugh. "It is January in Russia, even that far south it is never warm."

But she was talking to herself.

She cradled the phone to her chest and felt hope. Barely a thread wide, yet a mighty swath of cloth compared to what she'd felt lately. Not just Artemy. Nor since the crash of the American plane, no. Perhaps not in the three years since Murov had truly first favored Artemy.

Inessa's experience had taught her how easily a thread could break. She would nurse this one for everything she was worth.

First, she went to her rolltop desk and selected a piece of her custom note paper and a fountain pen. She would leave her note for Artemy by the coffeemaker. He would definitely need coffee after today's overindulgence.

My Dearest,

You were amazing last night. Thank you. You have inspired me. A "change of pace" is exactly what is needed. I have spent too long focused on the fashions I know rather than the ones I don't. I'm off on a quick tour to scout a few new fashion regions to collect fresh ideas.

I won't be gone for more than three days. I can't thank you enough for opening my eyes.

Or was that too direct? No, Artemy wouldn't see through this. Murov might, if Artemy showed it to him. But even that didn't matter. By then she'd be either fictionally or truly dead.

I'll be back in your arms ever so soon. Or at least her, hopefully fictional, ashes would.

She wanted him to feel riddled with guilt but that would show her hand. Instead, she settled for just a little guilt.

Yours for as long as we both shall live, The promise he had broken this afternoon.

Inessa

Creasing it neatly, she tucked it into an envelope and licked just the very tip of the flap before scribing his name across the front.

Next, she researched likely places to stop on her *tour*. After that, she hired a jet to depart before sunrise. Finally, she packed. Her laptop and handwritten address book were first— the only two things that could incriminate the ladies of her social salon. She would miss them all, but she'd miss them even more if she was dead.

After that, she focused on warm clothes, starting with sheep-fleece-lined knee-high boots. There was no reason that fashion couldn't be warm—especially if one lived in Russia.

49

"WHAT ARE WE FORGETTING?"

"Our sanity." Mike was sure they'd left that behind long ago.

"Okay, I'll grant you that much." Holly rested her head on his shoulder for half a second, maybe a whole one.

When had he gotten so pitiful that even such a small gesture brightened up his whole day? Maybe from the first moment he'd seen her six years ago. The Nevada sun catching her golden hair, a blonde beauty with her hip checked like a total babe—and sassing the crap out of a gun-toting and seriously pissed brigadier general in Area 51. Or maybe it was just the influence of the last day, thirteen hours of which had been on this plane.

"Didn't we wake up this morning at Taz and Jeremy's?"

"Only if you count days since we last slept. By the old American Pony Express method of timekeeping, that was yesterday. Maybe even two days ago, but I've lost track."

"That sounds like one of Miranda's weird rules."

"Pony riders said it was the next day after you slept at night or when the sun rose."

Mike didn't know why he'd asked. "I wonder what the sensible world is up to."

Holly flicked her seatback screen to the news channel. They were tucking *Air Force One* into a dry dock. Two massive wings rested on the pier beside it. Even as they watched, a helicopter lowered an airplane engine close beside the other three.

"They found Number Four."

"Miranda will be one happy little vegemite, totally in her element."

"What do you think she'll—"

"Mike," she stopped him. "I think we've got enough to worry about without her. She's got Andi, Taz, Jeremy, and all the powers that be in her pocket."

"Whereas we've got us."

"I wish you hadn't insisted on coming. This is going to be so damned risky…"

This time he was the one who shut her down. "It's not open for debate. Besides, what are the chances of this working without me. Repeat after me…"

"Less than zero," they said in unison.

But it didn't stop him from trying to figure out how much more than zero their chances were together. Not much. Last time, when he'd let her go on a mission alone, he'd aged by years. That was never going to happen again.

50

"You're back." Max, as voluble as ever, set a pair of beers on the bar. His black t-shirt left his GSOF—Georgia Special Operations Forces—tattoos on clear display. Holly took a long drink from her beer and sighed happily.

Mike tasted his, a nicely hoppy IPA. "That's nice. And, yep, we're back." He couldn't quite believe it, but they were. Two years ago, at the time of their last visit to the country of Georgia, they'd all been a mess. Andi and Miranda had been apart for a year, which had been killing both of them. And Mike had decided to walk out on Holly and get a life before they killed each other. Damn but the world had changed.

The Bunker hadn't. It looked no more reputable now than then. In World War II it had been an air raid shelter buried deep beneath Tbilisi, the capital city of Georgia. And probably again during Khrushchev's purges in the 1970s and the civil wars twenty years after that. Now it was a chain of brick-arched rooms with a dance hall and stage at one end, the main bar and tables in the middle room, and a small kitchen that pumped out American and Georgian specialties at the far end.

"Middle of the night." Past closing, there were only a few

lights making pools in the vast shadows. Or maybe it always looked like this.

"Middle of the night," Mike agreed, just like last time. And he felt every second of it, though it was still evening of some day or other back in the States.

Max's gaze flickered up over Mike's shoulder. Max had a small series of lights that indicated whenever someone was coming down the long staircase from the street to enter the bar. Mike didn't bother turning to look.

"Inbound?"

At Max's nod, Mike went and opened the door. As he did, Holly slid off her stool and disappeared into the shadows.

He recognized both of the newcomers. A glance at the bar revealed Holly reemerging from the shadows to head back to her stool. Her half shrug said that old habits died hard.

Soon they were all bellied up to the bar.

They caught up on the news in a few short sentences.

Pavle Rapava was fully installed as the head of the Georgian Intelligence Service. Max's wife Tamar was Pavle's chief assistant. But Tamar and Pavle's wife were both deep in pregnancy, so wouldn't be any part of this.

Tad Jobson, a retired Marine Corps helo pilot who'd chosen to stay behind on their last trip here, might as well be a local now. He'd married a Tbilisi chef and was still working as a consultant and trainer for Georgia's small helicopter air force.

"Yep, my boys are on it," Tad announced. "Last time you folks were here we had nine working helos and about as many pilots. We've got thirty of their thirty-eight airframes operational now, with another coming online next week. And I've got pilots coming outta my training program so fast I can't make birds fast enough for them. Couple are damned good. Not Marine Corps good, mind you, but serious skills." His broad grin said how proud he was of himself and them.

"Found your place in the world." Mike didn't turn to Holly,

but wondered what their place in the world was. Miranda's neighbors and on her NTSB team. He supposed that was enough to know for now. "Well done."

"Thanks, bro. So what drags your sorry asses back to Georgia and is worth us getting out of bed for?"

"Bit of a rescue mission. We need some help."

"Hey, you folks need anything, you're talking to the right guys. Right, boys?"

Pavle's careful nod said he'd learned a lot running the Georgian Intelligence Service. Max reacted just as little as Mike would expect—not at all.

Tad caught on and got serious. "So where is he? Downed pilot or something?"

"Or something. *She* is landing at sunrise. Needs to be gone by sunset. Needs to show up as dead along the way."

"Heard worse. Which airport?"

"Nalchik."

Tad's dark skin paled noticeably, even in the bar's dim light. "Nalchik?" He aimed a finger at one of the walls. "Like the one in Russia?"

"Exactly like that one."

"Well...shit, man."

51

———

Max was shaking his head.

Holly shouldn't have had the half beer. Or should have slept on the plane. Or followed that brief thought to go hide in her personal missile silo home back in Washington State.

"Max, it's the best we've got."

Andi's concept, that she and Mike had spent most of last night honing, had been only moderately ludicrous, making it vastly superior to anything else they could come up with. Get Inessa out on some frozen river, doing some kind of fashion photo shoot. Crack the ice so she goes in. Be waiting for her to fall through. Then, using a couple of diving underwater scooters (they'd brought a couple), drag her up-current to a pre-scouted hidden escape hole. Everyone else would assume the body was washed downstream to never be found. Conveniently the Nalchik River flowed right through the heart of Nalchik, Russia.

"First, it's January in Russia. The river is frozen."

"That's sort of the point, Max."

"*Reka Nalchik* is shallow. In most places it will be frozen to the bottom."

"Shit!"

"Second, they put in multiple cascades, what you call waterfalls, to stop it flooding the town in the summer. It chops the river into little sections."

"Okay, okay. I get the idea. I need something. We have to be in place by tomorrow and there have to be witnesses."

That shut the conversation down.

"Okay, let's one-step this," Tad was the first to break the long silence that threatened to crush her.

"Which means we ain't got shit!" Holly pushed herself upright, or tried to, but the Vicodin she'd talked out of the Coast Guard medic had worn off. She knew there was more in her pack, somewhere, but that would take too much energy to find. "Sorry, I meant that nicer than I sounded. Go ahead; take it from the top."

"If Pavle here can fake me some electronic Russian ID…"

Pavle raised his cup of coffee in a toast.

"Cool. Then I can get you in and out of the country. Georgia still flies a lot of the old Mil helos. I've got, uh, my boys, the, uh, Georgia Air Force have several Mil Mi-8 Hips and Mi-24 Hinds that would blend right in."

"We aren't invading Russia. I don't need a freaking gunship." Hinds were scary-as-shit gun birds. "And didn't Hips go out of style in the last century or maybe the one before that?"

"They still fly just fine, and Russia uses a ton of them. I have two in camouflage paint, so it wouldn't take much to add a Russian Air Force logo. Or would you rather I hop you into Russia on an American Bell Huey, Harper? I've got a double handful of those."

She conceded her battle, crossed her arms on the bar, and put her head down on them. "Okay, fine. You dump us in or near Nalchik in a repainted Hip, which is probably twice my age."

"They've only been making them for sixty years," he teased her.

"Fine, three times my age."

Only Mike laughed at her joke.

She managed to raise her head. "Then you fetch us once we have her, that gets us in and out. But what do we do between the time her jet lands at sunrise and takes off at sunset?"

"Did you say a jet?" Max was now leaning forward with both his hands braced on the bar. "How do you feel about snow?"

"White, which can be pretty. A bit on the chilly side so we aren't emotionally attached. What's your point?"

That's when she saw his smile. It was the one only a fellow Special Operations warrior could appreciate. It was a sure sign of a totally harebrained idea that would either be spectacular or get them all killed.

By the time they had it all hashed out, she was betting on the latter. Which was about normal at this point in an operation. Right on track.

52

Holly hadn't heard him approach, but she knew Max was there without looking up. Not behind The Bunker's bar, instead sliding silently onto a stool beside hers.

Pavle and Tad had gone to make preparations for Inessa's extraction. Done it simply because she asked without questioning who or why.

Mike was asleep on his jacket on the dance hall stage at the far end of the next room in the long bunker that was The Bunker. She should be getting what few hours she could...but even that had eluded her.

"At some point the cost becomes too high. That's why you can't sleep."

No need to ask, he was speaking a different language than before. This wasn't some mission planning language fit for people like Pavle, Tad, and Mike. This was between Spec Ops warriors. Holly could only stare at the glass of orange juice she'd poured but had yet to do more than wrap her hands around and hold on to like the line towing her away from the collective death on *Air Force One*. Yeah, only to kick her ass upon reaching the surface.

"Do you have to do this?"

Holly couldn't even find the energy to nod. "I made a promise."

"One worth your life?"

Holly no longer knew. "It's all I have to go by." Since the day her foolishness had killed her brother, she'd sworn to pay back his love by being the best. All through her life she'd reaffirmed that—for all the good it had done those around her. She'd sworn the same when she'd joined the Australian Special Air Service Regiment and again over the corpses of her team in a godforsaken Malay jungle. When she understood Miranda's challenges, yet witnessed her willing battle against forces she couldn't possibly understand, she'd stepped forward without a moment's consideration. If there was a way to turn aside from her present path, she'd left it behind at sixteen in that flash flood slicing across the Australian Outback.

"One worth Mike's life?"

And there was the question corroding away inside her since the moment Mike had given her Inessa's message. Her first extraction from inside Russia had been done by her alone. Mike had assisted but remained safe in a plane circling over Poland.

This time?

She should leave him behind. Or drug him and go alone. Or *accidentally* break his leg. Or...

But if she did any of the thousand other scenarios she'd thought up, she'd lose him as assuredly as if she got him killed. He would never trust her again if she shut him out this time. He'd walk away as he almost had two years ago—and she'd never get him back. If he did, *that* might be the one scenario she wouldn't survive.

Besides, he knew as well as she did that this time, if she went alone, she wouldn't be coming back. Either shot or spending the rest of her short days in some Siberian prison camp. Some missions simply couldn't be managed by a team of one. The only plan they'd been able to cook up in the limited time frame *required* Mike's skills to make this work.

"I made a promise." It was the only truth she had left.

"Made any to Mike?"

She had. "Only to spend the rest of my life with him. Never said anything about how long that life would be."

Spec Ops dark humor earned her the appropriate soft *Ha,* with no emotion behind it.

"You need to be thinking hard about your choices." Max's sigh acknowledged the trap she'd built for herself.

"Hello." Her tone said *Been there, done that.*

"Yeah." So had he. Except somehow he'd made it out.

Accepting her truth, Max finally slid off his stool. Rather than departing, he circled behind the bar. She knew he kept a Benelli M4 shotgun back there, because she'd faced it before— from the muzzle end.

"Yeah, shoot me now. Save them the trouble."

He didn't bother with a second *Ha* as that would have been over the top.

Instead, he tossed her a radio little bigger than the palm of her hand, but with a fat antenna that said *satellite capable.* Then he held up its twin and tucked it in his pocket before walking away into the darkness. "Go wake Mike. I'll make some breakfast."

Holly could only stare at the small radio. It made her want to weep. Max had gotten out, made it clear of the too-hairy-edge of Spec Ops-level missions. He had a bar and a wife with a baby on the way. But, knowing the odds better than anyone, he'd just offered to come in after them if she screamed for help. Or at least to try.

It was the nicest thing anyone had ever not said aloud to

her, except for Mike's killer smile when she'd said they'd spend the rest of their lives together.

She really hoped it was longer than sunset today.

53

Daiyu faced the President across the Situation Room table. She was still alarmed to be sitting in that great inner sanctum of American fiction...and found it mildly disappointing. It could have been any windowless conference room in any high-end office. It was beautiful in its simplicity and rich wood paneling. The lighting was gentle and indirect, but not dark and brooding. It was a place of business—though she hadn't missed the eight people stationed close outside the door at monitor-laden desks. They clearly were waiting for the least command from inside this room, whether for a file on someone or a nuclear-attack scenario.

Those of power sat here. The President, her Secret Service guardian, their most powerful military leader, and Taz for her deep connections both in and out of the Pentagon. Did Taz understand the tacit power she'd invoked in making this meeting a reality? Daiyu understood it. Daiyu discounted Mei-Li and Mui only because they were too young to have grown into who they would become.

Yet perhaps, just perhaps, Daiyu herself was the most powerful one in the room at this moment.

"Could you please turn off the monitoring of the room? What you do with the information after I impart it will be wholly up to you."

The first reaction was from the Indian woman who no one had introduced. There'd been no need, as like recognized like.

Daiyu faced her. "I promise you, warrior to warrior, that I wish no one in this room any harm. If you wish to secure me to this chair, I will not complain or struggle."

The woman studied her for several long seconds before turning to the President and nodding. She, in turn, reached out and tapped some control on the table.

"We're private now."

Daiyu nodded her thanks but made no other movement that might trigger the President's personal warrior. "To my second point, as we left the Old Ebbitt Grill to come here, knowing we would have a chance to meet you after all, I sent a coded message to my superior, General Liú Zuocheng."

The President glanced at the ceiling and the guard rose up on her toes.

"Ma'am?" the latter's voice was soft but tight, not quite an order.

The President held up a hand. "I don't wish to be slammed back into the PEOC. I only escaped it this morning."

"My communiqué was not for an air strike on the White House or other US soil. Nothing like that," Daiyu made patting motions for calm. "This is not Brunei."

The President nodded carefully, acknowledging that indeed Daiyu had been a part of that as well. Her warrior didn't understand and stayed braced for battle, her hand on her sidearm.

"In the message, I told him, using an historical reference that no one else would be likely to understand, that he has a traitor in the governing cohort of the Central Military

Commission. I did not name the man as I don't believe there is one."

Daiyu inspected the wall clocks. They showed the time here in DC, but also Moscow, London, and Beijing. One more clock matched the DC time but was labeled *POTUS*. Just like in the movies, it must be set to the President's physical time zone. She had been disappointed by the mundane conference room as the seat of such power as the United States wielded. But that simple clock said it was not so mundane after all.

"It is now five p.m. here; it is six in the morning there. He will have called an immediate meeting of the CMC. Except when the President is in attendance, they always meet in Zuocheng's office. That is all that is necessary."

54

———

Damn her!

Daiyu was supposed to be sending him good news about meeting with the American President. Instead she'd sent half a quote from Han Fei's twenty-three-hundred-year-old analysis of the *Dao De Jing* written three hundred years before that. Worse, it was a reference to an alternate translation that they had ultimately decided was appropriate to Fei's sentiments, but not his words.

Look for the Fei tiger by your side. Just that, no more.

Fei had been the first great philosopher to directly discuss traitors. Prior to his supposed writing of the rule-devouring tigers, other philosophers had only written of degrees of loyalty. They had written of spies and their uses and cautions in that use, but Daiyu had cited none of those references.

Into his ears alone, she'd shouted, *The CMC has a traitor.*

If she said it, there was nothing to question. Somehow she had found this fact and again proven her usefulness and loyalty. Perhaps some information she had wrested from the American President herself. Perhaps from one of her many contacts.

The source no longer mattered. This news threatened all he had built over the fifty-five years since he'd first joined the PLAAF. He'd worked his way from errand boy to pilot. During the Sino-Vietnamese War, he'd earned more kills that any other. For fifty-five years he had battled his way to the co-leadership of the CMC.

Who was he kidding? The *leadership* of the CMC. When a President was weak and solely focused upon consolidating power into his own hands for the sake of ego, he cared little for the most important aspect of power—the military.

And after all that work, to have a traitor in his midst made his hands shake with rage. It was good that his heart was robust or it would explode out of his chest.

Instead, he managed to occupy himself with a series of routine emails as the other five members of the CMC filed into the room and took their customary places at the conference table. It was all that kept him from pulling the Type 54 handgun out of his desk drawer—where he'd kept it close to hand for the decades since his service in the Sino-Viet War—and shooting them all.

Nobody was late. No trivial power plays. He'd said six a.m. and every man was here.

He knew them. He knew their history both military and personal. Their wives, mistresses, and the whores they were cheating on their mistresses with.

One was a traitor and before this meeting was over, he would know which one.

Zuocheng sent a message to Daiyu, *The ruler regards his ministers.* She would know the full quote.

55

Kali raised a hand to her mouth and whispered into her wrist microphone.

"What was that?" Sarah turned to look at the head of her protection detail.

Kali turned to Wang Daiyu. "The outer guards monitoring your phone say that you have received a message, *The ruler regards his ministers.*"

Daiyu spoke so softly that Sarah had to lean in to hear.

"*When the ruler regards his ministers as his hands and feet, the ministers regard their ruler as their belly and heart.*" Then her eyes focused back inside the room. "It is an ancient quote from Mencius about reciprocal loyalty—that which exists between servant and master. General Liú has completely believed the message I sent and believes he is thanking me." She pointed at the clocks. "It is now precisely six a.m. in Beijing. He likes to start his meetings punctually on the hour. It has begun."

"What has?"

"A hard lesson in precisely that—reciprocal loyalty. Especially when it is not earned but taken for granted."

56

General Liú Zuocheng pulled out his chair, but he didn't sit. Instead, he placed his palms flat on the table. "All hands where I can see them."

Everyone placed their own hands on the table without hesitation. Those who'd had their hands beneath the table had been cradling no weapon. So there was no immediate physical threat.

The lack of hesitancy, despite his frankly rude and abrupt command, offered him no insights. He inspected each man carefully. He knew no persons better except for the President and, of course, his Black Jade warrior/lover, yet he saw no deceit in their eyes.

He nodded an apology and sat in his chair, resting his hands on the padded arms. Perhaps the direct approach was the best.

"An unimpeachable source has informed me that one of you is a traitor."

Again no sign of anything beyond genuine shock—shock first, then denial. From a traitor he would expect the opposite—denial, then a sham of surprise.

"As I know it isn't me, that leaves the five of you. We are remaining here until I am certain of the truth." And he would find who threatened his life's work if it was the last thing he ever did. His fury ran so deep that his hands began to shake. Clutching the chair arms tighter didn't stop them.

A breath. A calming breath. He would not give them the satisfaction of him dying from a heart attack.

One of them wiped at their mouth as if they were feeling nauseous. Two were sweating. Others' hands were shaking.

He tried to speak...but instead clamped his jaw for fear he too would be ill.

General Liú Zuocheng managed to jab the button to call his bodyguard into the room. The man burst through the door with Zuocheng's secretary close on his heels.

Zuocheng tried to speak. To warn them. For now, at this moment, he fully understood. But unable to speak, he could only observe as his bodyguard and secretary touched him, his chair, the table—and sealed their own fates.

One of the committee members clasped his chest and collapsed face down onto the table.

Zuocheng remembered Wang Daiyu circling and circling the committee's conference table during her final trip to his office before departing for America. He had turned his back on her as she continued her course...circling to spread a nerve agent that would linger on every surface. She would know that he only used this table for meetings of the CMC. He'd otherwise preferred the commanding power of sitting behind his desk.

And he recalled her final question, as she stood in the doorway to leave for America with his blessing. She'd asked who knew of her relationship to him. They were all in this room and—he saw his bodyguard's hand begin to shake—they were all dead.

His final thought was that his Black Jade had indeed become a weapon too dangerous to wield. *She* was Fei's tiger turned to consume its master.

245

57

Daiyu looked away from the Situation Room's clocks. It was now three minutes after the hour in Beijing. Plenty of time.

"There is a saying often attributed to Sun Tzu, but it is actually from Mario Puzo in *The Godfather, Part II*, a text that General Liú did *not* study. It states: *Keep your friends close, and your enemies closer.* For three years I cultivated General Liú's attentions with this precise moment in mind. Though I did not anticipate where I would be sitting."

No one interrupted her.

"The enemy of everything decent and human in China is our current government. The President has surrounded himself with sycophants and is now ineffectual. The true power in China lies with the CMC. They were all General Liú Zuocheng's handpicked men, and he was anything *but* ineffective."

Again she glanced at the clock. Five minutes. The Novichok agent that she'd managed to acquire from Russia, rather than the American VX nerve agent, could kill in less than twenty seconds with dermal absorption of a few tenths of a milligram, less weight than a mosquito's wings.

"As of this time, they no longer exist. I used a Russian poison to further sow confusion. Perhaps it will harm any alliance that might have allowed those two fascist regimes to prop one another up to commit more atrocities."

She wanted to allow time for that to sink in but continued quickly as she didn't wish to be interrupted prematurely.

"I must warn you that the People's Republic is not Russia. The President is not quite so beholden to sycophants as some of your Presidents have been. He will replace them with men of skill, but it won't matter; they won't be men of competence. Not one will dare gainsay their President. Unlike General Liú, he has not studied Sun Tzu who said: *He whose generals are able and not interfered with by the sovereign will be victorious.* Instead, he will consolidate the CMC's power into his own control, losing flexibility and, with that, the power to act."

Daiyu inspected her hands. They had shaken badly after leaving Zuocheng's office yesterday morning. The fear of handling the Novichok had only been a part of that. Her worst nerves had been that this whole gambit would fail. But his final message said that his office in the Eight-One Building was now a bunker for the dead. Her hands were rock steady.

"Today I have paid him for that, for the crime of forcing me to marry an abuser so that I could spy on one of his own, for his future plans to use Mei-Li and Mui as weapons against their adopted country, and for many crimes far worse, including his unprovoked power grab in Antarctica and the attack on the US aircraft carrier *Theodore Roosevelt.*"

The room remained in stunned silence.

"I, Wang Daiyu, am the traitor to the CMC. No one still alive outside this room knows it. Their deaths will never make the news, but they are all dead by now." She turned to Mui. "My sole regret is any pain I may have caused you in killing your grandfather."

58

Mei-Li watched for Mui's reaction. But, as usual when Mui's mind worked hardest, Mei-Li couldn't read her at all.

They had often discussed the threat General Liú posed. Zhang Ru, Mei-Li's former owner, had been blatant in his actions and therefore predictable. Grandfather Zuocheng had been far more intelligent and very subtle in his machinations, making his actions impossible to predict. Though they were American citizens, neither doubted that someday Zuocheng's claw would reach out and drag them into his plans.

To have him gone? Mei-Li wanted to leap onto the Situation Room table and improvise her greatest-ever gymnastics routine. She wanted to dance, sing, shout, and cavort about like Fu Sang, the Dragon of the Pearl River who brought wisdom and prosperity. It—

But Mui continued to study Daiyu in the long silence until Mei-Li almost wished there was a mechanical clock here so that she could listen to the mechanism ticking. When Mui finally spoke, it wasn't to Daiyu, but rather to her.

"Your life's goal is achieved, Mei-Li."

And it was. How many hundred sleepless nights had images

of the CMC's fall swirled about her thoughts? And yet, like so many before, her hands were clean and she had, against all odds, survived.

"You are a fighter, Mei-Li, but you are not a warrior. Together, we will forge a new goal for you..." she managed a deep breath as Mei-Li could see her accepting her grandfather's death, "...for us. One of life, not death."

And Mei-Li could do no more than rise to her feet so that she could offer her most formal bow to Mui's superior wisdom and patience. It was Mui, not herself, who embodied the true spirit of the dragon, of all four dragons: wisdom, growth, beauty, and, most importantly, the harmony of Shen Long, the mighty Dragon of the Huai River.

Then Mui turned to the American President. "I believe that Daiyu mentioned there was a third question she would ask. A question if she was *not* to be sent back to the People's Republic of China to be tried for killing so many. I am certain that it is the same question that Mei-Li and I didn't dare to even hope for when we first came to America. So I will dare for her by asking it in her place. Madame President, for Wang Daiyu, I request asylum for her here in the United States of America."

59

"Wilson is dead. They're going to rule it as accidental. Killed by a stray golf ball." The voice on the other end of the call hesitated. "He was a good man."

"Well done. Good or not, he served his purpose and you're the one who said he could no longer be trusted."

"Yes."

"Second thoughts yourself?"

"No."

"Good. Keep it that way." He hung up. Let the man know that there were people willing to do to him what he'd done to that poor sap Wilson.

The President had cleared China as a likely suspect. He didn't know how that had happened so fast. He'd expected months of confusion, leaving him time to act.

Well, it couldn't be helped.

And there was still Russia to blame.

60

Holly hunkered behind the corner of the main terminal at Nalchik Airport. Thirty meters long, it was the best building of the place, which wasn't saying much. All the airport boasted were a pair of rusting Quonset huts without ends, presumably for servicing planes, and a scattering of job trailers that were probably leftover from the tsar. They broke into one of the trailers—not locked, just fighting the rusty hinge—that hadn't been used in forever. There they dumped their gear bags and pulled on orange work vests so that they'd look at least somewhat official.

Back outside, it was a mild January dawn: calf-deep snow, seven degrees below zero, and enough wind chill to turn a polar bear into a giant vanilla freeze pop despite being dressed in a cozy white rug.

"I requested somewhere warm."

"We're invading Russia in midwinter." Mike laughed. "Get a grip, Hol."

Not something she expected to happen anytime soon.

Tad had flown them through a low pass in the Caucasus Mountains that separated northern Georgia from southernmost Russia, landing them at a remote farm fifteen kilometers east of Nalchik. The farmer, a friend of someone or other in Pavle's Georgian Intelligence Service, had given her, Mike, and their gear bag a ride into the city. The Toyota wasn't that old, but the heater was on the fritz. It had trapped the midnight chill inside, far colder inside than the dawn outside.

Parts, the farmer sounded very annoyed. *Since himself,* he jerked his head to the north apparently indicating the Kremlin in Moscow, *invades Ukraine, nothing foreign keeps running. As if my car knows he is asshole, it breaks out of spite because it knows the parts now require the* chernyy rynok *to buy. More money in his pockets and his cronies' pockets as they are the ones who run the black market. I should have bought Russian car. Then I would not be so surprised when it breaks; I would be expecting it.* The farmer rolled down a window to spit out his distaste, which briefly raised the temperature inside the car but also increased its windchill. If he noticed, it didn't show; he hadn't bothered to zip up his parka.

He was glad to talk the whole way without asking any questions, which saved her from making up a bunch of lies. It also let her hear the local accent so that she could shift her own. Mike's Russian had improved over these last years, but even when he didn't mangle the syntax, he'd always sound like a Muscovite with a broken nose, so she'd told him to keep quiet whenever possible.

It had also given her a chance to watch the land emerge in the predawn light. Nalchik was a Russian city of a quarter of a million people, mostly Muslim. She'd never been in one like it before. It lay in a curved cradle of foothills leading to the Caucasus Mountains rising five hundred meters all around the city. But the mountains beyond the foothills, like Seattle's Cascade Range, kept striving skyward in sharp crags. And like Mount Rainier's abrupt quiescent volcano, which rose for fourteen thousand feet out of almost nothing, the icy twin peaks of the dormant Mount Elbrus punched up to eighteen thousand. Catching the first sunlight, the peaks shone like white beacons that defined the skyline to the southwest.

Holly forced herself to look away, but her thoughts didn't turn. Eighteen thousand feet high made it the tallest mountain in both Europe and Russia. Perched at forty-three degrees north latitude also made the peak one of the coldest spots in either. For every thousand feet higher up a mountain, it was like moving three hundred miles north. That placed the peak climatically about two thousand miles north of the North Pole.

Knowing what lay in their future didn't quite rise to a level of panic, but she seriously considered freaking out in Russia as the safer option compared to what they'd cooked up in The Bunker last night.

Nalchik city was also strange because it didn't have the gray Khruschevian concrete projects that every other city in the USSR had succumbed to. It had gotten its start as a resort town for spas, mineral baths, hiking, and skiing. For once, Nikita had left something alone. Instead of dismal gray, it boasted row upon row of white buildings with interesting and varied designs. But she saw more businesses closed than open, and restaurants were few and far between.

The airport was almost a relief as it made few pretensions. A peek through the front windows of the still-closed terminal building revealed fifty or so steel seats bolted onto a white linoleum floor that had seen better days. A pair of vending machines stood in the back corner, one with no lights showing. There was no electronic arrivals-and-departures board. Instead, there was a curling poster that had the days of the weeks and a handwritten list of flight schedules that hadn't been changed in a long time. One every day from and to Moscow, two a week from Kazan. By the schedule, neither spent much time in Nalchik. Bits of paper with a large red X on them were tacked along one edge of the board. One of these had been moved to X out tomorrow's flight. Or was it today's?

"What day is this?"

"Doomsday."

She elbowed Mike in the ribs, but his parka, down vest, sweater, turtleneck, and long johns layers made it strictly symbolic.

Except he wasn't looking through the window of the only decent building there was. He was looking up at the sky.

A sleek bizjet overflew the airport before entering the pattern and coming in to land.

"No flights today," Mike whispered. "That means—"

"We aren't ready yet. She needs to be *seen* here in Nalchik. I'll take care of it."

The jet landed cleanly and within a minute had pulled up to the terminal and was cycling down its engines.

"No, Holly. No. No! NO!"

"What?"

"You are not doing it to me again." He stabbed a finger at the jet.

She slapped his arm down as the pilot was looking at them strangely. "I'm not doing what?"

"That isn't Miranda's nice little six-seat Citation M2."

"You flew that bigger jet just—"

"Two years ago. I did it once to help you save Miranda and Andi. The miracle was that I didn't kill us. And that was a Citation 700, like a tenth the size of that thing."

Holly looked at the hundred feet of the sleek Bombardier Global 6000. "More like half. Besides, you have to give the woman points for style; that's a very nice jet. I have faith in you, Mike."

"I don't!"

"Shape up and keep quiet. Here we go."

The door's locking mechanism clunked, then lowered gently outward to make a set of stairs.

Inessa Turgeneva stepped out like the Queen on a visit to Australia, all regal and smiles. A huge smile. One threatening to turn into a burst of tears. Holly tapped her worker-guy vest. She'd only intended to blend in, but no one else was here to greet the unscheduled flight. So they'd be taken for airport workers and that could work. Inessa gave them an infinitesimal nod before schooling her face and continuing down the eight stairs.

Holly didn't waste time in greetings. "We need you to have high-visibility. Do your planned day in Nalchik. Be back here by midafternoon, at least an hour before sunset. Take the pilot with you."

"Pilots." Inessa didn't even blink, instead waving a hand toward the rear of the plane and raising her voice imperiously. "Fetch my blue sample case from the rear luggage."

Mike headed around the wing and Holly grabbed his arm before he could get away. "Inside access only, *glopyy chelovek.*" She'd pay for calling him a *stupid man* later but turned to Inessa. "You simply can't get good help these days."

"I never seen this plane model before." The tone of Mike's complaint clearly called her a bitch.

"Not so much with the bad speaking," she reminded him to keep his mouth shut. Inessa's smile struggled to stay hidden.

"Pilots. Plural," he whispered in panicked English.

"Yeah, I caught that," she answered in lazy local Russian. They definitely hadn't planned on that.

"*Kakogo chyorta!*" Mike never swore, but he nailed *What the Hell!* in Russian just fine. Except he wasn't looking at her, the plane, or the pilots.

An evil-looking jet-black passenger minivan rolled up to the jet in a big hurry. It *looked* evil even discounting the huge square grill designed like a prison door. Big enough for six or eight agents. The windows were tinted and the weight must be at least five thousand kilos based on how it shifted on the shocks as it came to an abrupt stop—definitely up-armored.

"We're screwed," Mike said in English.

It was Holly's worst nightmare on four wheels. Their cover was blown, and the FSB was about to grab them all. The driver stayed in the vehicle, but the passenger clambered down. He was a classic Russian bruiser of a guy, big even discounting his immaculate Russian greatcoat.

"Ms. Turgeneva?"

She nodded.

"I am Ivanovich, your bodyguard for the day. Do you have any bags you need?"

She covered Holly and Mike's gasp of relief by raising her voice. "You two. Wake up. Go and fetch my blue bag. Make sure you get the right one with the dress samples inside."

The bruiser nodded and moved back to the van and opened one of the side doors. No phalanx of FSB agents poured out to arrest them. Instead, he waved for Inessa to step into the luxury interior.

"I like to be comfortable." Inessa whispered then turned to the pilots even now descending the stairs. "You boys have been so nice about my whims. We will be here until the afternoon. Why don't you come and keep me company in the city rather than spending the day at this dreary airport?"

She didn't have to ask twice.

Mike and Holly climbed aboard the jet.

"Wow, not just style." The interior came right out of some luxury bizjet magazine. They entered into a galley complete with a marble counter and glass-fronted cabinets loaded with crystal and china. In the main cabin, a group of four executive leather chairs were split into two pairs by a deep-pile carpeted central aisle. Pairs of seats faced each other over shining mahogany tables adorned with lovely fresh flower arrangements despite it being midwinter. An identical four seats came next. The aft third of the cabin boasted a long sofa to one side and a big screen television to the other. The rear lavatory was done in dark stone and bright brass. The back wall, more mahogany, had a small brass handle that opened a tall door to the luggage compartment.

"She doesn't travel light." Six large suitcases were lined up in the rack along one side of the plane's rear luggage compartment. In the vertical wardrobe, a range of coats and dresses hung in suit bags. "She can't think we can take all this with us."

"We can't." Holly shook her head. "Besides, if she takes her wardrobe with her, that would be a huge alarm that she didn't die."

"You two!"

Holly resisted jumping in surprise—barely. The plane was so big that she hadn't felt it shift when the bodyguard boarded. Rather than bothering to come down the aisle, he shouted from the front. His pleasant tone to Inessa had gone walkabout. "Hurry the fuck up. And now she says not the blue sample case, bring the black one and the brown one. And she wants the red and gold suit bags. Woman has some goddamn dresses she wants to show to the shitty local clothing shops that even my girlfriend thinks are crap. Shit but it's a good thing this job pays well." Then he turned and stomped back off the plane.

While Mike extracted the suit bags, Holly snapped open the blue case as they'd initially been instructed. Inside was a fine selection of top-quality cold-and-foul gear, including a small knapsack. She showed it to Mike who smiled with relief, then she followed him off the plane toting the brown and black ones. Maybe she should lift weights more often, these things were seriously heavy. Inessa sure knew how to put on a show.

They did their best to look as uncaring as the bodyguard when they loaded everything into the van's rear compartment.

Then, just as they were about to pull away, Holly rapped on the bodyguard window's glass.

He rolled it down and scowled at them.

She looked past him into the rear. "Hey, idiot pilot. I need the damned key to set up ground power and turn on the heater. Unless you *want* the nice lady to have to sit in a giant freezer when she comes back? Eh?"

He patted his pockets, then, "It's in the cup holder by the right-hand seat. Do not damage my plane."

"Da. Da." She waved them away as bored as could be.

61

It took a bit of figuring out, but they found the connector for land power and managed to scrounge up an electrical cable to plug in the plane. After they fetched their gear bag, they climbed aboard and closed the door.

Mike went into the cockpit, seriously unhappy, while she took their gear aft and began sorting it. After a while, the heat came on and soon, thankfully, she could no longer see her breath.

"Well done," she shouted forward.

"Go jump in a billabong with a gang of your salties, Harper."

Mike actually cursing her with Australian salt water crocodiles as the threat? She wanted to go and hug him. Hell with that; she wanted to jump him. Mike never let her down.

Holly stopped what she was doing and stared at his back fifty feet away.

Seriously? She tried to remember and couldn't think of once.

Had she ever let him down? The knot in her stomach answered that far too well.

"Hey, Mike."

He didn't respond, but he probably didn't hear her. It came out as little more than a whisper.

She laughed at herself. He was busy trying to inhale enough knowledge to not kill them when he had to fly the plane. She'd tell him later.

Unless there wasn't a later. The odds on this working were still longer than a roo's tail.

Her walk forward turned into a trot, then a run though they weren't all that far apart.

When she reached him, leaning forward to study one of the screens he'd managed to power on, she grabbed his head and turned him to face her. Then she kissed him hard. Kissed him with all her apologies and fears and hopes. Slowly at first but, getting with the program plenty fast, his hands came up to frame her face.

After five years of living together, there shouldn't be new levels to something as simple as a kiss, but there were. It escalated and swirled about them. Not like sex, though there was plenty of that electricity between them. More as if, for the first time, she really meant it.

When it shifted from kiss to awkward embrace—he was deep in the pilot's chair and she was leaning over the central control panel that filled the space between the two cockpit seats —she nuzzled his ear and whispered.

"I love you, Mike. I just wanted you to know that."

"Love you, too, Harper." The first person to say it, who she believed, since the death of her brother.

"For as long as we both shall live."

He chuckled, actually chuckled. "Let's just make sure that's longer than today, okay?"

"Deal!" She slid back enough that they could shake on it. Then she pictured the couch at the very rear of the plane.

Shifting away, she didn't release his hand. He clambered out of the pilot's seat and followed her aft.

They didn't make it as far as the couch.

62

Inessa almost missed the text. She was half afraid it was Artemy tracking her down. There'd been no word from him, though he'd never been particularly good at communicating by phone when either of them was traveling.

No, it came from the secure number.

She had to read the text twice. *Get takeout from a restaurant in town for three: you and pilots. Don't eat until back on the plane. Blue pills in galley into both their sodas. Red pill in one. Close your window shade five minutes after they drink.*

Inessa had seen *The Matrix* when it first came to Russia. So both pilots were to receive unreality, or was it reality? She couldn't remember which was which and she supposed that it didn't matter.

All she knew was that she herself was shifting between the two—and she didn't know which way she was going either.

63

Inessa was exhausted from a long day of dissembling at the sad little clothiers she'd entered. And they'd been so excited at the prospect of having direct access to Inessa's designs that it almost broke her heart. If all went according to her hopes, they'd never hear from her again. If it didn't, well, they probably wouldn't anyway. No misfortune comes without a blessing in it. Perhaps they would find some inspiration from her visits today; they certainly needed it.

After reboarding the plane, Inessa had to dig deep for the energy to charm the two pilots into sharing a meal with her in the main cabin rather than retreating to the cockpit. They'd almost defeated her need to plate the meals for them, but she'd insisted they get comfortable. "You are Russian men. I know better than to let you in the kitchen." One protested some skill, which she waved away with a flick of her fingers.

In the galley, Inessa saw no sign of any pills on the marble counter. She checked the refrigerator and food storage cupboards below. Nothing. And no sign of Holly or her companion, though she was sure they were somewhere nearby. But there must be some reason they remained hidden.

She'd been in here too long. No help as her phone sat on the table in the main cabin by the pilots.

"Do you have need of assistance, Ms. Turgeneva?" one called out.

"You know my name is Inessa."

"Do you have need of assistance, Inessa?" she could hear the smile in his voice.

She looked up to the heavens for help. And that's when she spotted the line of tumblers through the glass-fronted cupboard. One glass with a blue pill and another with red and blue ones. She quickly filled them with sodas, then wondered if she was supposed to empty the pills first. Peeking at the bottom of one glass, she could see the outer casing dissolving away.

"Here," she took both glasses to them, "You must be so thirsty. Drink up."

"And what are you having?"

She'd gotten nothing for herself. "I am not flying the plane, so I am going to open a split of that fine champagne and truly enjoy the flight." She winked at them and took her time pouring a flute.

They were too polite to start eating without her, but their sodas were mostly drained by the time she returned.

The copilot looked decidedly green already, and both were weaving in their chairs.

Inessa closed her window shade.

Inside of thirty seconds, Holly and her companion were aboard.

"Please tell me I haven't killed them. They have been very nice to me."

"Blue pills of forgetfulness and red pill of being terribly ill," Holly snagged a barf bag just in time for the copilot to prove the latter.

"The blue pill is Midazolam," the man answered. "It's used by surgeons. It relaxes you, but rather than knocking you out, it makes it so that you can't form short-term memories. You literally can't remember the pain of the surgeon cutting into you...or anything else. This man won't even remember being sick." Which the copilot was still doing copiously.

"He, courtesy of the red pill of reality, is suffering from a heavy dose of ipecac syrup. You give it to a poisoning victim to make them throw up. It annoys the stomach lining, so he's literally puking up the evidence." He found a second bag and handed it to Holly. "The blue of forgetfulness should be out of his bloodstream long before they think to test for it. He won't remember much between sitting down at this table and waking up in the hospital."

"Less talk, more action." Holly interrupted.

Mike nodded. "Ms. Turgeneva, would you be so kind as to call emergency services? We want to get this man removed to a hospital, though he won't really need one. Hint that he perhaps had some street food and is likely suffering from a simple round of food poisoning. Tell them he has been throwing up for some time and you're very concerned for him. We hadn't anticipated two pilots in our planning and have to remove one of them. My name is Mike Munroe by the way, hello."

"Inessa," she managed weakly. Her head was spinning. While her hands dialed 103 and she asked for a single ambulance for a man who had fallen ill, she tried desperately to catch up.

His clear explanations and absolute calm made him the perfect counterpart to Holly's energetic efficiency. And it was easy to see the connection between them, even without the telltale signs of Holly's dishevelment. Mike, on the other hand, looked very smooth and handsome as he peeled off his working clothes. Beneath them, he wore a pilot's black slacks and white shirt. Stepping into the small crew rest area between cockpit and galley, he extracted the captain's spare coat and tie.

By the time the ambulance could be heard approaching,

Mike dressed as the pilot, and Holly the local airfield worker, were manhandling the ill copilot down the stairs. They gave him a glass of water that had a distinct pink hue.

The man was violently ill again just as the ambulance arrived.

Then, in an accent as backwoods as any Circassian farmer, Holly began griping about him. "This *kachok* from *otvali* Moscow, curse it's very existence, just puked all over the lady's plane. Now this fucking pilot want my sorry ass to clean it up, like I'm their *suka*. I'm no jock strap's bitch, especially not one who should piss-off back to Moscow." She spit on the fresh pile of vomit that had splashed on the copilot's shoes. "Let me say *that* about why I'm all of a sudden everyone's *suka*." She slapped the miserable man on the back of his head as his stomach rebelled again.

Inessa didn't know whether to be furious that she'd hit the poor man or laugh because he wouldn't remember it happening.

"One can't have two deaths," Holly started the proverb about being bold in one's actions...and twisted it. "But I wish this one had died before he puked all over the plane. Get him out of my sight before I clean the carpet with his face."

Under her continuing harangue, Mike never managed a word before the ambulance hauled the poor man away.

They returned up the stairs.

"Hi, Inessa." Holly said in a perfectly normal voice. "I would offer you greetings from your Little Sister—but she doesn't know you're coming yet. I didn't want to disappoint her if I got us all killed first."

<h1 style="text-align:center">64</h1>

"Inessa, you need to change." Mike seemed to be the keeper of logistics. "Get your blue case and dress very warmly. Put only what you *must* keep in that knapsack. Will there be plenty of other evidence that you were on this flight?"

By the time she nodded, Mike had disappeared into the cockpit. Holly ducked outside. As Inessa proceeded to the luggage area at the back, she could see Holly clearing the electrical cable from the plane, tossing it on a heap of others, then tossing aside a pair of wheel chocks. The outer door thunked shut before she even had the blue case opened.

She hurried through the change, though she stumbled many times as the plane maneuvered along the taxiways. The pavement had been bumpy on arrival, but not this bad. Maybe Mike was using a different taxiway.

They sat still at the end of the runway long enough for her to put on every layer until she felt as fat as a sumo wrestler. She would soon expire of the heat if this took too long.

Back in the cabin, she pulled her laptop and her black address book from her handbag and put them in the knapsack. When she began to add her phone, Holly shook her head.

"Anything critical on there?"

"No. Just my normal list of addresses and phone numbers."

"You're dead, you don't need them anymore. But, they need to see your phone never move again after this flight."

Inessa set it back on the table with great care. She set her favorite handbag next to it.

Holly was giving the pilot another bluish drink.

"Will you overdose him?"

"I don't think so. My friends were fairly clear on what I should do."

"Your friends?"

And Holly didn't answer. Of course not. Because Inessa had taken neither the blue nor the red pill, neither illusion nor reality. Instead, she had crossed into a limbo land where assistance came from people she'd never met and whose names she would never know.

She finally nodded her understanding. The only sound was the idling of the jet's engines and a soft adenoidal snore from the pilot. "Is there a reason we haven't departed yet?"

"Mike!" Holly called out.

"Yeah. Yeah. Okay. I'm going already." But still it was thirty long seconds before she heard the engines begin their spin up to full speed.

"Nerves," Holly rolled her eyes.

"Nerves?"

"He's a bit freaked out by your plane. He's never flown one this big before."

"He—*what?*"

At that moment, he released the brakes and the plane jerked forward. She waited through the long takeoff roll, but the climb out was smooth. Wobbly, but smooth.

"Well, I hope that's the worst of it."

Holly's smile said quite the opposite. "How much do you know about parachutes?"

"All I know is that people use them to avoid plummeting out of the sky."

"Precisely." Holly's smile grew bigger.

65

THEY WERE UP AT THEIR PLANNED ALTITUDE BY THE TIME HOLLY came up to the cockpit. Mike had chased the sunset aloft. Exactly as planned, the sky was still golden, but the direct sunlight had fallen below the horizon, the worst possible time for seeing if anyone was watching the icy mountain peaks and the plane climbing into them.

Holly tapped his ear to remind him to put in the encrypted radio earbuds. He slid them in and she pulled a fleece headband down over them, then a thick woolen hat. Before he'd taken the seat, he'd changed out of the captain's clothes and layered up with the gear they'd brought.

"Test one, two, three. You're the best lover this woman ever had." Holly whispered into his ear.

He clicked the mike switch already taped to his wrist. "Right back at you, Hol." He'd needed every second, and about three additional weeks, to figure out how to do what they needed to make this plane go. But after hauling him out of the pilot's seat earlier before she'd turned and grabbed him in the galley... Then he'd taken her up against the forward bulkhead. And the things she'd done to him in one of those fancy leather passenger chairs...

Well, he'd regret the time if he ended up killing them for lack of study, but that was the only part he'd regret.

"We all set?"

She stuck a thumbs-up out in front of him. "You?"

He doubted it but didn't say so.

"Say when."

Mike nodded, watching the course plot and autopilot carefully. When the timing matched the plan Max had laid out on the top of The Bunker's bar, he began the countdown.

"Five."

"Four." Oh God, had he ever done anything so stupid?

"Three. Holly, are you positive?"

"Say two, Mike."

He said, "One."

Holly hadn't been merely giving him a thumbs-up. She pressed her thumb down on the small trigger he hadn't noticed clenched in her hand.

The plane gave a god-awful thump.

The Number One engine, mounted on the plane's left side just ahead of the tail, didn't give any alarms. It didn't give any readings either.

Holly had just blown the engine off the tail.

Also, if she'd done it right—and if there was one thing Holly knew, it was explosives—the flight data and cockpit voice recorders had ceased to exist in any meaningful sense of the word in that same instant. No data from this flight would remain, including the odd directions he'd given the autopilot, though it still had more work to do before it too died.

He transmitted a Mayday call, Holly had rehearsed him on the tone and accent until he could say it properly in his sleep. What he hadn't expected was Inessa to come rushing forward.

She grabbed the microphone from his hands halfway through the call.

Then she *screamed* into it in Russian.

"This is Inessa Turgeneva. Someone has blown up my airplane. You must come save me. Now! Hurry! Hurry! Oh my God, we're going to crash and die, don't let me die! I don't want to—"

Holly wrestled the microphone from her and handed it back to him. He glanced back to make sure that Inessa wasn't going to try to grab the controls or something truly dangerous. Instead, she offered him a brief smile and a pat on the shoulder before Holly shooed her back into the cabin.

"Could have warned me." Mike's heart rate would be a while coming down from that.

"Where's the fun in that?" And she too headed aft.

Women. They were absolutely going to be the death of him. Which, this time, just might be true.

The air traffic controller was shouting for more information, which he ignored.

Mike checked the autopilot one last time. The big plane was following his laid-in course just fine on one engine. Holly had added a small additional item to the electronics that would massively over-volt the autopilot during the crash. Any local memory would be permanently lost as well.

To all appearances, the plane had been sabotaged and that had caused the upcoming crash with no slight against the manufacturer. Allowing that would have made Miranda very upset. And it was true, the plane had been sabotaged as they'd been the ones to do it.

Sabotaged!

Right!

Mike popped his safety harness and raced for the back of the plane.

They were waiting for him. Inessa stood by the couch. Her

face spoke of terror, but her actions of calm. Mike shrugged on the parachute harness that Holly held out for him. In seconds, he was in and they'd both checked everything twice.

Then he stepped up behind Inessa. He'd never been trained in tandem jumping, especially not as the lead, but now was apparently the time to learn. He and Holly clipped and locked the four large D-rings that connected the front of his harness to the back of Inessa's. Her small knapsack was sandwiched between them.

She'd already pulled a balaclava down to protect her face from the bitter winds and Holly slid a pair of goggles over that.

He pulled down his own balaclava and goggles, then they stepped up to the hole in the side of the plane. They'd raised the cargo net to keep her suitcases in place on the side opposite the gap. Dresses and coats still flapped in the wardrobe area. Yet more proof that she'd been here as if the radio call wasn't sufficient.

"Ready?" He had to shout to be heard over the roar of noise coming in through the gap where the engine and the other side of the luggage compartment used to be.

She shook her head no. He couldn't tell through all her gear if there was a humorous shrug in there or not.

"Excellent! Three, Two—" he stepped out of the plane on One rather than giving her a chance to brace back against him in case she really meant no.

Mount Elbrus towered to the northwest of them. Eighteen thousand feet of snow and ice shone deeply orange in the last of the day's light. Like a mighty beacon of sunset fire.

He steered them southeast. It was a rugged no-man's-land between the back of the mighty mountain and the border of Georgia. They'd jumped at fifteen thousand feet where the air would still provide enough oxygen for clear thinking.

At twelve thousand, he released the big tandem parachute, which opened with a clean hard snap and elicited a squeak of surprise from Inessa. Max from The Bunker had scrounged these up from his old Spec Ops buddies. The coloring of the chute and their outermost coveralls would make them nearly invisible in the sunset light.

He aimed for the Georgia border. They wouldn't get that far, but they'd get close. Then he'd call in Tad and his Russian helicopter for an extraction.

Mike wasted a little distance to turn the parachute enough to see behind him, but there was no sign of Holly or the jet. Not that he'd expected to be able to see them. But still—

66

With Mike safely away, Holly felt she could breathe again. Sort of. The air at fifteen thousand feet was thin and bitterly cold, fifty Fahrenheit below zero. Time to get out.

Besides, she had to jump precisely twenty seconds after Mike did for this to work.

She double-checked her attachment points to the drugged pilot, still counting time in her head, and waddled him to the hole she'd blown in the side of the plane. When her brain ticked nineteen, she stepped forward.

And fell backward.

The pilot wasn't conscious—at least not fully, she hoped—but he managed to get a foot up against the side of the hull.

Twenty-one.

Twenty-two.

With each passing second, she was a hundred meters out of position as the plane continued on its course. Its *crash* course.

By twenty-three, it was clear that he was coming around and she didn't have time to dose him. He braced a foot again.

At twenty-seven, she twisted hard to whack his head against the wall. It didn't knock him out, but at least it dazed him for a moment. Then she turned around, and the two of them fell backward out of the hole at twenty-nine. Nine seconds, almost a kilometer late.

She did what she could to fly south, but she couldn't open her chute too close to the plane. The human eye, and hopefully any radar, would be following the plane. Once it was well clear...

Holly waited ten seconds, watching the ground approach far too fast as it rose higher here than her intended drop zone, before she popped the chute. Mike had three thousand meters, almost ten thousand feet of descent to get down the mountain along his planned path. She'd planned on half that, lost a third of that to the changing mountainside, and had just used up two-thirds of what little she had in getting clear of the plane.

She considered dumping the asshole right here, which would give her the lift—maybe—to get clear of the ridge to her south. But Inessa would be saddened and Miranda, even though she'd never hear about this escapade, would be truly livid.

So Holly didn't pop the emergency release on the pilot.

Instead, she bled out every meter she could, finally targeting a tiny gap in the trees, and plummeted down into the deep snow.

67

The Bombardier Global 6000's autopilot performed precisely as designed.

The autopilot advanced the jet's throttles from the slow cruise that Mike had selected to ease the jump. With only one engine, it was slow to climb, but it reached five thousand meters, sixteen thousand four hundred feet, as it circled wide around the massive double-mountain's south peak. The arc was big enough that it was like a girl wanting to make sure every eye was on her and her alone. Mike had gotten the idea from watching streetwalkers when he'd been conning on the streets of LA as a teen.

It leveled out only five hundred meters below the twin peaks but didn't ease the throttles. The Rolls Royce BR710 engine still had enough power in the relatively thick atmosphere at five thousand meters. At its normal cruise altitude of fifteen thousand meters, there was only a quarter as much air to work with. This allowed the airplane to accelerate strongly as it continued its wide, circular route. Soon, it was racing along at nine-tenths the speed of sound, over nine hundred kilometers per hour.

Covering the length of three football fields per second, it headed directly toward the glacier that capped Mount Elbrus.

Alarms sounded in the empty cockpit.

Low Terrain warnings blatted.

These escalated from audible to painful. The control yoke shook mechanically to get the pilot's attention, but he lay deep in the powdery snow fifteen kilometers away on the other side of the mountain—instinctively swallowing the blue pills Holly had just shoved into his throat.

The autopilot tried to correct the situation, except Mike had disabled that function. A detail that had been erased from all human knowledge except his by the destruction of the black boxes.

In full view of several Russian radars, sixty-million-dollars' worth of luxury business jet slammed into the large crevasse field on the northwest face of Mount Elbrus. As Holly's last charge fired off and destroyed the electronics of the autopilot, the thirty-meter length of jet didn't crumple or break. Instead it collapsed on itself from nose toward the tail, like a crash-test car slamming into a four-foot-thick wall of unyielding concrete without even an engine or structural steel to buffer the impact.

By the time the front ten meters of the plane had been accordioned to a two-meter-thick pancake between the wings, the wings themselves had split open spilling thousands of gallons of jet fuel over the snowfield and pouring down into the crevasse.

Still driving ahead at full RPMs as the plane abruptly ceased all forward motion, the remaining engine broke free from the tail. It launched forward into a large puddle of fuel. Below its flash point temperature of a hundred degrees Fahrenheit, it did not immediately explode. But, because the engine's inner turbine normally operated above the melting point of aluminum, an area of the fuel was heated well past its autoignition point of four hundred and ten degrees. Once it started to burn, the fuel still streaming from the ruptured tanks heated rapidly.

The initial fire, spreading over the spilled fuel's surface, accelerated the process. From ignition to widespread fire required seven seconds. From raging fire to a devastating fuel-air explosion required only two more.

The fire that raged for half an hour afterward created a brilliant beacon of true fire in the night, making the crash easy to locate. Though it would be a long time before any rescue crews could approach it. That evening, it was deemed too dangerous as there were no high-altitude assets in the area beyond a few park rangers. The hundred-knot storm that slammed into the peak the next morning lasted for three days.

By the time the crews managed to reach the site—losing two people into crevasses during the ascent—nothing but the scorched tail section and a scattering of luggage across the snowfield remained. The rest had disappeared into the depths of icy caverns that would not reveal any secrets for decades or perhaps centuries.

On the fifth day, Inessa Turgeneva was officially declared dead.

Artemy Turgenev's mourning and deep guilt was partially assuaged by the woman from Club Cloud 99. Tania entered his daily life soon after that announcement.

68

If everything had gone according to plan, Holly would have packed the chute and harnesses, stripped the jump coverall off the drugged pilot, and given him a small push.

Their original landing zone was supposed to be fifty meters above the Mt. Elbrus ski area. He would stumble or slide down onto the ski slope and truthfully claim for the rest of his days that he had no memory of his final flight, how he'd survived the crash, or how he'd come to be where he was.

Now, it was a hard hike over a steep ice-and-snow-coated ridge to get there.

Holly considered letting him come fully conscious, make a deal with him, and help him hike to the ski slope. But then he'd know that perhaps Inessa had been rescued and wasn't dead after all.

So, before he could gain the wherewithal of a hamster to argue with her, she dosed him again—double—as one should have kept him under for the whole escape. Except he was a big guy and she hadn't compensated for that. Might have a higher metabolism too. She then made a hauling sledge by tying him up in the parachute but leaving the long lines hooked to her body harness. The advantage was that the long swath of slippery nylon kept him from sinking into the deep powder, making him relatively easy to move.

The disadvantage was that it did nothing to help her.

They'd crashed at sunset, near enough 1645 hours for her not to care about the details. The problem was that, instead of getting rid of him this evening, she must deliver him to the top of the ski slope before anyone else arrived tomorrow morning. Sunrise was around 0730.

Fifteen hours to hike a kilometer was laughably easy. Doing it over a ridge at twelve thousand feet through deep snow and subzero temperatures? Not so funny.

She purposely drank her water bottle dry, loaded it with snow, stuffed it inside her coat to melt, and ate a piece of chocolate after wrapping him in his cocoon.

"You're a bastard, Boris." She hadn't bothered to learn his name, which might be a bit crass for drugging someone, wrecking his plane, and dragging his ass over a mountain, but she certainly wasn't going to waste time digging around in his coveralls.

"Couldn't you have been a svelte Natasha? A petite Svetlana gymnast I could toss into a backpack? Oh no! You had to be a Russian Ivan." After unlimbering a set of foldable hiking poles to steady herself and test for random crevasses, she checked her GPS heading, reminded herself to do that frequently, and set off.

After the first twenty meters of wading through snow up to her waist, she considered the wisdom of calling up Tad to come fetch her on *this* side of the mountain. Then they could drop Igor at the ski slope and keep going. Except every radar facing this side of the mountain would now be scanning for any detail.

The only answer was to walk around to the mountain's back side.

She wanted to call Mike and gripe at him as she fell into an under-snow pothole up to her shoulders and had to crawl back out. Max and Pavle had reported that there were no big crevasses on this face, but they hadn't said a word about woman-deep potholes.

But she couldn't call Mike. Though their radios were encrypted, the Russians would be able to triangulate the transmission point. If she was alone and on the lower slopes like she was supposed to be, she could transmit and move along quickly. Right now, she'd be lucky if she could make ten meters headway between a transmission and someone hunting her down.

They'd agreed to a minimum of twelve hours silence, giving the Russian surveillance some time to calm down. But for now it was just her and Alexey, trudging through the Russian wilderness.

Don't think. Just do. The voice of her old SASR trainer resounded in her head.

"Sure. When the hard get going, then the going gets hard." Duh! Nobody harder in the head than a SASR operative. Stubborn was a virtue. Or so they'd taught her. *No easy day,* according to the US SEALs. Same, same.

Shut up and lean into the traces.

"Not a goddamn farm horse."

But as there was no other solution, that's what she did. One foot at a time, if she never stopped, she'd never arrive. Or was it if the never started, she'd arrive too soon?

Loopy. Had she taken any of the blue drug?

No. She wasn't *that* hardheaded.

Altitude. Oh, right. She had plenty of that. At five thousand meters, someone had stolen half the oxygen along with half the air. Who should she call about such a mountainside robbery? The Ghostbusters? No, that was for something else. Yeah, like busting ghosts. She could use some of that. A lot of past ghosts seemed to be out crossing the

Mount Elbus snowfield tonight. Too bad she didn't have their number.

What else hadn't she taken? Any don't-do-thats from Miranda, because if she had, she wouldn't be here. Same with any smart advice from Max. Any water…

She checked her phone for the time. Off track. No, that was her GPS. And it was on track…kinda…but mostly not. The time said, she had to wipe the snow from her eyes, five hours gone. Maybe being hardheaded did work.

Holly checked the GPS again. Definitely not the right time. Or location. She was…

That didn't make any sense.

She pulled off her goggles and squinted at the display. She was four hundred meters upslope. Not up the ridge she had to cross, but straight up the mountain. She and Ilya, snoozing away all cozy in his rip-stop nylon cocoon, were still on the wrong side of the ridge, but far above the ski area.

Holly beat down a big enough circle of snow that she could sit without being inundated by the powder.

Water. Right. She fished out the water bottle, drank it dry, again packed it full of snow before tucking it back inside her jacket. *Survival 101, Harper. Get your shit together before it kills you.*

"Yeah, Sarge. I hear you. Nothing worse than being killed by shit." She ate another piece of chocolate, which almost broke her teeth as she'd left the bar in an outside pocket. She tucked it in a middle layer pocket, hoping her body heat didn't melt it into goo. Then she checked on Anatoly. Sleeping like a giant Russian baby. "Yep, they grow their babies big here in Russia, Sarge."

Once she felt the water and chocolate kicking in, she studied her GPS map again. Not as bad as she'd thought. If she cut a forty-five degree downslope as she climbed the ridge, she'd be walking along a level terrain line.

"Hold your altitude, Harper. Seriously." Because if she trended too far downslope, she doubted she'd ever manage to drag Fyodor back up it. Getting him this high on the mountain had taken everything she could give.

No such thing as that. A SASR warrior can always make it the extra mile.

"Sure thing, Sarge." It would be easier to argue with him if a) he wasn't so damn decorated for achieving the impossible, b) he was here, or c) both of them were tucked in a nice warm pub arguing over who owed who the next pint.

Since scenario c) wasn't going to happen as long as she sat here cooling her ass on the side of Mount Elbrus and it was her favorite of the three choices, she struggled to her feet and began to walk level on the level. It turned out to be much easier than going straight upslope—until she fell into another hole.

69

Holly waited in the sunrise until she saw the top of the highest lift start spinning. That meant that some operator or ski patrol would soon be riding up. It was a battered old chair lift. Every third or fourth chair needed some serious repair, but it was moving.

She'd run out of Russian names, so she freed Big Bird from his nylon cocoon and propped him up against the top stanchion. Then, finally back on plan, just sixteen hours late, she stuffed the parachute into its bag and retreated upslope into the brushy trees to watch.

The chairlift stopped two or three times before finally delivering someone. Not a big guy, except for the heavy coat he was swaddled in to survive a day at the top of the lift.

"Really can't get good help these days." The man literally tripped over Kermit's outstretched legs.

A lot of shouting, a couple rounds of shaking, and a bit of cheek slapping woke Elmo from his torpor to start the conversation.

Holly didn't bother sticking around to see more, she'd had enough of the guy.

She had to continue another twenty to thirty degrees around the mountain before heading downslope unless she wanted to walk back into Russia. Covering two kilometers at this elevation before heading down would get her where she needed to go for her rendezvous. Heading down to the base first would slam her into twenty kilometers of exceedingly rough country to cross to the rendezvous with Tad.

She covered the first of those two kilometers, then looked up to gauge the position of the sun. Some survival instinct was beginning to worry about things. So much of it had been worried for so long that she hadn't been paying it much mind.

But its sense of alarm finally busted through all the aches she'd picked up since slamming back-first in *Air Force One* and the impressive lack of sleep, even by SASR standards as she'd been whipsawed from the ocean to Georgia to Russia.

Not the time, she'd kept an eye on that when she remembered. Nor her GPS track—she'd only gone astray twice more in the night, but only by a hundred meters one time and seventy-five the other. Not the sunrise, she'd delivered the Stay Puft Marshmallow Man—or was he the Michelin Tire Man?—to the head of the lift by sunrise.

Sunrise?

It had gotten brighter, but there'd been no sunrise.

Holly tipped her head back to look aloft again and fell over backward because she didn't have the burden of Viktor's harness steadying her. It would have been okay to fall back, except she once more traversed through deep powder. The walls caved in, covering her in a soft, cool world of white.

So pretty.

Don't you dare stop moving, soldier.

"Yes, Sarge." She beat a hole in the snow and gazed at the sky. The gray sky. The dark, like evil-dark, gray sky.

Hadn't she jumped out of the plane during a beautiful, clear-sky sunset?

She had.

Hadn't she done stellar navigation last night?

Oh, that's what had gotten her in trouble. She'd started that way. Until a high layer of cirrus clouds had hidden random parts of the sky in a sliding pattern—before finally closing down hard and forcing her back to her GPS that insisted on telling her she was stupid.

Some snowflakes landed on her face, and she raised an arm to block another collapse of the powdery wall onto her face. Except the wall didn't collapse.

She opened one eye, which got pithed by a snowflake for its trouble.

Holly sat up and surveyed the situation. The snowfield continued for thousands of meters downslope. She was still on the wrong section of the mountain to start her descent by a good kilometer.

Once more she inspected that sky. The peak was already hidden, and features were disappearing fast around her. She'd blundered through a night without killing herself, but hiking through a whiteout was just asking to have her ass kicked in a very permanent fashion.

Holly found a big outcropping, big like divert-an-avalanche big. Then she began digging and packing at its base. When she uncovered large rocks, she incorporated them into the walls until she had a respectable snow cave—okay, a smallish snow bivouac—but it was enough. Her view of the Caucasus Mountains of Georgia, which had looked so close she felt she could reach out and touch them, had disappeared while she'd been building. She built the entrance smaller and smaller, until it was little more than a slit. Maybe she'd retain more of her body warmth that way—Australia forces, even SASR, wasn't exactly big on ice-and-snow survival training.

She did another round of water and snow-in-the-bottle, then sat with her back against the rock wall at the back of her tiny cave and thought. The first thing she thought of was Mike —which sounded kinda pitiful but it beat thinking about whether or not she'd killed Francisco while towing him all over the mountain.

Then she thought of her radio and pulled it out.

Oh God, she was so stupid. Outside pocket, battery drained by prolonged exposure to frigid cold, dead as a doornail.

So many of her skills had gone stale. She didn't even know who she was anymore.

Holly could only sit there with her back to the rock wall and watch the thick waves of snow blasting past the slit. Nothing to do but sit here on the ice hard floor. The lumpy ice hard floor.

She shifted to one side, then the other—and the lump moved with her. She shifted well aside and checked. No lump on the floor, she'd made it well, expecting to sleep out the storm in here. Then she felt for the lump on her ass.

Something was there underneath all those layers of clothes.

70

A RADIO CRACKLED TO LIFE, AND HE HEARD A FAINT VOICE.

Mike grabbed his off the bar. "Holly! Holly! Can you hear me?" Nothing. He tried again. Still nothing.

Max looked at him oddly.

"What?"

Max looked down with some surprise and reached into his own pocket, pulling out a tiny radio as if it might explode. Then he keyed the mike and asked, "Holly?"

"Hey, Max. Did you get them?"

Mike grabbed for the tiny radio and Max let him have it. "They got us. Where are you? Ready for us to come get you?"

"Uh, not quite."

"Why not? What's up?"

"From here? Not much. Maybe a thousand meters of glacier."

He looked at Max. It didn't make any sense.

"She's still high on the mountain."

Mike looked back at the radio. "Why?"

"Nothing better to do."

"Holly, goddamn it. Give a straight answer for once."

"For a couple crooked people like us, I think that's cheating. No, I *really* have nothing better to do. There's a major whiteout blizzard going on. I'm dug in. I'm safe. My other radio battery is dead. So I'm going to turn this one off to save it until the weather clears. I delivered the pilot. You deliver Inessa."

"I already did. I had Clarissa send a plane. Andi is going to get Miranda to escort her in to see Sarah. I want you to check in every twelve hours."

"Good boy. This storm is going to last a lot longer than that. Love you, Mike. Over and out."

"Love you too."

But he got no reply.

Max took the radio from his nerveless fingers and inspected it. Then he reached under the bar, grabbed a charger cord, and plugged the radio in.

"But— Did she just say goodbye?" The last word out tried to choke him.

Max was shaking his head. "You know she's got skills, right?"

He nodded because he couldn't speak without whatever pain was choking him blasting out.

"With our kind of training, hers and mine, if she says she's dug in safe, it means just that and no more. She delivered her man, assessed the weather, the state of her comm gear, and chose to shelter in place. Was even in good enough shape to remember that little radio I gave her. She'll also know that the Russian presence on Mount Elbrus is going to heat up high for the next little bit. You won't hear from her until she decides it's safe to emerge. Waiting sucks, but at least you're warm, fed, and know she's alive."

Over the next four days of silence, that gave Mike exactly seven and a half seconds of comfort.

71

———

"Harry! Wake up!"

"Sure. Yeah," he mumbled from where he had sacked out on the cot they kept in their office. Neither of them had left their stations for the three days since the crash of *Air Force One*, no longer than was sufficient to grab a shower in the CIA gym locker room.

Heidi knew Harry was nowhere near awake. "Sorry guys." She began plucking tiny rubber dinosaurs from her station and tossing them at him. Tyrannosaur to the chest, raptor to the ribs—the Stegosaur barely longer than her thumb caught his nose. That woke him up for real.

"What?"

"Someone's booting up *SAM 28000.*" Unsure of quite what the signal would be, they'd hacked their way into a lot of the US Air Force 89th Airlift Wing's systems. At least it gave them something to do. Everything else they'd done had led a grand total of nowhere.

At the moment, the maintenance log was open and a new entry stated the date, time, and: *Routine power-up test.*

In her prowling about, she'd stumbled on a backup copy of

the plane's software. For lack of anything else to do, they'd been poking through it, with a complete lack of insights. She'd had no idea it took so much code to make an airplane fly, even ignoring all the complexities of its service as *Air Force One.*

With the plane coming online, maybe they could grab the code loaded there and compare it to the backup. Asking the USAF to power up the plane for them would have tipped their hand if someone knew something of what had happened. The CIA's poking around in USAF's world also would have pissed them off but good, which had been attractive in its own right.

Heidi liked that last thought. It felt like some of her hacker mentality was coming back online.

They grabbed a full copy of the plane's live code stack. The big problem now? It was all in flying-ese, not a language either of them spoke.

But she knew who did.

72

Jeremy barely had time to show his ID at the CIA's front desk before Harry whisked him down into the basement and dropped him in front of a computer.

Harry and Heidi pulled up chairs to either side of him. Harry began explaining before he finished sitting down.

"We found two major code discrepancies between *Air Force One's* master backup we scammed and *SAM 28000* when they booted up the plane. We tried reading it, but it just doesn't make much sense."

The first one was a block of barely smart AI code. It took him longer than it should have to figure out what it was doing because he hadn't expected it to be doing something so simple. He could have coded that in a hundredth the space. Someone had taken a very polite piece of voice recognition software that could easily handle a vast knowledge base and formulate intelligent responses to a wide range of questions—and forced it to perform one small task.

The second piece of code was much shorter. And once he'd read it, it was dead obvious what it did.

"Uh, what was the date of the backup?"

"Why? What does this thing do? November 11th."

Jeremy felt that was important. But he didn't see quite how it fit in.

73

"Yes, Madam President." Elizabeth and the others had risen as Sarah stepped into the Situation Room.

"Then how should we be meeting?" Trust Miranda to ask one of her questions, killing Sarah's light greeting. Three others and a dog were in the room. Andi leaned over to whisper that it was a joke and Miranda made a soft *Oh* in reply; Sarah appreciated the buffer.

"Clarissa, to what do we owe the honor of a visit from the D/CIA?"

Uncharacteristically, Clarissa stayed silent and merely indicated the room's other occupant. She was a lovely woman, older than any of them, but not by much. Her dark hair looked elegant and her clothes were very high end.

"And you are?"

"That is a good question, Madam President. At the moment, I don't have a name."

"A woman of mystery?"

"A woman without a past. Holly Harper, who I understand is still trapped high atop a Russian mountain by a snowstorm, and Mike Munroe, below and nervously awaiting her recovery, went to some trouble to ensure my apparent death. I feel that I would gainsay their efforts if I were to use that name ever again, and it somehow leaked out that I survived." Her voice was mesmerizing...perhaps soothing was a better word. Just enough of a Russian accent to sound dark and lush.

"If you have no past, why are you here?"

"Oh, I have a past. It is a present and a future that I currently am lacking."

Clarissa found her voice. "She has been providing the CIA with extremely high-level intelligence for the last few years."

"So this was an operation to bring you in from the cold."

"Not precisely, Madam President. Though it was a rather chilly departure, even by my Muscovite standards. My circumstances changed rather abruptly for strictly domestic reasons. General Mikhail Murov, the head of the FSB, is grooming a new President for Russia."

Though she didn't move, Sarah felt as if she'd been thrown back in her chair by a hard punch to the chest. How was she supposed to assess such a wild statement?

"I know this," the woman read her far too easily, "Because the man being groomed is my, ah, an interesting playing of the words, my widower. The man I widowed by dying before I could be executed."

Sarah punched the intercom connection, isolating the room. "No one can hear us now. You'll need to explain that last statement."

"Of my dramatic death?" She waved a hand at the blank screen at the front of the room. "Search on any news channel that covers Russia and you will find it. My fame has risen dramatically in the last forty-eight hours, regrettably both enhancing my ex-husband's image as the poor man left behind, and the sudden fortune from my fashion house that sadly will also benefit him. My former business will grow greatly for some time after the tragic news of my death, though I shall no longer benefit from it. You will want to be researching General Artemy Turgenev of the FSB. I had to die. I stood in his future's way."

Clarissa laughed. "Do you realize how little we know of FSB internal operations? It has been decades since we had anyone with insider knowledge there."

Inessa merely smiled before raising a hand and tapping her own chest. "I have spent most of three decades getting to know them intimately."

"It's true. She worked with my parents." Miranda spoke for the first time.

"Your parents?" Sarah could barely keep track of the many strange connections, from Wang Daiyu in China to this woman in Russia, that Miranda and her team could claim.

"Yes. They were CIA agents until they were murdered for aiding Boris Yeltsin. Some say it was by his enemies. Others say it was by Boris Yeltsin's own order, because they knew too much about him. How can it be both? I don't understand."

"It's one or the other," Andi explained. "But we will probably never know. Right, Clarissa?"

Sarah glanced at Clarissa, who was nodding. "The answer is not in our files, though the manner of their deaths is accurate."

So this wasn't some Miranda fantasy. How was it that everything seemed to connect through her? Whether she understood how or not, it certainly confirmed Roy Cole's advice to always listen to Miranda, even when it was hard.

Sarah focused on the Russian. "If you know so much, was Russia responsible for the murder of President Roy Cole and others?"

"I had little time to investigate, as my life fell into imminent danger that same evening. Artemy certainly did not know of it. And no rumors or hints reached me, though they absolutely should have for an action of such magnitude and importance. I am unable to make guarantees, but I would deem it to be exceedingly unlikely that your *Air Force One* was attacked by Russia."

"If it wasn't China or Russia, then who the hell attacked *Air Force One?*"

"It wasn't attacked," Miranda was shaking her head. "It was sabotaged."

"What's the distinction?"

"The former is a distinct action of aggression. The latter is a carefully planned and executed task to achieve a specific aim."

"How do you know?"

"Each engine failure was caused by the burnout of a master control chip and both of its backups. I considered it as a possible manufacturing fault, though it seemed unlikely. This was confirmed by the black box information Jeremy analyzed. The control chips for each engine were burned up precisely thirty seconds apart. Engines Four, Three, Two, One. This precision implies human, not mechanical causes. Hence sabotage."

Sarah felt sick to her stomach. "All to kill Roy?"

She scanned the others' faces but saw no answers.

"You have determined the how, Miranda. Thank you. Well done. Everyone else, let's start going with the why. Who would be most upset by Roy's final goodwill tour?"

74

Miranda didn't even try to follow the conversation that swirled around her. Andi, Clarissa, and Inessa all made suggestions. Sarah also called in Felicia, her Chief of Staff.

The phone in front of her rang.

All conversation stopped and everyone turned to face her.

It rang again.

She picked it up and turned so that the phone hid most of her face. But that placed her facing the corner of the room, something her mother did to her as a child each time the world overtook her with too much sensory input. It was actually the right thing to do as it limited her overwhelm. Only now as an adult did she understand that Olivia Chase had probably meant it as punishment for a child she couldn't control.

"This is Miranda Chase. This is actually her and not a recording of her." She twisted herself further around, but then the phone cord brushed against her neck. Spinning back the other way, she faced Inessa. But Inessa had kept trying to talk to her until she'd had to pretend to be on the edge of a meltdown to make her stop. Luckily, Inessa didn't know to check on Meg's attitude to indicate if her panic was real or not.

"Hey, Miranda."

"Jeremy!" She liked talking to Jeremy.

"I'm with Heidi and Harry. We just uncovered some code updates to the software on *SAM 28000*. They're root cause, designed to destroy the plane only if the President was aboard and too far offshore to make it back."

"That is bad." No one in the Situation Room was speaking. Which meant they were listening to the conversation, *her* conversation. Or at least her half of it. "Jeremy has confirmed that it was sabotage."

She waited.

Rather than getting her less attention, now they were all watching her even more intently.

"It was added to the plane's software."

They still didn't look away.

She turned back to facing the corner. But the phone cord... She reached behind her, without looking, and moved the phone enough that the cord no longer touched her neck. That was better.

"Yes," Jeremy agreed. They rarely disagreed, which was also very nice. "But there's something that seems important, though I can't pin down why. It was done on November 11th."

"Oh. Well, that predates anything in my investigation timeline."

"What does?" Sarah asked from somewhere behind her.

Andi leaned close. "Use the speakerphone, Miranda."

"Will everyone stop looking at me and start looking at the phone then?"

"More of them will."

Miranda turned and selected speakerphone. But Sarah had asked a question. "The sabotage of the VC-25A aircraft occurred on November 11th. The earliest date on my investigation timeline up until this moment has been the initiation of planning for Roy's trip on December 9th."

Again nobody spoke.

She leaned over to whisper to Andi. "No one is looking at the phone."

"Just wait."

To distract herself, she coaxed Meg from the chair she'd chosen, over into her lap. She liked petting Meg. Meg's happy sigh and collapse across her legs was nice too.

"Why is that relevant?"

Miranda shrugged. "I can only confirm what and how. You know I can never answer Why or Who kinds of questions."

"Your death, Madam President." Clarissa and the Russian said in unison. With Elizabeth close behind. Andi was nodding as well.

"But Roy was the one on the plane." Miranda protested.

It was Andi who explained. "First, there was the election. Then the plane was sabotaged. It was after that when Roy planned his final trip."

"But," Felicia spoke, "President Cole would have used the plane for his final trip home."

"The failure parameters..." Jeremy spoke from the phone.

Finally, everyone's attention shifted there. Andi was right, as usual; she just had to give it enough time.

"...the ones set in the software to disable the engines, required both an unrecoverably dangerous distance from shore *and* that the plane was flying using the *Air Force One* ID over the radio. Without that, say once he retired, President Cole could have flown anywhere."

"But that means..." Sarah's skin had turned a surprisingly pale shade.

"Oh, yes," Mirand understood now. "That means that you were the target. If Roy hadn't spontaneously added that trip, you would have been the first to fly internationally aboard the plane using the *Air Force One* call sign."

Sarah's skin didn't return to her normal coloring. Miranda

had no references in her notebooks about the meaning of skin tone changes.

"Is that a Why?" Miranda asked Andi. "Did I actually figure out a Why?"

Andi wiggled her head in neither a shake or a nod that Miranda could interpret. "Why they sabotaged the plane, yes. Why they wanted to kill President Feldman, no."

Miranda looked at Sarah. "All that leaves is who wants you dead badly enough to kill a whole airplane."

Sarah spoke very softly, as if talking to herself. "Well, isn't that just too perfect?"

75

—————

Icing your bruises was supposed to make them feel better. Holly had been icing her ass with an entire glacier for three days and it didn't feel one bit better.

She hadn't come prepared to sit high on Mt. Elbrus through a big storm. Yet more of her training that had slipped away unnoticed. When selecting her gear at The Bunker, she'd opted for fast-and-light mission profile, with no secondary prep if it ended up being a stay-low-and-slow. Worse, she'd apportioned the bulk of what she did bring into Mike's gear, expecting him and Inessa to be the ones to get into trouble if anyone did.

For three days the storm raged outside the slit of her snow cave. When it covered over, she let it. She started her snow vigil with a dead battery in her radio. By Day Two, her phone followed in its discharged footsteps. Now she no longer knew the time because who wore a watch in the age of smartphones besides the fashion conscious like Mike? Not her.

So she tracked time by whether she could see the walls of her dim Holly-sized hole-in-the-snow: daylight, or could not see the walls of her ice-bound Hobbit hole: night. A bare nine hours of daylight in mid-January meant she spent a whole lot of time in a world darker than a dingo's butthole.

Day Two saw the end of her energy bars, even rationed into single bites. She didn't mind being hungry, but running out of chocolate on Day Three had seriously hurt. Mostly she dozed to conserve energy and stayed hydrated with melted snow.

Day Four, it was the quiet that woke her. Either she was finally buried deep enough to no longer hear the storm's howl or the damn storm had finally abated. She could almost make out the vague outline of her gloved hand, so she waited.

The cave's brightness eventually rose to normalish levels, which meant that if she was buried, it wasn't avalanche deep.

Then she heard it: the heavy thud of helicopter rotors, muffled by the snow. She could feel the pulse of the deep bass notes. The weather had cleared, but the skies hadn't. Until now, it had only been nature trying to kill her. Now it would be the Russians.

If the crash had gone according to plan, the plane should have impacted on the northwestern face of the peak at five thousand meters. Her best estimate placed her on the south side at four thousand. Even though she'd retained her white coverall from the jump, the passage of the helicopter overhead told quite how big the rescue operation must be. Probably not the best time to go out for a stroll, even wearing white on a snowfield.

Three more helo passes confirmed the wisdom of her decision. But, dozing in and out, she couldn't tell when they stopped until the cave darkened. All of the overflights had been in the morning. At least half a day since the last one.

She punched a hole—or rather tried to. The snow cover extended beyond the length of her arm. Hard decision: wait through another long night or start to burrow? The first would leave her that much weaker and perhaps trap her for another day if they resumed patrols this far afield in the morning. The latter had only one problem, her snow cave had no spare room. If she started to burrow out, much of the extra snow would have to be backfilled into the cave. That meant no retreat once she'd started.

Well, it wasn't the biggest risk she'd taken on this mountain. And she actually wanted to see Mike—the bastard. One lousy *I love you* had changed nothing and everything. But she wasn't going to see him anytime soon if she stayed perched up here all winter. *Burrow out* it was.

After three meters, she stopped to check the feel of downness to make sure that she was still moving horizontally. At five meters, she wondered if she was digging in circles; she'd set out moving directly away from her protecting rock. It was now dark enough outside that any attempt to look behind her didn't reveal a thing. Besides, the tunnel was exactly the size of her body.

At eight meters, by which time her entire body was encased in impacted snow, the powder working its way in through every crevice in her gear, her fist broke through into free air. Was it mountain free air or had she circled back into her snow cave, in which case she just might cry some icicle tears. The shivers were setting in from all the snow melting inside her clothes. A very bad sign.

Packing the snow to the sides as much as possible, Holly dragged herself forward until she could see out the hole. Not the cave. High, horsetail cirrus clouds blurred the half-moon. It didn't take many seconds to note that the direction of the clouds ran west to east—fast. Another weather front moving in. So it was a good thing she hadn't waited until morning.

She froze with her body half out of her tunnel. She was looking down...a *long* way down. A glance behind her showed why. The big outcropping she'd built her cave against had caused a massive snow drift. Had she exited her cave and turned right or left, she'd have punched clear in the first few meters.

Here, she'd tunneled straight out through the long-axis of a snow drift that reached to a towering cliff's edge. Or...was she lying on only more snow suspended over the abyss. Fit to crumble at any second.

Holly tried to retreat, but she'd plugged the hole behind her as she'd wormed along. Going to the right wasn't an option either because of the cliff not having a top there either, though that was the direction of her escape route. Out of choices, she edged to the left out of the drift and did her best to disturb nothing until she was well back on firm ground. Or at least firm snow.

After moving once again close to the massive outcropping and away from the vertiginous drop, she faced the massive snowdrift across her route. She unzipped her coverall and parka to shake out what snow hadn't already melted. The bitter wind took the opportunity to make her wet inner gear several degrees cooler.

Ordering herself to think wasn't helping matters.

"Damn it, Sarge! We ever get to that warm, cozy pub, *you're* buying! Not this girl."

Sealing up everything as well as she could, she plunged through the drift. The passage from east side of the drift to the west side was both disgustingly easy and brutally cold. All the snow that she'd cleared out of the gear was replaced by a fresh load of snow looking for somewhere to perform its spring-melt magic act—transforming from lovely glittery stuff that caught the moonlight to freezing cold water running down her back, arms, and legs.

But she was through.

A kilometer more at altitude, then descend in a straight line. She doublechecked her GPS. Except nothing happened.

She looked at it again through one eye. And then the other. Still nothing.

Oh, right. It was on her phone. And its battery was dead. No backup battery. No dedicated unit. No nothing.

Well, she still had the moon. Except not for long. Those clouds were moving in faster than she was moving out. She eyed the drift behind her. So far she'd made good about four meters from her cave.

She leaned back into ritual. Drain the water bottle. Pack with snow. Inside pocket. No colder than the rest of her.

Screw the one-more-sideways-kilometer plan, she needed to get down. Except there was a reason not to. Oh yeah, the abyss at the end of the snow drift. One kilometer. In deep snow, that was about two thousand steps. Somewhere in her escape from her icy-Hobbit-hole-of-doom, she'd lost one of the hiking poles.

It required a very careful concentration to get the strap around her wrist. It turned out the trick was to remove the heavy outer glove first. But when she set it on the snow to focus on the strap, the wind took the glove over the cliff.

"Well, isn't that just dandy." Holly finally decided to remove her other glove and put it on the hiking pole hand. She jammed the half-bared hand in her pocket.

Then she poked the pole into the snow in front of her. When she found no crevasse, she took a step.

One.

Poke. Two.

Three.

76

"I'VE GOT HER ON THERMAL."

Mike didn't wait for Tad to fully land the helicopter, he jumped out as soon as he dared.

"Hey you." She blinked at him like a zombie affronted by the predawn light.

"You look like shit." And she did. Not just her lips were chapped white, but most of her face. Her golden hair was matted and soaked by the rain falling at Mount Elbrus' base. She had an outer snow glove on one hand but only an inner on the other. All that kept her propped upright on the boulder she sat on was a single bent hiking pole.

"You've said that before." Holly's voice came out as a dry croak.

"Most goddamn beautiful thing I've ever seen." And he wrapped his arms around her.

"Mike. You swore."

"Damn straight."

Her hug started tight and hard, but within seconds it faded. He shifted back, and almost lost her to the ground. Finally safe, she'd passed out.

Finally safe. Because she was with *him.*

God. Damn. Straight!

77

US Air Force Colonel Taz Cortez didn't know whether to laugh or be as creeped out as all hell. It had taken only two weeks since Miranda solved the crash of *Air Force One*. Placed in charge of the final phase by the President, what Taz had done was both elegant and terrifying.

With Clarissa's help, a feeling Taz would never manage to scrub off in the shower, she and General Elizabeth Gray-Nason, now Senate-confirmed Chairman of the Joint Chiefs of Staff, had built a spy network—one *inside* the Pentagon.

They'd chosen each person carefully, with the aid of an AI computer—run by Heidi, Harry, and Jeremy and buried deep within the CIA.

Their AI wasn't some genius self-aware machine, but it had offered perfect tracking of every person's activities and provided instant secure communication from each to the very top without revealing who they were reaching out to—all without the ability to betray any other members. The AI also scanned the complete social media, email archives (both personal and professional), and all phone and texting records captured by the NSA for each person prior to their recruitment. That's how they'd recruited everyone so quickly and not suffered a single leak.

The problem was that they'd confirmed far more than the one crime she'd expected to discover. They had uncovered a second, far greater conspiracy as well.

Taz now stood at the door to the PLC2 Building, at the sole door that had been opened into the Pentagon's underground auditorium outside of E-Ring, Corridor 8. She'd been a naïve eighteen when she'd first arrived here. Actually, she'd been a street savvy fifteen-year-old Mexican immigrant with a stolen identity making her three years older, but the military had never figured that out. Street-smart and Pentagon-stupid. But that was twenty-four years ago, and she thought she'd have seen it all in that time.

Apparently not.

"What's going on, Colonel?" She was known and the people invited to this meeting kept asking the question.

Her reply was the exact same every time. "Special meeting, sir. Please swipe in."

The first arrivals were mostly in the lower ranks of colonels like herself, lieutenant colonels, and a few majors. The turnstile beeped green as they came in. As word got out about the invite-only secret meeting, the turnstile beeped red more often. She would double-check their ID card against the list on her tablet —but that was only a courtesy—turning away those who tried to slip in uninvited. Some she knew too well and wouldn't mind frying their asses, but this wasn't personal. Not on the list? She turned them away.

The generals all tried to arrive at the very last second to show how important they were. Those who arrived with their typical entourage of assistants complained bitterly about which of their people were admitted and which ones were turned away—twice she had to signal to the Marine Corps guards waiting to either side of the door to settle the matter.

She managed not to smile about how they'd feel as soon as they were inside. A squad of Coasties were in there scanning and disarming each individual who entered. Their personal invitations to the meeting had said to bring no weapons, which only seemed to have encouraged them. Being scanned by Coasties was like a slap in the face as they were Department of Homeland Security, not Department of Defense. They were also one of the only two branches of the service, along with the Marines, to get a clean bill of health from Taz's investigation.

She took care to not meet the eyes of any of her spies dragged here as part of some entourage because it would be too dangerous to refuse their commander. The turnstile took care of turning them away, saving her from doing so. She had done the final recruitment of each one personally, wanting to get a personal feel for them first—twelve of the forty-seven had failed to cross that final hurdle. She would thank the ones who did for their service later.

"What's up, Vicki?"

Taz jolted. The Chief of the Air Force had been a good friend of the general she'd served for nineteen years. "Not for me to say, sir. Please swipe in."

His grimace said that was poor payback for treating her decently over all these years.

"Sorry, sir."

The turnstile turned green for him, his deputy, and three of the five assistants he'd brought. Once they were through, she double-checked her list. Gods but she was glad whoever had known that the chief was on the list hadn't told her ahead of time.

She managed to keep her face calm as the Chief of the Navy swept by, though neither his deputy nor any of his assistants were admitted. Vice President Carl Crawford, a former Lieutenant General of the Army, followed close behind and was greenlighted through.

Five minutes after the hour, she sent the five missing names to the Marine Corps honor guards posted throughout the Pentagon for this purpose. Due to the building's unique layout, which let a person walk from any room to any other in under seven minutes, the five stragglers were all rounded up in under ten. One felt he was too important, three too busy, and one had simply forgotten.

That's everyone we identified, Jeremy texted to her tablet as soon as the last one had swiped his ID through the turnstile.

Unsure what to send back, a smiley, a frowny, a weeping emoji—they were all jumbled up inside her—she sent a K for *okay.*

Then she signaled the Marine Corps guards. They all stepped through and lined up across the exit facing inward. The Coasties guarded the other doors from the inside. She locked the entry door behind her and stood in the gap they'd left for her.

The auditorium's stage was empty...and remained that way.

78

———

"Do I have to?"

Andi nodded. "Who else? You're the one who figured it all out."

"No television cameras?"

"We talked about this, Miranda."

Miranda covered her face with her hands. They had. How did she keep forgetting? She'd even written it in her notebook so that she wouldn't. Since she never forgot anything, that must mean her subconscious was blocking it, which wasn't saving her at the moment. They stood backstage of the Pentagon's PLC2 auditorium but she could feel them lurking out there, just waiting to pounce on her like...nasty...evil...leopards! Except you could trust a leopard to do leopard things, like chase and eat other animals. People like these couldn't be trusted.

"After this, no more television cameras, okay?"

Andi pulled her hands down, held them until Miranda opened her eyes, and nodded.

"Ever. Promise?"

"I'll do my best."

If Andi's best wasn't good enough, then no one could do better. She could only hope that her skills sufficed. "Come with me?"

"Anywhere."

For the second time in as many weeks, out in the world, television screens everywhere were flashing with a bright red *Breaking News* banner. She could only hope it didn't break her. An analogy! They weren't as tricky as metaphors, but she was encouraged at finding one.

Maybe, with Andi beside her, she could do this. Maybe.

She tried calming breaths. It didn't help. She tried picturing baby bunnies safe and snug in their bunny den—and imagined a stoat with a camera strapped to its head invading the safety of their underground lair. When she—

"The longer you wait to start, the longer until you finish."

"That's true!" Once again, Andi had the right of it. She looked down at Meg, "Are you ready?" She wagged her tail and grinned. Miranda could always rely on Meg too. She turned on her heel and hurried to the podium with her dog close beside her.

Andi followed her out of the wings onto the stage, wearing the same uniform she'd worn at their wedding to stand beside Roy and await Miranda's arrival. As this was sort of the wake for Roy, it seemed appropriate. She stopped two steps back and two to the side, dropping into a parade rest stance.

As long as she was nearby, Miranda didn't care if she stood on her head. That image almost made her smile.

Almost, until she looked at the room.

She faced the two hundred-and-fifty-seat auditorium, counting quickly though she already knew how many should be here—eighty-three seated military personnel. Curiously, it was the exact number who had died aboard *Air Force One*. Also, just another one-third of a person and it would be exactly one-third full. Was thirty-three-point-two percent capacity more rational that thirty-three-point-three repeating forever? She'd never liked numbers repeating forever; they were so untidy. So this was better than the implied yet deceptively false elegance of one-third capacity.

Miranda put up the first slide.

"My name is Miranda Chase, I'm the NTSB Investigator-in-charge for the investigation of the crash for *SAM 29000*, flying as *Air Force One* at the time of the incident. We ask that you keep your questions until the end as the first part of this conference is being nationally televised. You will be informed when the cameras are turned off."

Just in case anybody had a question, she purposely didn't look up to check for raised hands.

"On December 18th of last year, President Roy Cole decided to travel on a final goodwill tour as President. On January 3rd of this year, his aircraft departed for the hastily arranged tour. Hastily, but including all standard security protocols." She clicked to a map showing the final flight route. "His aircraft's engines all failed two hundred kilometers from land. Unable to make landfall, *Air Force One* crashed into the ocean fifteen kilometers offshore of Delaware, killing both the plane and all hands aboard. Everyone knows this much."

There were no sounds from the audience. With the lights focused on her, she wouldn't be able to see a raised hand anyway, even if she could bring herself to look up from the podium. That functioned as a satisfactory safeguard.

"The engines failed in reverse sequential order at precise thirty-second intervals: Four, Three, Two, One. There was no reason for them to have done so that could be attributed to any normal factor such as: fuel contamination, ice formation in fuel filters, manufacturing faults, bird strikes, or..." Miranda looked at the long list she'd made of known causes of engine failures. She hadn't thought to alphabetize them or order them by frequency of occurrence. She closed her eyes and changed her planned speech without opening them to look at her notes, "…or any other known direct cause."

Then she opened her eyes and peered at the page. Nothing essential had been skipped. It shortened the time she had to stand here by approximately nineteen seconds. That was good.

"The precision of the thirty-second intervals was indicative of a non-systemic cause. I've been asked to keep this simple. That request itself was not complex as the ultimate cause itself was simple as well."

There were several chuckles from the audience, though she was unsure as to why.

She glanced back at Andi, who tipped her chin upward.

Miranda tried it…a couple times. "Oh, you mean like keep going?"

Andi nodded to more laughter.

"Okay." Miranda tapped the next slide. "Two alterations were made to both of Roy's and now Sarah's VC-25A aircraft during their most recent maintenance cycle prior to the incident."

"Presidents," Andi whispered to her.

Miranda turned to her, "Yes, I meant the Presidents. I don't think I know any other Roy personally and the last Sarah I knew was in horse camp the summer before my parents died and were buried in TWA 800's crash."

"Never mind," Andi's whisper barely reached her.

"You know I'm not good at that."

Andi nodded and then did the chin tilt thing again.

"Oh, right." There were yet more laughs, again she didn't understand why, so she went to the next slide. "During that maintenance, this line of code was inserted into the airplane's command-and-control stack. For those of you who can't read even such simple computer code, it sets a number of parameters when the aircraft's systems are booted up. If these parameters are met, it runs an infinite-loop command into the key control chips successively in each engine at thirty-second intervals. In lab tests, identical chips exhibited a mean failure time of nineteen seconds with a standard deviation of only two-point-four seconds to overheat and reach failure. On *SAM 29000*, the VC-25A operating that day as *Air Force One*, it initially appeared to be little more than a series of burned-out chips with merely a curious timing coincidence. This would indicate that there'd been a manufacturing fault in the chips."

She put up a photo of *SAM 28000* still parked in the Andrews Air Force Base hangar.

"The next time *SAM 28000* was powered up for maintenance, the attack code was uncovered."

The tech sergeant who had died shortly after *Air Force One's* crash had been the first clue—at least to the others. Their attempts to explain it to her had left Miranda with a headache. She didn't put it in the presentation because she still didn't understand it.

"The parameters," Andi whispered.

"Oh, right," she selected the next slide. "They were actually quite simple. First, the aircraft had to be flying at over thirty-thousand feet; it was flying at forty. Second, it had to be doing so at least three hundred kilometers downrange from departure on an overseas route, placing it over two hundred kilometers offshore. And third, it required a true state from this section of code," she brought up another slide. "Which is a little more complex. It is voice recognition software that had to register a back-and-forth radio call including the phrase *Air Force One*. The aircraft would never be called that unless the President was aboard. This was clearly a case of sabotage with intent to harm Roy or Sarah."

When she paused this time, there was no laughter or other noise. Actually, it was an ideal environment for testing the qualitative measure of a room being so quiet that you could hear a pin drop. She almost pulled out her notebook to remind herself to bring one if she ever presented a national broadcast like this again. Then decided that she'd rather not do one again —ever.

"This concludes a verbal summary of the detailed report that I will be submitting to the Air Force Accident Investigation Board and the NTSB. I will add a strictly personal observation that will not be included in my report: whoever did this to *Air Force One* is a very bad person."

This time she had no doubt that she could have heard a pin if she'd had one to drop.

"The last thing," Andi prompted.

Miranda hadn't forgotten, but she'd been reluctant to put up the last slide as she wasn't the one who'd done it.

The guilty have been identified and arrested.

"This ends the national broadcast."

She couldn't gauge the sounds of the audience this time. It sounded like a gasp of relief from a few individuals, which didn't make any sense.

79

"Thank you, Ms. Chase," President Feldman stepped onto the stage. During the campaign, Sarah had learned that thinking of herself as *the next President,* had placed her in a presidential mindset for appearances. But some things took precedent. "You may call me Sarah at any time."

"Then why did you just call me Ms. Chase?"

"Miranda, then."

"But—"

Andi Wu came up, looped an arm through Miranda's, and led her away before she could ask more questions. Miranda always had more questions. Her dog trotted along beside them.

Sarah waited until they were off stage. Then she turned to face the audience though she didn't step to the podium. It was enough that she was here, the President visiting the Pentagon.

It was enough that she could see the two Chiefs of Staff in the first row, their initial gasp of relief returning to cautious silence as they eyed the armed sailors guarding each exit. They now suspected and would soon know. She glanced at the now-dark cameras that had been broadcasting Miranda's analysis to the world. Soon they too would know, but not yet.

Chairman of the Joint Chiefs of Staff General Elizabeth Gray-Nason crossed from the wings to the podium and introduced herself. After that, Elizabeth didn't waste any words.

"Every person seated in this audience is hereby accused of one of two illegal actions. Fourteen of you are to be charged with conspiring to murder the duly elected President of the United States, Sarah Feldman. Due to his hastily planned final trip and the unanticipated use of *Air Force One* before his retirement, you also stand accused of being complicit in the murder of President Roy Cole, First Lady Rose Cole, and Chairman of the Joint Chiefs of Staff General Drake Nason in addition to the other personnel on that flight. Further, you will all be charged as felony accomplices for the destruction of property, specifically the multi-billion-dollar military asset commonly called *Air Force One*."

Sarah couldn't look at Carl Crawford. They'd campaigned together, both fought for their country; she'd thought they'd become more than colleagues—friends. Yet he had recruited a team as carefully as Miranda's team had recruited their spy network—almost as carefully.

"*All* of you will be charged with agreeing to support Vice President Carl Crawford in staging a full military coup after he had attained the Presidency through President Feldman's death."

Taz Cortez's spy network had unraveled that it wasn't merely the unstoppable ego of a single man wanting to command the Oval Office by killing her. Her team had revealed a far more dangerous plot. Crawford believed that the military should run the nation with him as the commanding general—all power concentrated in one man's hands.

When this arrest first reached the news, it would look politically motivated. As if Sarah was the one consolidating power. Only when the charged were revealed would it become clear that she was stopping a military coup rather than staging her own Executive Branch one from the Oval Office.

Elizabeth continued as steady as a rock. Sarah assumed they would both weep later, each in the privacy of their showers.

"The evidence of your crimes has already been collected. In the last fifteen minutes, it has been submitted to the Judge Advocate General's Corps for each of your appropriate military branches. Your offices are currently being stripped. Do not bother erasing your phones—by a legal warrant, we have already copied every text, email, and image from each one. Fourteen people in this room are to be charged with murder and all eighty-three of you, per the US Attorney General's interpretation of the Constitution Article III Section 3, treason. You will be tried by general courts-martial. The Attorney General has already decreed that there will be no bail before trial. No deals will be struck."

Sarah couldn't stop the tear that escaped and rolled down her cheek. Not for the threats to her own life, but for the threat to her country's democratic core.

"Per Article 31 (b) of the Uniform Code of Military Justice," Elizabeth hesitated. She and Sarah had laughed together, briefly and bitterly, when planning this moment. The civilian equivalent to the military code was known as the Miranda Rights. The sheer irony of it all—for Miranda Chase was the ultimate champion of justice, but for her airplanes, not people —was galling.

Elizabeth cleared her throat and continued.

"You all have the right to remain silent. Anything you say…"

80

Nataliya Turner, no longer Inessa Turgeneva, stood in the courtyard between the Old and New Headquarters Buildings of the CIA. Her dark hair, now dyed silver, hung long about her face, hiding her cheekbones and jawline from facial recognition software. Unlike many, it hadn't aged her appearance but rather elevated her to the heights of elegant sophistication. Her clothes were no longer her own designs, but she was enjoying an exploration of Versace, McCartney, and others, without the pressure to create anything beyond her own personal style.

Her escort / armed bodyguard waited quietly off to the side. The CIA courtyard was a lovely space in many ways: a small park, a peaceful place between the storms within the two buildings. The March morning was chilly, but so much warmer than a Moscow winter that she hadn't bothered to button her full-length Prada cashmere coat.

She sat on a stone bench and faced the enigmatic sculpture that stood there. A great bronze wave three meters—ten feet high, she corrected herself, she was in America now—and twenty *feet* long. No more than seven or eight centimeters thick, whatever that might be in their arcane inches. Like a great sheet of paper stood on its long side, then pressed in from each end until it made a soft S-shape, it dominated this end of the garden. The entire surface was riddled with hand-tall letter-shaped perforations.

Kryptos. She remembered Miranda describing how her father had attempted to hone her curious brain into a cryptography machine. Pushing her to decipher the codes the artist had embedded there, sections of which still stumped cryptographers thirty-five years later. What a strange childhood that must have been.

Her multiple attempts to speak with Miranda had not gone as she'd imagined. Rather than bonding over Miranda's parents being her mentors, each tale she told to Miranda drove them farther apart. It was hard to imagine they were talking about the same people.

Nataliya was used to understanding people, easily becoming fast friends and confidants. Not this time. She was no code breaker but, unlike Miranda, she could appreciate the metaphor of *Kryptos* standing between them—her and her *Little Sister*—a wall that she didn't know how to breach.

Hidden codes applied to her future as well. Stepping into the world of the American's Central Intelligence Agency was an opportunity with a thousand hidden ramifications as complex and full of subtle meanings as the sculpture before her. At least this was a terrain she understood well.

Though no longer a billionaire, she'd extracted the bulk of her wealth from Russia before the international sanctions and her *death.* She could afford a life of luxury anywhere in the world. But luxury beyond her clothes had never driven her, except as a tool to engage others. No, it was the beating heart that fascinated her; the pulse of humanity that might be shifted or used to make the world a better place to live in.

She had maintained a delicate thread of communication with the head of the CIA's Russia Desk, Valentina Mills; a connection originally set up by Holly Harper. And, starting today, that connection would become side-by-side offices within this mighty bastion of clandestine knowledge. She knew precisely who to reach out to of her former contacts, never revealing who she truly was, of course, but perhaps *Inessa's Salon* would live on under another name. By some impossible path, her training by Miranda's parents and the resulting connection to her *Little Sister* Miranda had led her to sitting here before *Kryptos*.

"She loves this damn thing." Nataliya didn't turn at Director Clarissa Reese's approach, letting the symbols of the curious path opening before her play across the sculpture's surface.

"Miranda loves *and* hates it, I believe," she said as Clarissa sat beside her. Over these last months of debriefings and the pursuant negotiations about Nataliya's possible work at the CIA, they had come to appreciate each other as sparring partners.

"Loves and hates. Much like this place."

At that she turned and saw the weariness on Clarissa's face. She might be able to hide it from others, but Nataliya knew it too well from observing their sparring...and from her own mirror.

She also saw the pain. The pain of so much being ripped away. Of being a woman standing alone against all comers. Miranda had her Andi. Holly had her Mike. Who did Clarissa have with the death of her friend Rose? Who did she herself? Some questions were too hard at the present. So she chose another.

"Tell me about the parts you love."

A few minutes' planned welcome became a quiet hour. To Nataliya's surprise, Clarissa's passion for her country matched her own for Russia. Except, her own passion had been misplaced; her beloved country was past saving. She hoped, oh how she hoped, that Clarissa's was not.

81

Tim Andrews rolled into the Palomino and eased up to the bar. "Hey Jenny. An Ivan when you get a chance."

"Wet cat drag you in, hon?" She'd been pouring beers here at least since he'd come in for his first-ever legal pint, most of two decades back—and probably twenty years before that. Woman wasn't a barmaid; she was an institution. One of Ma's besties besides. He liked the small-town feel of this being his regular place, even if Jenny working here meant he couldn't get away with shit. It was also close by the Missoula, Montana, smokejumper base, which was a big bonus.

"Feels like." He nodded toward the windows he'd sat with his back to. Outside, March was coming in just like the proverbial lion. Freezing rain slashing down out of the Bitterroots that would turn to snow in the next couple hours. "Parts for that worn retardant pump came in."

"And you couldn't wait for clear weather to fix it, could ya?" She tossed a coaster on the stone bar top and set a pint of Ivan the Terrible Russian-style Imperial stout on it. Patting his hand, she winked at him. "Always were a good boy, Timmy." She made him feel about twelve, but the beer tasted just fine.

327

"Usual buffalo burger?" Wasn't a local she didn't know down to their bones.

"Maybe in a bit."

She eased on down the bar to tease a couple of the old timers—they'd been holding down those stools since long before he'd had that first brew. Doug fir paneling, dark with age, covered the walls. Behind the bar were photos of planes new and old that had flown to fires from the nearby airport. Some t-shirts commemorating the worst fires. Even a few hardhats and fire axes hung there. But mostly were framed pictures of each summer's team all the way back to the very first in 1940. Photos of folks he'd fought fire with and ones long buried and forgotten—except by folks like him and Jenny.

Tim closed his eyes and let the quiet seep in. The rain had pounded on his slicks all damn day until the drumming was the only sound in the whole world. But he'd gotten the damn pump running. Wouldn't need it until June, July if they were lucky, May if they weren't. Or sooner. There was no predicting the firefighting season anymore. That big Colorado burn where they couldn't get water because all the lakes and rivers had frozen over. Pacific Northwest was a mess all down the Cascades for six, seven, eight months a year now. Alaska had started their first burn in April last year, not July. California never stopped burning at all.

He didn't have time to move slowly. It was his job to make sure the Zulies' air tankers, smokejumpers, and hotshots were ready when the first burn hit.

Tim shook his head to clear it and focused on the sounds of the bar. In here, there was talk, laughter, stories, and the smell of good food. This was the right speed to wind down on a cold, wet, winter's day. For now he was warm and dry, and that felt plenty good.

"Retardant pump?" Woman's voice. Odd accent, not much, but nowhere near Montana.

He looked over two stools. Two stools and six inches down. Had she been sitting there when he came in? If so, he musta been blind. Not a whole lot of Asian women hanging out in Missoula, Montana. Her black hair fell in lazy curls to the shoulders of her fleece vest, like she was just letting it grow. A thin slick hung on the hook under the edge of the bar. Good gear, though not much of it for a Montana March. She didn't look like she was cold though her damp hair showed she'd been out in it.

"Yeah. Stuff we use to fight fires. A couple hundred thousand gallons of that sludge will wear a pump plenty fast. Parts were back-ordered to hell; was half afraid I'd start the season with a wonky pump."

She was drinking a Big Sky IPA by the color. Turning half to face him, she propped her elbow on the bar and her cheek on a raised fist. "You their fix-it guy?"

"Chief cook and bottle-washer, too. At least in the off-season. Run the outfit when the season's on."

She widened those up-turned narrow eyes for just long enough to see they were darkest brown, not black like he'd first thought. "When are tryouts?"

He laughed.

She didn't. A slight smile tugged at her lips, like she wasn't laughing with him or at him but found something else entirely different kinda funny. It made a man notice her face; her damn nice face that went fine with that nice hair. He couldn't pin her age but there was something in that gaze that made him revise his estimate well upward. It was a look he'd seen in some of his best crew.

"Did you serve?" He himself hadn't, but he'd learned to appreciate the skills and drive that a person picked up from doing military time.

"Long time. Done now."

Didn't look old enough for that *long time* to be true. Except maybe those eyes.

"You got a card?"

She fished out a wallet and set her card on the bar top. It was a simple white Incident Qualification Card that everyone called a Red Card because of the red letters on the section headings. Under Qualified Positions it had just one entry: FFT2.

"Firefighter Type 2? You a newbie? The Zulies aren't a beginner's outfit. Top crew in the US all battle for a slot with us."

She tucked the card away, sipped her beer, then rested her cheek back on her raised fist. "So teach me."

This time when he laughed, she smiled along at the joke. Steady. Didn't take offense easily. That was one key factor. "You got sticking power?" That was another.

"Till the end." It was a voice that said she knew *exactly* what that meant and reminded him of the chill rain slashing against the windows. The hardest thing to teach a civilian was that you didn't stop until the fire was beat—no matter how many days or weeks it fought back, you did *not* stop. He couldn't doubt her words, not with that tone.

"Why forest fire?"

She stared somewhere way beyond the beer taps before answering. "I was up in remote mountains one time—not like these, really remote. Didn't understand that too much of my life had been in the city until that moment."

More remote that the Bitterroot Wilderness? That seemed unlikely. Then he noticed how her expression shifted and knew he'd just picked up a trainee. Every wildland firefighter knew that look. It had a lot of different names: Nature's Call, Call of the Wild, Tree Lover, Earth Warrior. Didn't matter what you called it; it was the key factor in any wildland firefighter because the pay certainly didn't compensate for the risk and pain. But she had it—the mad passion for the wilderness.

"Got a lot of gear needs sorting and fixing."

Her shrug said that menial work didn't bother her.

"You got a name, girl?" He should have read the card when he had the chance.

"Wang Dai—," then she stopped and really laughed. It wasn't the bright giggle he'd expect from a girl with such a face, but instead a woman's throaty laugh that just might have a seriously bad moment or two...or three...behind it. "Jade." She managed a steadying breath, nodded to herself, and held out a hand. "Jade Wang."

She didn't have some gentle handclasp, and her calluses weren't faked either.

"Tim Andrews. Why do I think this is gonna be an interesting season?"

Jade raised her glass in a toast. He clinked his to hers and they both drank.

82

———

THE FUROR HAD BEEN SLOW TO ABATE AND MIRANDA HAD DONE everything she could to hide. Living in an unmarked missile silo in rural Washington State had made that easier. She left only for the crash investigation call-outs that she couldn't refuse.

The warm May had brought blossoms to the small grove of cherry, apple, and pear trees that she'd planted along the driveway. It also brought the spring birds to the feeders and fawns to romp through the meadows.

She'd watched each of her friends go through grieving after the crash and resolution of *Air Force One*...but still didn't know how she felt about it. Yes, now and then she wished Drake would call with some impossible crisis. Not because she wanted the crisis, but she did miss the sound of his voice and his patience with her.

This morning she sat with her back against a big-leaf maple, Meg asleep in her lap, and a book resting on Meg that she couldn't seem to focus on. Instead, her attention followed the breeze playing with the bright green new growth of the conifer woods that started along one edge of their property and continued far up the slopes of Tiger Mountain.

Mike and Holly were in Seattle investigating the downing of a Twin Otter float plane that had run into a houseboat to avoid a sailboat.

Andi was busy in her own vegetable garden, attempting to prove that she didn't kill plants with her mere presence. She still wasn't allowed into Miranda's garden past the bench she'd installed close by the gate. Andi had yet to disprove Miranda's hypothesis about Andi's black thumb, though she remained determined to try.

As Miranda sat quietly, Meg's ears twitched toward the nearby tall grass. Sure enough, the stalks began to weave about. Miranda had set out a handful of dried corn when she'd arrived and her rabbit friend soon emerged to nibble at it.

Except he'd changed. His coat was all matted down one side with dried blood. And he was definitely favoring his right front paw. One of his eyes had a big gash over it as well.

"Oh, you poor thing," she whispered to it. It twitched one ear in her direction, but the other was badly tattered and must hurt to move.

The fawn-colored Eastern Cottontail had grown accustomed to her and ate the corn within easy reach. When Miranda brushed a hand over its fur, she could feel the shiver of muscles beneath.

"You need help."

In answer, the rabbit finished its corn and began trying to clean its injured paw.

Miranda took off the floopy sun hat that Andi made her wear whenever they were outside and scooped the rabbit gently into the bowl of the inverted crown. It watched her intently, but made no effort to escape as she cradled it in her arms. As she hurried back to the house, Miranda could feel it twitch whenever a wound was bumped. She hoped that her apologies helped. Meg trotted along eager with curiosity at her heels.

"What do you have there?" Andi looked up from inside her fenced garden where the surviving plants were a quarter the size of the ones in Miranda's.

"My rabbit friend is hurt. It looks like he got in a fight with another rabbit. A fox would have done more damage and a coyote would have killed it. Maybe he fought off a hawk." She didn't stop until she was inside.

She had assembled an animal medical kit to replace the one that had been burned up along with her island home but never had occasion to use it since their move here. She rolled it out on the counter and set the bunny beside it on a clean towel. Then, step by step, Miranda went through every needed procedure she'd learned on an isolated island filled with wildlife: trimming fur, applying Blood Stop Powder to deeper wounds, and antiseptic to shallower ones. Binding his injured paw had required some negotiation, but they'd managed it together.

When Andi came to watch, she lifted Meg onto one of the bar stools. Miranda had been so concerned for the rabbit that she'd forgotten that Meg would want to watch too. As she moved from paw to rump to ear, Andi wandered away and Meg curled up on the stool to nap. When she was done, she shifted the rabbit into Meg's carrying kennel with several leaves of chard and a small dish of water. He ate a little, nibbled at a bandage but without any real effort, and then went to sleep.

She followed the sounds of a screw gun out to the workshop. Andi was covered in sawdust but she was mounting a hinged door on a brand-new rabbit hutch.

"It looked as if that rabbit needs to stay safe for a while. I hope this is okay."

Miranda hugged her despite the sawdust. "It's perfect. You're perfect."

"Only on Thursdays."

She'd learned this was one of Andi's jokes and, after a bit of explanation, had decided it was funny, so she laughed whenever Andi used it. She hurried back inside to fetch the injured rabbit as Andi set the hutch under a blooming cherry tree. She gave it fresh spinach from her garden.

"Oh, she'll like that. It's so pretty here."

Once the rabbit was situated, she and Andi stood with their arms around each other's waists and watched it eat.

"Should I build another?" Andi nodded toward the hutch because she couldn't mean the rabbit or the cherry tree as neither one required building.

"Why?"

"Are you going to start rescuing more rabbits?"

"If they need rescuing."

Andi's grip tightened about her waist in an encouraging way. "And fawns? And birds?"

"And abandoned fox cubs."

"Lost ducklings."

"Hurt elk." A herd of Roosevelt elk often wandered across the property, which had required stout fences around each garden and orchard. Though she'd never noticed a hurt one.

"Injured raptors. The birds of prey, not the dinosaurs."

"Right, because the latter are extinct. It would be illogical to try and rescue those."

With each one they named, Miranda could see the property as if in double vision. One, her childhood home on Spieden Island and all the wild animals that had been left behind from its brief time as a hunter's game park. The other, here, a home for animals that didn't have a home or couldn't survive in the wild.

"It's as if all my years chasing air crashes were..." Miranda sighed. "I wish I was better at metaphors."

"A side track?"

"Like a train that got on the wrong track and was stuck there? Yes, it was."

"So what track do you *want* to be on?"

Miranda had to think hard about that one. The first thing outside her family that she'd enjoyed in a while had been helping the injured rabbit. "Enjoyed! Hey, I did *enjoy* that." Emotions were so tricky.

"What was the last crash investigation you enjoyed?"

Miranda had to sit in the grass and stare at the sleeping rabbit for a long time while she sorted through them. There'd been hundreds in the twenty-two years since her first investigation. Yet...enjoyed? "Is one supposed to enjoy a plane crash?"

Andi lay down beside her and used a long piece of grass to tickle the back of one of Meg's ears. "Well, maybe enjoy isn't the right word. Fascinated by? Energized by?"

"I'm fascinated by whatever I'm working on at that moment. It's part of being autistic. Energized by?" She again considered each of the crash investigations she'd worked on over the last twenty-two years. Andi understood and waited for her to review the entire catalog mentally. "I can't think of one."

She'd been more energized by their belated trip to Chincoteague Island to see the wild horses than by the crash of *Air Force One* that had occurred just fifteen kilometers out to sea from there. The fire chief on Assateague Island, who technically owned all the horses, had offered fascinating stories of the care of the ponies, the annual swim across the channel, and offered many insights into herd management and care.

"I was energized by helping our bunny."

Meg twisted and managed to snatch the grass stalk from Andi's grasp. As soon as she turned away, Andi plucked another.

"Would you be energized if we turned this property into a wildlife sanctuary?"

And her double vision of her childhood animal friends whom she'd studied so carefully and the lone bunny happily nibbling on his chard merged into a single vision on this property as if coming into focus for the first time.

Miranda managed a nod. She could imagine looking forward to each day tending those like her childhood friends. Autistics tended to have a strong affinity for animals and she could feel the joy of dealing with them daily. They weren't like humans, always filled with a dozen conflicting emotions. Instead there was a purity of simply being what they were.

Except she wasn't alone.

"How about you, Andi? What do you want?"

Andi lay in silence for as long a time as Miranda had before speaking. She didn't even tease Meg's ears. "I think Drake's death was somehow one too many. I lost my copilot to a Russian grenade in Syria. I had lost teammates in Syria, Afghanistan, Iraq, and other places before that. I've been crawling around wrecks with you for almost five years and we've seen a lot of dead people. I wouldn't mind spending my time with things that are alive."

"Animals die too, you know."

"Yes, I know. But that bunny," she pointed her grass stalk at the hutch, "is going to live longer and healthier because of what you just did for it. I like that."

She sat and Andi lay as the occasional pink cherry blossom fluttered down against the blue sky.

"What are you going to name it?" Andi asked after a while.

"Who?"

She pointed her grass stalk at the bunny.

Miranda didn't have to consider. The bunny's calm demeanor on what must have been a very trying day settled it.

"I'm going to call him Drake."

AFTERWORD

If you enjoyed Air Force One
please consider leaving a review.
They really help.

More Miranda coming soon.
In the meantime,
keep reading for an exciting excerpt from:
Night Stalkers Reload #1, Guard the East Flank

Be sure to visit:
https://mlbuchman.com/fan-club-freebies

- *Bonus Scene/Story*
- *Recipe from the book*
- *Character list, place maps, plane pictures, and more*

NIGHT STALKERSRELOAD #1 (EXCERPT)

IF YOU ENJOYED THAT, YOU'LL LOVE…

GUARD THE EAST FLANK (EXCERPT)

"WHEN WAS THE LAST TIME YOU FLEW?"

"Yesterday. Or was it Tuesday, Emma?" Mark glanced her way, but didn't give her time to respond. "Yep, thinkin' it was Tuesday." He pointed westward at the abrupt upward break of the Montana Front Range. Their twenty-thousand-acre ranch ended there and the million-acre Selway-Bitterroot Wilderness began.

She, Mark, and Colonel Cassius McDermott had stopped their horses in the shade of a white birch copse atop a crest of the rolling landscape. It was one of Emily's favorite views. They were on a lazy afternoon ride a couple hours from the ranch, and this would be their turnback point.

The sun glinted off the sharp peaks of the Lewis Range, emphasizing the alternating light and dark strata that slashed through the mountains like the insides of mile-tall layer cakes. Being born and raised in DC, even six years living here hadn't decreased Emily's wonder at this vista rising in her backyard.

"Took a couple of fat-cat tourists on a spin out there, in our little Bell JetRanger helo. We spotted bear, moose, a couple herds of elk. Gonna be some good hunting for the larder this fall. Good photo safaris, too—we're marketing those heavy this year. You should come on out, Cass. It'll be a good time here at the ranch."

"I don't think that's what Cass is asking, is it, Colonel?" Emily gave Mark the hint, but he missed it. "Six years since the last time we flew a mission."

Then she caught the look in Mark's eye. He'd known exactly what he was doing. Instead of scowling at her for spoiling his game, he offered her one of his broad conspiratorial winks, including her in his play. He'd always enjoyed his games but never been particularly attached to the winning or the losing. Less so with each passing year. The ranch had mellowed him so much that it was occasionally hard to spot the former 5th Battalion D Company commander of the Night Stalkers' regiment.

He pulled out a hip flask. After taking a sip, he offered it to Cass seated on Rollo, reaching over from atop Wind Runner. His big black gelding hadn't slowed with age, but the years had made Mark a better rider—at least he rarely fell off anymore.

"Sorry, didn't get you were talking about *flying,* not flying. Well, why didn't you say it plain, old son?" His horsemanship may have improved; his phony Texas accent hadn't.

Cass was looking at the flask as if there was something wrong with it, or the fact that it was still early afternoon. The early summer finally warm enough for no more than a light jacket.

"None of us on duty out here, Cass, and 'tain't poison. Licensed distiller from just down the valley a piece. All local: water, grain, even the oak for the casks and the cooper who knocked them together—seriously hot, by the way. I'd introduce you, but don't want to tick off your wife." Well, his Texas was a little better, even if she'd never understood why a Navy brat turned Montanan kept toying with it. As far as she knew, neither he nor his SEAL father had ever been so much as stationed there and his mother was pureblood Cheyenne from Wyoming.

"He also has a beard down to his solar plexus, except when he singes it while charring a barrel. You might object to that even more than your wife would." Emily felt it was only fair to warn him.

Cass laughed and took the flask. The whiskey was too harsh for Emily's palate, any whiskey was, but Cass seemed to like it well enough to take a second taste before returning it to Mark, who tucked it away.

It might be Mark doing most of the speaking, but it was Colonel Cass McDermott she watched carefully. He hadn't brought his wife on this trip, which meant he was here on business—the Army's business.

"Did you say six years, Emily?"

"You're thinking eleven." She kept her smile to herself.

"I admit I was."

"The last five were under a different classification, Cass." Meaning operations that her former commander hadn't been cleared for. Always a bitter taste, one that showed clearly on his face.

"Yeah," Mark said in his normal voice. "Classified mission compartmentalization sucks. I always found it as annoying as hell, too."

Cass made it halfway through a nod of acknowledgement when a rabbit bolted from practically under the nose of Cass' horse. When Rollo ran, he had a habit like no other horse she'd ever seen. The gray dropped low and bolted so fast that Cass looked as if he floated in space for a moment before plummeting to the thick Montana grass.

"Goddamn it!" Mark swung his reins over and gave Wind Runner a hard kick. He didn't need it; his horse also loved to run, and he was the fastest on the ranch—because, of course, that's what Mark had insisted on when they moved here, not realizing as a rank beginner what he was asking for.

Rollo offered an easy ride, good for a beginner like Cass—usually. Wind Runner? Not so much. Mark and the two horses raced out of sight over the bluff.

Knowing her own level of incompetence, she'd requested the friendliest of mounts and never regretted her choice. Chesapeake watched the others race away as she chewed her latest mouthful of the lush grass before reaching for another bite. Emily patted her on the neck.

She hoped that she wouldn't have to go rescue Mark next.

Dropping the reins over her mare's neck, she slid to the ground. Nothing much bothered her horse, and she wouldn't run off even if it did.

"Anything hurt other than your pride, Cass?"

"Not much." He remained seated in the foot-tall grass of the July prairie.

The rains had come late—late enough in June to strike fear into every rancher's heart, even a Jane-come-lately like herself. But the so-called million-dollar rains had finally come on strong and set the crops. It had also turned the entire Front Range into a magic carpet of bluebells, buttercups, and windflowers. Their bright colors danced on the air lush with the scent of green. July's typical dusty dry taste had been pushed out into August, making every Montanan walk a bit sprightlier, whether from the prairie or the town.

Cass picked up the cowboy hat they'd given him against the sun, but he didn't put it back on. Instead, he worried the brim around in a slow circle through his hands as he remained seated on the grass. "Six years? Thought you were flying to wildfires."

"That's one way to look at it." They'd also been flying black ops missions under the cover of being helitack firefighters, reporting only to the President and the Secretary of Defense.

She sat down on the grass beside him. Emily felt Chesapeake come up behind her, but she didn't react.

Her mahogany mare picked the hat off Emily's head without catching her long blonde hair in its teeth.

"See? They don't tell me squat simply because I'm the 160th SOAR's commanding officer."

She let her silence tell him that it was going to stay that way, too. Her years flying for the Night Stalkers of the Army's Special Operations Aviation Regiment had been the highlight of her career, but that hadn't been the end of it by a long stretch.

Chesapeake flapped Emily's hat up and down, laughing through clenched teeth. It was an old game between them, since back when they first met and the only thing Emily rode was Black Hawk helicopters. She waited for the horse to hang her head over Emily's shoulder so she could scrub Chesapeake's cheek. The horse sighed happily, dropped Emily's hat in her lap, then turned her attention to ripping up grass.

Cass was thinking hard about her flying career...and something else as well. Didn't matter, Emily was dug in here, but she was curious at what had dragged him all the way to Montana from Fort Campbell, Kentucky.

Picking up her hat, she slid it on. Not for Chesapeake to steal again, but her light blonde hair and matching complexion didn't offer any defense against the Montana summer sunshine even wearing a serious SPF number and sitting in the broken shade of the swaying birches.

"Six years is still too long for us to go airborne again, Cass. A single month off blunts that fighting edge in a top pilot. Six years..." she let that hang.

It would take a minimum of half a year of retraining to regain that edge, if she even could. Flying a Night Stalkers helicopter into a battlespace was *not* a bicycle that your body simply remembered how to fly.

"You knew that before you came here. What's really going on?"

Rather than answering directly, he appeared to be watching the snow-capped ranges behind her. "I saw that you're still listed as active duty."

She was. Mark had finally retired when he'd hit his twenty years—*Same as Dad is plenty good enough for me*—his final four years as a trainer at the nearby Malmstrom Air Force Base. He'd flown and taught leadership courses before finally standing down as a lieutenant colonel. Getting the silver oak leaf had tickled him no end. But when she'd pointed out that a few more years' service might get him a bump to being a bird colonel, he'd scoffed.

Think I'm after Cass McDermott's job? Not even a little interested.

And he hadn't been.

Done my tour.

In the two years since, he'd settled in as if he'd never been anywhere else. His dad still ran the place. Though pushing seventy, Mac was a retired SEAL and wouldn't stop until he was six feet under the sod, if then. But Mark and the ranch had started to fit each other in ways he'd never managed even as commander of the most elite SOAR company.

As the commander of the 5th Battalion's D Company, he'd been a driven hard-ass. The only quality that was good enough for Viper Henderson was perfection—setting the gold standard himself. On the ranch, he was the one behind the scenes making sure everything kept ticking along. It was easy to miss where he slipped in unless she watched for it.

He was also Superdad. Tessa and Belle loved her, but they worshipped their dad—two seriously daddy's girls. Which was okay, she worshipped Mark a little herself.

Cass *knew* Mark had retired; he'd come out to the ranch for the retirement party. Whatever he was after...

I saw that you're still listed as active duty.

"Oh, no. Wait a minute, Cass. I don't want back in the service."

"Saw you earned the same silver oak leaf as Mark, same year too, though you're a couple years younger. Don't seem to recall any invitation to *your* retirement party...unless there never was one. Still on active duty without any missions or any posting showing up in your records at all, at least not any I get to see."

Emily had already answered that one. Five years technically flying to fight forest fires. At least that was the wider perception. By which time, she'd had it running so smoothly that she was able to hand it off.

For the six years since, she'd created and led a clandestine intelligence operation at the behest of the former President. Though now that she thought about it, that operation had finally matured as well. There was little that Lauren, Claudia, and Michael actually needed of her anymore. She been chomping at the bit for a while now, worse than Chesapeake when she scented the barn coming in range after a long ride.

Fully retire like Mark? Leading yet another trail ride didn't exactly fill her cup past a quarter full. Chasing down yet another attack on the Executive Branch sounded equally uninspiring no matter how good she had become at it.

She'd always been a pilot first and last.

Cass smiled. "Eddie Arnson wants to make you an offer."

"Then why are you here?" The Chairman of the Joint Chiefs of Staff, the top-ranking military officer in the nation, knew how to find her. He was Mark's uncle, after all. Only the second Marine Corps general to ever be named to the post. She still wondered what crowbar the President had used to pry him loose from his beloved HMX-1 post commanding the Marine helicopters responsible for Presidential-lift missions.

"Because I asked to make the pitch."

"So pitch."

The ground vibrated slightly beneath her butt. A discontented snort from Rollo announced that Mark had caught the runaway horse unfairly and far too soon into a glorious gallop over the thick summer pastures.

Cass waited for the two of them to come up.

"You hitting on my wife, Cass? Gotta warn you, Emma gets *more* dangerous with age. And she started out plenty dangerous to begin with." He rubbed his jaw where she'd planted his face into an aircraft carrier's ready-room table for stealing a first kiss. A dozen years and a lifetime ago.

Though he never missed an opportunity to mention it, they shared a smile at the memory. She remembered the kiss with searing clarity but had to take Mark's word on what she'd done to him after that.

He also kept the outer bezel of his watch permanently set to the precise minute of that first kiss. She'd tested him a few times; he never had to hesitate longer than a single breath to tell her years, days, hours, and minutes since.

Despite the memory, Emily's smile felt tight on her face.

"Can't say that my missus would take it much better than yours," he winked at Emily, but kept looking up at Mark on his horse. "How do you feel about being outranked?"

"You've always outranked me, Old Man. Simply being older seems questionable grounds for such a thing, but..." Mark shrugged it away.

"You can double that barely concealed envy now. They're bumping me upstairs, commander of USASOAC, giving me a star for my troubles." He tapped his shoulder where it would go.

"Head of the whole Army's Spec Ops Aviation Command? Very fancy, *General* Cassius McDermott, sir." Mark offered a salute sloppier than a recruit fresh through the gate. "Congratulations, Cass, seriously. You're a hundred percent the man for that job. Who's taking over the 160th?" Command of the 160th SOAR called for a colonel, not a brigadier general.

Emily felt the blood drain from her face. Robbed her of the power to speak.

"Funny you should ask that." Cass pulled a small box out of his pocket and tossed it at her.

Emily caught it by reflex. Though it burned against her palm, she opened it. Then turned it to show Mark the winged silver collar insignia of a bird colonel.

He slid down off his horse but didn't say a word. Instead, he stepped up and rested one of those big strong hands on her shoulder. That was good, or the gentle breeze rippling over the grasslands might waft her away easier than an errant bumblebee, never to be seen again.

"There's the pitch. You going to be making the catch, *Colonel Beale?*"

Emily couldn't react as Chesapeake stole her hat again.

The only comfort she found was that, for once, Mark was struck as speechless as she was. Not a single Texas drawl to be heard on the wide Montana prairie.

The sole sound on the wind? Her horse's laughter.

———

Buy now at fine retailers everywhere to continue reading
Guard the East Flank

ABOUT THE AUTHOR

USA TODAY AND AMAZON #1 BESTSELLER M. L. "MATT" Buchman started writing on a flight south from Japan to ride his bicycle across the Australian Outback. Just part of a solo around-the-world trip that ultimately launched his writing career.

From the very beginning, his powerful female heroines insisted on putting character first, *then* a great adventure. He's since written over 75 action-adventure thrillers and military romantic suspense novels. And more than 200 short stories, and a fast-growing pile of read-by-author audiobooks.

PW declares of his Miranda Chase action-adventure thrillers: "Tom Clancy fans open to a strong female lead will clamor for more." About his military romantic thrillers: "Like Robert Ludlum and Nora Roberts had a book baby."

His fans say: "I want more now...of everything!" That his characters are even more insistent than his fans is a hoot.

As a 30-year project manager with a geophysics degree who has designed and built houses, flown and jumped out of planes, and solo-sailed a 50' ketch, he is awed by what is possible. He and his wife presently live on the North Shore of Massachusetts. More at: www.mlbuchman.com.

353

Other works by M. L. Buchman: *(* - also in audio)*

Action-Adventure Thrillers

Kate Stark
Final Taste
Ice Burn
Knife's Edge

Miranda Chase
*Drone**
*Thunderbolt**
*Condor**
*Ghostrider**
*Raider**
*Chinook**
*Havoc**
*White Top**
*Start the Chase**
*Lightning**
*Skibird**
*Nightwatch**
*Osprey**
*Gryphon**
*Wedgetail**
*Air Force One**

Science Fiction / Fantasy

Deities Anonymous
*Cookbook from Hell: Reheated
Saviors 101*

Contemporary Romance

Eagle Cove
Return to Eagle Cove
Recipe for Eagle Cove
Longing for Eagle Cove
Keepsake for Eagle Cove

Love Abroad
Heart of the Cotswolds: England
Path of Love: Cinque Terre, Italy

Where Dreams
Where Dreams are Born
Where Dreams Reside
*Where Dreams Are of Christmas**
Where Dreams Unfold
Where Dreams Are Written
Where Dreams Continue

Non-Fiction

Strategies for Success
Managing Your Inner Artist/Writer
*Estate Planning for Authors**
Character Voice
*Narrate and Record Your Own
Audiobook**
*Beyond Prince Charming: One Guy's
Guide to Writing Men in Romance*

Short Story Series by M. L. Buchman:

Action-Adventure Thrillers

Kate Stark Stories
Miranda Chase Stories

Romantic Suspense

Antarctic Ice Fliers

US Coast Guard

Contemporary Romance

Eagle Cove

Other

Deities Anonymous (fantasy)

Single Titles

The Emily Beale Universe
(military romantic suspense)

The Night Stalkers
MAIN FLIGHT
The Night Is Mine
I Own the Dawn
Wait Until Dark
Take Over at Midnight
Light Up the Night
Bring On the Dusk
By Break of Day
Target of the Heart
Target Lock on Love
Target of Mine
Target of One's Own
NIGHT STALKERS HOLIDAYS
*Daniel's Christmas**
*Frank's Independence Day**
*Peter's Christmas**
Christmas at Steel Beach
*Zachary's Christmas**
*Roy's Independence Day**
*Damien's Christmas**
Christmas at Peleliu Cove

Henderson's Ranch
*Nathan's Big Sky**
*Big Sky, Loyal Heart**
*Big Sky Dog Whisperer**
*Tales of Henderson's Ranch**

Shadow Force: Psi
*At the Slightest Sound**
*At the Quietest Word**
*At the Merest Glance**
*At the Clearest Sensation**

White House Protection Force
*Off the Leash**
*On Your Mark**
*In the Weeds**

Firehawks
Pure Heat
Full Blaze
*Hot Point**
*Flash of Fire**
Wild Fire
SMOKEJUMPERS
*Wildfire at Dawn**
*Wildfire at Larch Creek**
*Wildfire on the Skagit**

Delta Force
*Target Engaged**
*Heart Strike**
*Wild Justice**
*Midnight Trust**

Night Stalkers Reload
*Guard the East Flank**

Emily Beale Universe Short Story Series
The Night Stalkers
The Night Stalkers Stories
The Night Stalkers CSAR
The Night Stalkers Wedding Stories
The Future Night Stalkers

Delta Force
Th Delta Force Shooters
The Delta Force Warriors

Firehawks
The Firehawks Lookouts
The Firehawks Hotshots
The Firebirds

White House Protection Force
Stories

Future Night Stalkers
Stories (Science Fiction)

SIGN UP FOR M. L. BUCHMAN'S NEWSLETTER TODAY

and receive:
Release News
Free Short Stories
a Free Book

Get your free book today. Do it now.
free-book.mlbuchman.com